HIGHEST BIDDER

GEORGIA LE CARRE

ACKNOWLEDGMENTS

Many, many thanks for all your hard work and help:

Leanora Elliott
Elizabeth Burns
Nichola Rhead
Kirstine Moran
Tracy Gray
Brittany Urbaniak

Highest Bidder

ISBN 978-1-910575-91-8

FREYA

"Excuse me," the woman said loudly, as I turned to leave the table.

That tone usually only meant one thing. I'd messed up. With a sinking stomach, I turned back and faced her.

She was using her knife to dig around the rocket leaves and cherry tomatoes on her plate. "Didn't I *specifically* say I *didn't* want parmesan shavings on my salad?"

I showed her my apologetic face. "Oh, I'm so sorry. I'll take it back and get you another one."

"What kind of waitress are you? It was just a simple salad and you couldn't even get that right."

"I'm really sorry. I was sure I made a note of it. There could have been a mix-up in the kitchen. I'll just get another one for you. It won't be a minute, I promise." I picked up her plate and turned away.

"Er … excuse me," she calls, her voice now not only loud, but sarcastic as well.

Keeping my expression polite and solicitous, I turned to face her.

"Shouldn't you take my husband's meal away too and put it under one of those hot lights to keep it warm?"

The man opposite her spoke up for the first time, "No, it's not necessary to take my lasagna back. It looks so hot it will probably burn my mouth if I eat it right away, anyway."

She threw him a death glare before looking up at me and snapping, "Take his meal away, and keep it hot."

"Yes, of course." I flashed her husband an apologetic smile, picked up his plate, and carried both plates back to the serving station.

"What's up?" Alfredo the Second Chef asks as I put the two plates down.

"Table twenty-one. She asked for no parmesan. It might have been my mistake. I can't remember if I wrote it down."

He glanced at table twenty-one then completely lost his cool. "It is that fucking bitch again. Every time she comes here, there's always something wrong with her order." He crossed his arms over his chest, and demanded, "What about the other dish then? What's wrong with that?"

"Nothing. She just wants us to keep it hot while we make her another salad."

"What a stupid bitch," he cursed. Muttering ferociously to himself as he shoved the lasagna under the warmer, he walked away with the salad.

Taking out my pad, I flipped back to the order and saw from

my carbon copy that it was my fault. I didn't note it down. That was the third mistake I'd made today.

Maya, one of the other waitresses stopped next to me. "What's up? You look like someone stole your last dollar."

I winced. She had no idea how right her observation was. "I messed up table twenty-one."

"Don't worry about it. She's never happy, that one. I don't know how her husband puts up with her nonsense. I would have divorced her on the wedding day itself, if I were him. He always looks so unhappy as well."

"It was my fault, Maya," I admitted. "She told me and I didn't write it down."

Maya touched my hand. "Hey, it's okay. Don't beat yourself about it. We all make mistakes."

Yeah, but three mistakes in one shift. I took a deep breath. I needed this job. I needed to concentrate.

Alberto came back with the salad, his face still black with rage. "Here you go. Santini salad without its most important ingredient."

"Thanks, Alberto."

I carry the two plates back to the table. "Santini salad without parmesan and meat lasagna. Sorry again, for the mix-up."

"Sorry, is no cure," the woman muttered under her breath, as if she was a kid in a playground.

When I came back to the serving station Maya said, "Look, I only have five tables left and the guys on table seven look like

3

they're going to be here forever finishing that bottle of wine, so if you want to leave, I don't mind taking over your two tables."

I really could do with leaving early. An hour and a half ago, the university called to say my mother's check to pay for my fees had bounced. I needed to go through my mother's financial records and find out why. "Are you sure?" I asked her hopefully.

She grinned. "Sure. You've done it for me before."

"Thanks, Maya. You're a star."

She patted me on the back. "Don't worry so much. It will be alright, you'll see."

I took off my apron, grabbed my bag, and ran all the way to the bus stop.

FREYA

Twenty minutes later, I arrived at King's Road, jumped off the bus, and walked briskly towards my mother's boutique.

Martin, the bald-headed, spectacled man - who had been my mom's loyal assistant during her socialite days when we had lots of money - had morphed into her new retail assistant. He was peering through the display window with a frown on his forehead. "What are you doing here, Missy?" he asked as I walked into the store.

"I need to check out something that's in Mom's office," I said, and hurried towards the back of the store.

Closing the door, I almost tripped over a stack of samples in my rush to get to my mom's messy desk of receipts and letters. I sat in her swivel chair and pulled open her drawer. I was actually looking for Mom's bank statement, but as I opened the second drawer, my eyes connected with a strange document. Curiously, I picked it up, and I thought my heart had come to a stop in my chest.

No, no, no. I reread it and I still couldn't believe what I was seeing.

I fished my phone from my pocket and dialed my mother.

She picked up on the fifth ring. "I'm at the Food Hall for some groceries," she said cheerfully.

"Mom, I'm in your office," I said to her.

"Why are you—" She paused when she realized what my statement meant. "What are you doing in my office?"

"Did you mortgage Grandma's home to open the boutique?"

For a few seconds there was silence. Then she spoke, "Yes."

Her voice was so soft I had to strain to hear. I could feel the blood pounding in my ears. "But you told me that you had some savings ... that you sold off some of your jewelry."

"I did, but it wasn't near enough to get a location on King's Road."

"So you mortgaged off the only property we had left?" My voice rose, even though I was trying to keep it down. "That is the only home you have to live in, and it's Grandma's apartment. Dad never touched it even when everything was falling apart."

"Freya," she said with a heavy sigh. "I did what needed to be done. You know, there's no point opening in some dreary area. Even my own friends wouldn't dream of coming to see me if I had opened in Brixton or Peckham—"

Suddenly, it was too much. The university calling me, the Santini Salad woman looking at me as if I was a total idiot, and now this. My voice broke as tears rolled down my cheeks. "H-how could you—do this without telling me, Mom? We talked about it and I told you opening a boutique at a time when everybody is shopping online is pure madness. I even offered to move in with Ella. You could have moved out to a slightly cheaper area and rented out the apartment. You could have used the difference to slowly pay off our debts. That was the safe option, but of course you had to go and throw every penny we had left into this stupid store. And now we have no more assets left. What are we going to do if the boutique fails, Mom?"

"Freya, come home, let's talk."

"Yeah sure," I said, and disconnected the call. I took a few deep breaths and tried my very best to calm myself down. I didn't want to upset my mother even further. She was already going through so much, but I felt like I was suffocating in frustration and despair.

A n hour later, and relatively calmer, I walked through the door of our apartment in Chelsea, which was technically no longer ours. I could hear her moving around in the kitchen. After dropping my things off in my room, I went to meet her.

"Hello darling," she chirped brightly as though we had never had the earlier conversation, as though there was absolutely nothing wrong in our lives. "I'm making dinner. I got you your favorite. Beluga caviar and I'm steaming those small potatoes you like so much so you have them together."

Whatever bit of calm I had worked so hard to claim was gone. "Mom!" I yelled.

She turned to me. "What?"

I couldn't believe her. I gazed at my forty-five-year old mother and I could have sworn she was the most naive person that I had ever met. "What part of we are completely broke, don't you understand? We've defaulted on several monthly payments already. We'll be foreclosed on at any moment! And you bought caviar?"

"It is your favorite and," she said, looking confused, as if she couldn't understand why I was being so unreasonable.

I couldn't hold back the agony any longer. "Yes!" I screamed. "When dad was alive. When we were bloody rich, and when we weren't on the brink of being fucking homeless."

"It is only a thirty-gram tin," she muttered.

Gazing at her small frame and bedazzled turban made me feel a strange mixture of admiration and exasperation. She refused to cower down to the lowly status my father's death had brought us to. She looked nothing like an impoverished widow. Her robe was of the finest silk, her ears glistening with diamond studs, and her house slippers were made out of some kind of special material that was imported from llama growing country.

"*Mom,*" I wailed, not knowing what to say or even think. "Mom!"

I felt so sorry for her, but at the same time, I felt even more sorry for myself. This past year had been a nightmare beyond compare and it seemed as though we weren't done falling yet. I wanted to break down, but I couldn't. It would finish us both.

So, I turned around and stormed out of the kitchen.

"Freya ..." She came after me. "Where are you going? Freya!"

I banged the door shut, and half ran all the way to the bus stop.

FREYA

I had run out without even a coat over my jeans and jumper so when my best friend, Maddie opened the door I was standing on her doorstep shivering like crazy.

Her eyes widened in shock. "What are you doing?"

"Visiting you," I said through chattering teeth.

She pulled me into the house and shut the door.

When she turned around, I threw my arms around her body.

Automatically her arms went around me and for a while neither of us spoke. Then she quietly asked, "What's the matter, Freya?"

When I didn't respond, she went on. "Did something happen to your mother?"

I shook my head.

She scowled. "So what happened? Why are you like this?"

I tried to hold the tears back, I did everything I could, but instead they rolled helplessly down my cheeks.

She didn't ask any more questions. She pulled me toward her warm living room and together, we plopped down on her couch. Then she held me in her arms, whispering again and again, "It's okay. It's okay. Whatever it is we'll work it out together."

The doorbell rang suddenly, making both of us jump.

I jerked away and we stared at each other.

Her brown eyes widened in the warm light of the lamp on the single book shelf behind her. The bell rang again, this time more insistently.

I sniffed. "Are you expecting someone?"

"No." She stood up and headed towards the door.

I wiped the tears off my face and grabbed the remote to her television.

A few moments later, I heard Ella's high-pitched voice, say, "Freya's here? Just the person I wanted to see." Seconds later, she appeared in the doorway wearing a fantastically skimpy dress. "Hello, babe."

She peered at me. "Why are your eyes red?"

"Why are you dressed like that in winter?" I asked back.

"Have you forgotten?" she asked airily. "I'm on a mission to find a stinkingly rich idiot."

"We're still on that project?" I asked, looking away.

11

"Bagging a rich guy so I don't have to lift a finger for the rest of my life? Yes, we are."

"You know that was what my mom did," I commented quietly. "Twenty-four years later, she's a struggling widow about to be homeless."

The room turned so silent I could hear the winter wind as it blew past, and footsteps of strangers passing on ground level above the basement apartment.

"Um," Maddie began.

I turn just in time to see her share a perplexed look with Ella.

Ella immediately joined me on the couch. "You're about to be homeless?"

Maddie came over to sit at my feet.

"It's almost certain. Mom mortgaged the apartment to open the store six months ago."

"Noooo!" Maddie gasped in horror.

"How did you find out?" Ella asked.

"The university called to say Mom's check had bounced so I went to her office this evening to look at her bank statement. While I was there, I saw the mortgage documents."

"What did your mom say?"

I shrugged. "What could she say? Anyway, I am convinced she is deliberately refusing to understand what is going on. Like she is still shopping at the food hall in Harrods. And when I called her, she knew I'd be pissed so she went all out and got me Beluga caviar and steamed eggs to appease me."

"Damn." Ella used a hand to hide her smile. "Your mom is adorable."

I looked at Ella in astonishment, but Maddie concurred. "Yeah, she is the best. Every time I go to her store I walk away with something new. I've already told her I'm in the market for a new mom whenever she's tired of you."

"Well, you can have her," I replied, frustrated that both my friends could not see how bad our situation was. We were thousands and thousands of pounds in debt, and I would almost certainly have to leave university and get a full-time waitressing job, and Mom would probably have to declare bankruptcy, lose her home, and maybe even move into a Council flat. It would kill her to do that.

"Why?" Ella demanded loyally. "What did she do? I don't get it? She just tried to make you feel better. You're the one sounding highfalutin now."

"We're already broke," I said tiredly. "Why spend perhaps our entire eating budget for the month on Caviar?"

"I still don't get what the problem is," she argued.

Maddie turned to her. "Stop being so dense. Caviar is rich people's food. Not for the broke and struggling."

"Are you joking? Caviar is not that expensive."

I stared dumbfounded at her, but I shouldn't. Ella's parents are moderately rich and she has had little luxuries all her life. Even now she lives with her parents. Maddie is from a firmly working class background.

Maddie held her hand up to her forehead. "I think she does this purposely." After a few seconds, she moved her gaze to me. "How bad is it? Are we talking repossession anytime soon?"

"I don't know. I haven't looked too deeply, but I know the boutique is struggling."

The room went totally silent again until Maddie took my hand. "You'll get through this, Freya," she assured me. "You'll be fine."

"That's what you all said to me when—" I still couldn't bring myself to say it. Sometimes, I could have sworn that it was all still just a dream. Some cold distant dream that I was bound to wake up from. I straightened my spine and went on, "It's been a year, and I'm still not fine. Nothing is *fine*."

"You've smiled again," Ella pointed out. "Remember we watched Sex and the City for days after to get through it all, and you asked the same question Carrie did. *'Will I ever smile again?'* Well, you have."

My smile was dark. "It was the wrong question. What I should have asked was, *will* I ever stop crying? Big didn't die, my father did."

Maddie rubbed my knee in calming motions.

I shook my head to push it all aside. "There's no point for any of this," I said. "I'll have to give up Uni and get a full-time job."

"You can't give up Uni!" Maddie protested. "I already had to give it up and our dear princess here is barely thriving in hers. We both need you to graduate, get a good job and help us out."

"I'm not even offended," Ella said, and rose to head into the kitchen. "I didn't sign up for this goddamn tough world."

We both turned to watch her dancing to the music in her head as she poured some of Maddie's table wine into a plastic cup.

"How I wish I was that carefree," I muttered.

"She can afford the luxury," Maddie replied, in a hushed tone. "She still has her parents. We both don't."

I began to stretch out on the sofa to sleep.

Maddie pulled me back up. "You can't sleep. We have to figure out this home repossession thing."

"Not tonight. I can't take any more of life's bullshit today."

Ella returned with her wine and kicked the sofa in agreement. "Get up. Let's brainstorm. We're good when we put our heads together."

"How much does your mother's apartment cost?" Maddie asked.

I popped one eye open. "Why? You want to buy it from my mom?"

"Sure, let me just make sure I can pay my rent this month first."

I smiled weakly.

"No, really," she insisted. "How much did your mom borrow off her home?"

"I don't know. I was too shocked to take it all in properly. I'll look tomorrow."

Maddie looked at me sadly. "I think I'm going to cry."

"It's alright," I consoled both her and myself. "It's not a big deal, just a small hiccup. I'll get through it. I'll drop out of Uni and it'll all be fine."

That was when Ella suddenly dropped her bombshell, "I know how you can get at least fifty thousand pounds overnight."

FREYA

Maddie sat up from her bean bag, while my eyes narrowed with a mixture of skepticism and dangerous hope. For the longest time, none of us said a word, Maddie and me because we didn't know what to make of Ella's statement and Ella because she was milking every last drop of drama from the situation.

"Are you joking?" Maddie asked, finally.

"Why would I?" Ella shot back.

"How?" I noticed the slight vein bulging in Ella's temple. That was her mark of honesty. She wasn't kidding.

"Yeah, how?" Maddie asked, her eyes filled with curiosity.

If Ella had any hope of using the same method for herself, they were immediately dashed by Ella's next words, "You can't participate, Maddie, and neither can I. Only Freya can."

"Why is that, then?" Maddie asked, her tone had become cynical.

"Do I have to sell a lung or something?" I asked.

"Not exactly."

I immediately sat up. "Then what *do* I have to sell?"

Ella hesitated, her gaze roving between Maddie and I. "Think. What is it you have that Maddie doesn't?"

"Fucking talk, for the love of God!" Maddie exploded.

"Calm down." Ella chuckled. "It's just a virginity auction."

"What the hell are you talking about?" Maddie asked.

"Haven't you heard? It's a big thing now. Instead of just giving it away, lots of girls are selling it at auction." She got up and headed to the refrigerator.

"Hang on a minute," Maddie squealed suddenly. "Freya's still a virgin?"

Both Ella and I turned to frown at her.

She covered her mouth with a hand in amusement. "Sorry, I always thought you were messing about."

Ella returned with a bowl of grapes.

"Can you please stop giving it to us in dribs and drabs and just spit it out," Maddie said, her eyes flashing with impatience.

"Hold your horses, girl … I'm just about to do exactly that. The auctions are held in this very exclusive club. It's called the Blue Butterfly. I heard of it from a friend."

I immediately lost interest at the hearsay tag, but Maddie's interest diminished not a bit. "Fifty thousand just for a night? You're exaggerating."

"I'm not," Ella replied. "Thirty thousand is usually what an intact hymen goes for, but some girls, the really beautiful ones, have walked away with fifty, sixty, even seventy grand. The sky's the limit. Just depends on the girl and how badly the guy wants her. With Freya's figure and looks, I don't see why she shouldn't achieve a high sum either."

Maddie was stunned speechless.

Whereas, I didn't believe a word of this. "This actually happened to your friend?"

"No, to her friend's sister."

"Yeah, right 'a friend of a friend'," she said, making air quotes.

"I know it sounds totally unbelievable, but honestly, she's a straight kind of person. I wouldn't mention it otherwise."

"What exactly does it entail?" Maddie asked.

Ella plopped a grape into her mouth. "It's a club owned by this mysterious and secretive billionaire. You have to be someone in the inner-circle to be a member. Its main activity is to promote *experiences of extreme pleasure,* whatever that means, but that of course has nothing to do with the virgin thing. That is a special, I believe, once a month event at the club."

"The girls go through an auction?" Maddie asked.

"Yeah," Ella replied.

Maddie inched closer to her, and hung onto her every word.

I fished out my phone to check the message coming through.

It was my mother apologizing. I put the phone back into my pocket. I was beginning to feel slightly ill in the pit of my stomach. I looked up and saw Ella watching me intently.

"Girls can auction off their virginity to the highest bidder. All they have to do is set a reserve price, and from there onwards, the price can get as high as the market decides. An ex-Ukrainian beauty queen walked off with one hundred and fifty thousand. An Arab prince bought her."

"An Arab prince?" Maddie asked. "So after you're bought, what happens?"

"Okay, I don't know all the details, but from what she told me, you spend the night with the man, soil the club's sheets, and leave when it's over. It's in the club's rules that you can't be forced to do anything sick or violent unless you both mutually agree on that. You are also advised to use a condom. Since the whole affair takes place at the club, security is provided, unless of course, both you and the client insist on taking it elsewhere, which is not recommended and you have to sign a document releasing them of all liabilities if anything should happen to you."

"And after that one night …"

"You never have to meet up with him again, unless you want to, of course. Oh, and because it's all celebrities, billionaires, and royalty that attend these auctions, you sign an NDA."

Maddie nodded. "So, I'm assuming a doctor's physical exam is involved somewhere. Otherwise, anyone could just lie that they are a virgin, right?"

Ella turned to her in surprise. "You're surprisingly detailed in mischief."

Maddie sighed miserably. "It's a gift and a curse."

"You're beautiful, Freya," Ella said in the softest of tones. "You could easily come away with at least fifty thousand. It could really help you out, but think about it long and hard. Don't force yourself into anything you'll regret one day. There are other routes to take to help your mother. They'll just be slower and full of painful sacrifices, like giving up your education and moving into a housing estate."

I clasped my hands together. "What would you do, Ella, if you were in my shoes?"

Her answer was simple. "You both know I was basically raped for my first time and it hasn't been all that wonderful most times since then either, so I would be the first in line at that club. Especially, if it would help my mother."

"Mine was with that bastard, Derek," Maddie said. "He was only special until after the fact. I still can't believe he jumped out of bed after the bloody ordeal and said he had to meet his mates at the pub. Fucking demon."

Ella covered her mouth to contain her giggle.

"Anyway, Freya," Maddie continued. "I know you've always wanted your first time to be with someone special, but in my opinion, perfection is overrated, or perhaps doesn't even exist. I'm not saying you should do this, but speaking from experience, don't let such an old-fashioned and stupid idea hold you back. I've yet to meet a girl who told me her first time was special. It's awkward, messy and a bit painful too. As feminists, we own our bodies. We can do whatever we want with them."

I blinked a couple of times to be sure that it was Maddie

speaking, then I shook my head. "The two of you can dress it up any way you want, but this is just prostitution, pure and simple."

Ella turned to me. "Actually, Freya, most relationships between men and women have an element of transaction to it. It may not be hard cold cash, but excuse me, what is dinner and a movie, an all paid for weekend in Paris, or even a wedding ring? I would have no problem doing it, especially for such a noble cause, but you are different than me and I don't want this to taint you. If I'm being honest, then I have to admit that your first time is probably going to be a billionaire weasel who looks like Carlos Sim or Warren Buffet, or worse, the living dead himself, George Soros. There isn't a muscle to share between the three of them."

Maddie and I stared at her.

She took a deep breath and went on. "I guess what I'm saying is, I don't want this thing to change you, so I'm sorry I even brought it up in the first place. You'll have to make some painful sacrifices, but you and your mother will get through this."

I didn't need Ella to tell me. I knew in my heart from the moment she mentioned an auction—I was *never* doing something like that.

FREYA

By the time I went home, it was late and my mother had already gone to bed, but she had left the caviar out for me and a sweet little note telling me she loved me. It had little love hearts drawn all over it with red ink.

I sat down at the kitchen table and looked around me. We lost our fine home and it looked as if my mom was almost definitely going to lose this little apartment too, but I wasn't going to allow myself to be sad. I was determined I would find a way to solve our problem … without selling myself to the highest bidder.

I decided then to quit university and find a proper job that would help support us. I also intended to go through the accounts of my mother's boutique. I would either try to revive the business, or if the situation was too bad, tie up the loose ends and get rid of it. It was time my mother stopped living in fantasy land and woke up to the reality of our new situation.

Once I had made that decision, I felt better, freer than I had since Dad died. I made a slice of toast, spread the caviar on it and ate it. I knew it was the last time I was going to be eating anything this luxurious for a long, long time. When it was all gone, I wiped the table clean of crumbs and went to bed.

By the time I woke up Mom had left the apartment. She left a note that she had a hairdressing appointment. I put the note down and sighed. Obviously, I was not begrudging Mom a trip to the hairdresser, but her hairdresser cost nearly a thousand a visit.

We were both going to have to make a lot of changes and sacrifices.

Just before I headed off to Uni, I called Martin to find out if my mother was at the boutique. He said she had just popped out and told me to come over as there was some leftover cake, Marie, the cleaner, had baked and brought to work. I loved her baking so I headed there.

I arrived at the store and felt a pang of sadness at the sight of it. We were in this mess partly because of me. In the heat of the moment, I'd forgotten that I hadn't put up much of a fight when she wanted to open this place. I guess we were both reeling from my father's death. The way he died. I just wanted to make her happy again.

I had known that owning a high-end boutique had been one of her dreams when she was younger. It was only superseded by being married to a wealthy man and playing the part of a socialite.

As I waited for the pedestrian light to turn green, I saw a woman walk in. With her bright red heels and long black coat, she seemed like just the demographic that my mother's store aimed to cater to. Perhaps my mother was seeing her customer of the day, that is what my heart hoped.

I saw Martin hurrying up to welcome her, but at the sight of her, he came to a dead stop and actually began to retreat.

The light turned green, and keeping my gaze on the store, I crossed the road and stopped by the window. I don't know why I didn't go in. I guess I knew I was about to witness something important.

With his hand up, he appeared to tell her to wait. Then he hurried away to the back.

I watched, wondering what was going on.

Then my mom showed up, her reading glasses on her nose. My mother was the vainest person I know so she loathed them and only put them on when no one could see her, and for her to forget and come out into the front shop with them on, must mean something extremely serious was going down. She went towards the woman and listened as the woman launched into an animated monologue.

My mom tried to speak, several times, but the woman would cut her off and eventually her voice rose, and despite the bustle of the people around me, and endless stream of vehicles passing by, I could still hear her voice.

And that was *not* okay.

My mom was watching her with a placating, almost bewildered look.

I couldn't take it anymore. I took a step forward, ready to barge in and give the woman a piece of my mind, when she turned and began to go through the racks of clothes. As she did so, she began to snatch dresses and blazers off the racks.

My mom went after her, trying to speak and hold on to the clothes to stop the woman from taking them away. It was then I realized what was happening. I froze and took a step back so I was hidden by one of the large potted plants on either side of the door.

Although, it hurt so much to do so, I forced myself to wait. My mom had to be the one to handle this on her own, or I might make matters worse. The woman was probably a supplier whom my mom had defaulted on payments to.

My heart ached as the woman piled a heap of clothes in her arms. The whole time, my mom followed behind her pathetically pleading with her as she went through the store.

I couldn't take it anymore, but yet, I couldn't bring myself to move because I knew that it would hurt my mom more than anything to know that I was a witness to her humiliation. I blinked back tears for my mother. How life had changed for her.

Then suddenly, my mother rushed towards the woman and tried to pull the clothes back.

I watched in disbelief. *Oh, Mom! Just let her take them and go.*

But my mom wouldn't let go, until the woman got tired of the tussle and threw the clothes at her. At that moment I forgot my earlier intention to let my mother handle the situation. I stormed into the boutique, and I was just in time to hear my mother's plea.

"They've been paid for," she cried pitifully, her gaze to the ground. "The clients will be coming tonight to pick them up."

"That was what you said last month," the woman screamed into my mother's face.

I couldn't move.

"Catherine," my mother begged the woman. "We need this sale to be able to survive this month."

"Evelyn!" she called my mother by her first name, and my mouth fell open. "If I don't get these clothes back to the office, I will not have a job by the end of today and there is no way I'm getting fired because you're in over your head."

My mom placed her hands together as if in prayer. "Please, Catherine. Please? Give me one more day. The credit card sales will register tomorrow and I'll give you the money in cash if you want. Please. The client who bought these is a huge one, and it will bring us the opportunity of more business, which just means more business for you. They will be coming for a fitting at lunchtime, and if these clothes aren't here, I might as well close down the shop right now and go out of business. I'm begging you, just give me today."

Catherine ignored my mother and bent down to begin gathering the clothes. "That's impossible—" she began, but stopped suddenly.

My mother had dropped down to her knees and grabbed the clothes. Catherine was so shocked she let go of the clothes which made my mother tumble to the ground. She was lying on the ground clutching the clothes to her chest.

FREYA

I was in shock, the kind that made me so angry I started to shake. I didn't remember moving across the room, but in an instant, my hand was locked around my mother's wrist and I was pulling her up with all my might. I fought it, but the tears blinded me, and made me delirious with fury.

"Get up!" I yelled.

My mother was so surprised to see me, "Freya," she whispered.

I hid my face from hers, as I pulled her up then turned around to the woman. "Get out!" I screamed at her. "Get the fuck out of here, and you can take your damn clothes with you." I was shaking so hard my words were incomprehensible. "How fucking dare you treat my mother like she was a piece of shit you stepped on? Just because she has fallen on hard times doesn't mean you get to treat her like that."

My mom held my arms to pull me backwards to stop me.

The woman's gaze roved between the both of us. Finally, she

shook her head. "I'll give you till tomorrow afternoon," she said coldly. "After that, we're done. I'm pulling all our stock out."

Then she walked out of the store.

I glared after her, wishing that I could hurt her arrogant ass, even half as much as she'd heartlessly just hurt my mother. For a second, I shut my eyes to calm myself, then I wiped the tears away from my cheeks and turned around to meet my mother's white face.

"What are you doing here?" she asked, as though nothing had just happened, even though her lips were quivering. "Don't you have to be at class?"

I watched my mother fight with everything she had in her, to keep standing, to make me believe that her pride had not just been shattered into a thousand pieces at how deeply and completely she had been humiliated in front of Martin and me.

She couldn't hold on to that composure for long though. Before she could fall apart in front of us, she turned around and rushed back into her office. "I need to make a quick call, give me a moment." Her voice sounded strangled and thick.

I gave her several minutes while I quietly joined Martin in hanging up the clothes that had been thrown to the ground.

When we were done, Martin nodded at me. "Go on. Go to her." I had never heard him sound so sad.

I headed to her office, then turned back. "Have you been paid, Martin?"

He shook his head silently.

I knocked on the door.

"Come in," my mother called.

I opened the door to my mother's bright, plastic smile. I didn't smile back. I couldn't.

Her smile faltered. "Don't you have class?" she asked. "You're not meant to be here."

I walked up to her and enveloped her in a huge hug. Poor thing was shaking like a leaf. "Oh, Mom, I'm so, so, so sorry," I sobbed.

She patted my back as if I was a child. "It's okay, darling. It'll work itself out. You'll see. I just need one big sale. Then everything will be fine. I don't know why I behaved like that."

I drew away from her and looked into her eyes. She was begging me to play along. To pretend that nothing was wrong. To pretend that I hadn't seen her abject humiliation. Now, I felt beyond sorry that I had lost control … that I'd been unable to hide myself, so she wouldn't know I had witnessed her in such a state.

Somehow, I made my mouth move. "I'm sorry for interfering," I apologized. "I do have class, but I just dropped by to apologize for last night and to say I don't have to work tonight so I'll cook. We can have your favorite."

"Oooo … chateaubriand with bordelaise sauce?"

I smiled at my mother. In a way, you had to admire her. The bubble she had built around her was made of Teflon. "No, not that. I was thinking of green curry and rice."

She grinned. "That would be wonderful, darling. I'll pick a bottle of something nice to have with it."

I bit my tongue, but I didn't say anything. Let her have her bottle of something nice. "Okay, Mom." I reached up to her face and took off her glasses.

She tutted. "Oh, I can't believe I went out wearing them." She touched her glasses.

"I love you—Mom." My voice broke.

My mother's eyes filled with tears. "I love you too, my little button. Now I want you to go to class and stop thinking about our finances. I'll sort everything out. I promise. We will be fine."

I nodded my agreement with a smile, and echoed her words, "We will be fine."

"That's my girl," she said approvingly.

"See you later, then," I said and walked out of her little back-room office.

In the past year, we had lost almost everything: my father, our status, our homes, our cars, a good proportion of our 'friends', even our peace of mind. Not anymore. My mother was going to keep her pride. I determined right then I was going to ensure she would be able to hold her head high again. She was not going to lose the apartment that my father had bought for her when they first got married.

When I exited the boutique, I did not head to Uni, instead I pulled my phone out and called Ella.

"So, did you speak to your mom about dropping out?"

"I didn't," I responded. "There was no need."

Her voice became quiet. "Why?"

"We're not going to lose anything more, Ella. I'm not dropping out of Uni, and she is not going to lose her shop or the apartment either. I'm going to participate in the virginity auction."

"Uh, actually, I don't think that's a good idea, Freya. I was annoyed with myself today. It was so stupid of me to even bring that topic up last night. You're not like that and you shouldn't have to do things that you will regret for the rest of your—"

"Ella ..." I stopped her in her tracks, "... my mom went down on her knees today. She knelt down and pleaded with some fucking bitch close to our age who wanted to seize some of her stock because she hadn't been paid. This is now beyond my going to Uni. I'd rather die than watch my mother lose her dignity that way again."

"What about her? Will she be okay with the way you're about to lose yours?"

"That's not my dignity," I argued stubbornly. "My dignity is in my ability to care for my mother."

"Freya, you don't have to—"

"I can't believe you're saying this to me right now. When your mother went to jail, you dropped out of school to support your entire family. "

"That's dropping out, I didn't sell myself to some fat, old billionaire."

"Ella, I'm going to do what I have to do. My mind is made up."

"There's no billionaire club. I lied."

I stopped in my tracks. For a few seconds neither of us spoke, then I yelled my frustration into the phone, "Fuck you, Ella! This is my damn life and I want to make my own choices."

"I won't forgive myself if this goes awry, Freya ... if this damages you."

"I won't forgive you if we lose everything," I growled. "If once again, my mother has to get on her knees to save our lives, I won't forgive you. And if she breaks and does something stupid, that'll be her blood on your hands. Send me your friend's number right now."

FREYA

And with that I ended the call. My breaths were coming in short spurts, my heart thumping in my chest, and my hands were shaking from everything that had happened. I felt bad, I had never spoken to Ella like that before, and I hoped she would forgive me. I looked around then and saw a bench. Walking over, I perched at the edge and tried my very best to settle my swirling mind. Anxiety had slowly crept into my life over the last year and remained.

I shut my eyes and thought of my father. His smile. His lofty pride. He'd loved us, but he loved himself just a bit more. He spent all that money and left my mother unprotected. For that, the bitterness towards him remained in my heart.

My mother and I would not have been in this state if he had only paid for an insurance scheme. Our hearts would not have been so broken, and we would not have been thrust into this pit of humiliation with no means of escape in sight.

My eyes opened.

Until now, I corrected. *No means of escape ... until now.*

I watched the world go by, the babies in strollers, office workers carrying their lunch with them; the pigeons pecking at the ground, then flying off without a care in the world. I would have given anything to be one of them.

The buzz of my phone startled me. I didn't expect a response so soon. Ella had sent a message with her friend's phone number. I stilled my heart, then unlocked my phone to access it.

I didn't allow myself to think. Only when the number was already dialing did I realize I hadn't even mapped out what to say.

It was answered after a few rings.

"Hello?" a smooth male's voice came through.

I did not expect a man and for a second I almost ended the call, but I gripped the phone hard and went for it. "Hello," I began, "I was given this number by a friend of mine.' At that moment, an elderly woman joined me on the bench so I quickly rose and began to walk away.

"Yes?" The voice went on. "How can I help you?"

"Um I'm interested in the – uh … the sale? I mean the auction."

"Could you please clarify which service—"

"The virginity auction," I blurted out.

"Ah … right," he responded as though I was doing nothing more significant than ordering a takeout. "Send a selfie of yourself to this number, and we'll proceed from there."

"Okay," I responded and the call was abruptly disconnected.

For a while, I could only stare blankly at my phone, then a text message came through startling me out of my daze. Nerves rattled, I immediately clicked into action and looked through my phone. I was filled with a sinking feeling that I didn't have even a half-decent picture of myself to send.

Over the last year, I hadn't taken many pictures of myself. It had been a bad time in my life, filled with moments I most definitely did not want to capture. I turned on the camera hoping perhaps my current state would be passable, but upon the self view of my makeup free white face, and my windblown mess of a ponytail, I knew I couldn't send that.

I opened my messenger and sent a text to Maddie. My eyes caught the time. I was already so late for school. I had just arrived at the underground station when her response came.

Why do you need a selfie of yourself?

My reply was deliberately vague. I *don't know, but I need one now.*

She messaged back. *Why don't you just take one?*

I called her. "Because I look like shit."

"You couldn't look like shit if you tried. Again, why do you need a selfie? What's it for?"

"Look, I'm going underground, so I'm going to lose reception. I'll speak to you later okay."

"Let me search," Maddie's reply came. "You used to give me some to edit for you when you still used to care about your Instagram page."

Yeah, that felt like a lifetime ago. "Thanks, Maddie." I tucked away my phone and ran down the steps into the subway. The train arrived just as I got onto the platform and I went in. It was just about noon and the carriage looked fairly empty. I let my gaze skirt to the only other occupant. She was wearing particularly unique skinny-heeled boots. Her white collared blouse was tucked into leather trousers, and her short elegant hair with wavy bangs completed the sophisticated look.

For some reason, it made me feel just a bit sadder. She turned and looked at me and I immediately looked away to my dirtied converse and oversized puffy coat. I looked a mess and I knew it. All I looked forward to each day was end when I would once again, be in bed, shielded from everything. I couldn't wait for this day to end too.

As I arrived at Uni, Maddie's message came in.

How about this one?

She sent me a picture of a day the three of us had gone zip lining in Lancaster.

The selfie was of me seated atop one of the hills we had climbed to, while the background was of mountains and a dull sky. It had been taken just when the sun had hit me at a perfect angle, and although there hadn't been much makeup on my face either, my hazel eyes looked as if they'd been set ablaze, and my skin was flushed with an ethereal glow. I looked happy and attractive. This would have to do. If I was rejected, then oh well, my mother and I were basically doomed.

It'll do, I responded.

Then I sent the picture to the number given to me.

Forty-five minutes later, I arrived at Ealing Broadway and caught the bus to the University of West London. The lecture theatre was already filled and the lesson on auditing already underway. I settled in a vacant seat on the second to last row and tried my hardest to concentrate, but my hand remained clenched around my phone in anxiety. About half-an-hour later, when the last break of the session had just been announced, my phone beeped with a new message.

I peered down at my screen, surprised that I was the girl in the picture. I looked so carefree and happy.

FREYA

As it turned out, Mom went to bed early with a splitting headache and since she didn't feel well, I didn't bother to cook. I was rummaging through our refrigerator for something to chew on when Ella's call came through.

"How did it go?" she asked excitedly.

I found a half-eaten avocado and the leftover heel from a loaf of bread. My mother tended to avoid crusts like they would undo all her best anti-aging efforts, so I brought them to the counter and laid them on the cutting board. Going hands free with my airpod, I popped them into the toaster, then began to spread butter on them. "They asked me to go to a studio in Islington tomorrow to have some professional photos done."

"Professional photos?" she squealed. "Does that mean you've been accepted?"

"I think so," I responded cautiously.

"What? Without a physical examination?"

"He did briefly mention it, so there will be one down the line."

"Hmm ... right," she said thoughtfully, probably thinking of me with my legs in a stirrup.

"What are you up to?" I asked, as I sliced off the few brown spots in the avocado.

"Worrying about you and folding my three-week old laundry. I really should stop chucking them all in the corner of my room. They look worse than when I took them out of the dryer."

The recollection of my friend's disdain for domestic work made me smile.

"Anyway," she went on. "I inquired a bit more and it seems an auction will be taking place this weekend."

I inhaled deeply, surprised at how rapidly it was all moving. "It's once a month, right?" I asked quietly.

"Yeah."

I swallowed. "I'm just in time then."

"You can still change your mind," she pleaded. "I don't want you to do this."

I ground black pepper on the sliced avocados and carried the plate up to my room. "Is losing my virginity to some pot-bellied swine with an empty soul that bad?" I asked, and for some reason we both laughed out loud at the image I'd just drawn. I stopped suddenly and dashed away the tears that had welled up in my eyes. An awkward pause followed.

"I just feel you haven't really thought it through, and I'm worried you will regret it for the rest of your life."

"I'm yet to hear about anyone who had a blast their first time," I pointed out. "So it shouldn't really matter."

Ella pressed on, "It does regardless, because *you* will always remember it."

"Then so be it," I said. "I'll also remember that it gave me enough to settle our most immediate debts and make life a little easier for my mom, at least for a little while. Maybe it will buy enough time for me to finish my education and get a proper job. That's not such a bad thing, is it?"

She didn't say anything.

"Stop worrying," I said. "It's just a one-time thing. Beggars can't be choosers. I'll suffer through it and move on with my life. Plus, I think I've gone beyond the childish idea of keeping my hymen intact for someone special. Who really cares? It's not at all important in the big scheme of things. There are children dying of starvation in the world."

"I know there are children starving, but that doesn't mean you can't designate certain values to yourself and keep them special."

"Let me tell you, Ella, the only thing that would be more painful than watching my mom being humiliated in her own store will be knowing I could have done something to help her and didn't because I thought my virginity was more precious than her wellbeing. She took care of me all those years, Ella. And now it's my turn to do something for her."

"Alright," she conceded. "If it helps, I would have done the same thing."

"Thank you, Ella," I said, my voice choking.

"Remember our motto. This too shall pass."

"It shall." I smiled. "My only hope is that it's worth it. You said I should get at least thirty thousand, right?"

"Well, that's what my friend said, but if things do go wrong, or the money is not worth it, just get out of there. I'll be coming with you anyway, so I'll handle it."

"I don't think I can get out that easily. The guy who called made it a point to ask me if I would be okay with signing an NDA."

"If they don't let you go, then I'll call the police or … something."

I sighed. "I am not an ex-beauty queen, Ella. Even if I go for fifteen thousand pounds, I'll take it."

At 10:56pm, on the third Saturday in December, Ella accompanied me to the club, dressed all in black in her role of my bodyguard. Her no-nonsense military boots, baggy outfit, and sinister visage promising to do damage to anyone who manhandled me - beyond what they would pay for - had been exactly the comic relief I'd needed to get my legs working and out of the house.

The Blue Butterfly club was so well hidden in an obscure street in the city that we had to go into a dingy umbrella shop to inquire about the address I had been given. An Oriental woman smiled sweetly at me and said we were indeed already in the club. She pointed at a black door that led to the back, but told us only I could go on through to the club, though.

Ella immediately dragged me out of the shop onto the sidewalk. "I really don't like this cloak and dagger stuff. Are they a club, or an umbrella shop? I mean, why is it hidden at the back of an umbrella shop? Heck, I'm beginning to think there is something very fishy about it all. I don't even know if this is legal."

"It has to be if billionaires and celebrities are taking part," I countered reasonably.

"I don't like secretive things," she huffed.

"I'm here now, and I'm doing it, Ella," I insisted stubbornly.

"If you don't text or call me in three minutes that all is well, I'm calling the police," she fumed, before turning her face towards the surveillance camera above us and yelling, "I'm calling the police on all of you if you hurt her. I'll be waiting right here until she comes out." She turned back to me. "And I'm not joking either!"

"Look, you can't wait here for hours. Just go home. I will be okay, I promise. I'll call you if anything seems out of place," I reassured her, then I went back inside.

The Oriental woman pressed a buzzer and the black door opened.

To my surprise, the door opened to a luxurious space with a Renaissance-style painting on the ceiling that would have rivaled any fine house in England. The walls were painted in eggshell blue and decorated with intricate white moldings. The floor was made of glistening checkered marble.

A woman wearing a long black dress was waiting for me. She smiled at me and addressed me by name. She opened one of the small locker doors and asked me to leave my cellphone in it since no photography was allowed.

I quickly sent Ella a text to say all was well and put my phone into it.

She locked it and gave me the key.

I could see two lifts. She called one and we entered it. It travelled smoothly and noiselessly downwards. It opened three floors down.

Silently, she led me down a brightly lit corridor to a room that looked like a standard hotel room. "You are not allowed to wander around the club on your own, so please do not leave this room. Someone will come shortly to prepare you for the auction," she instructed before she left.

I thought she was going to lock me in the room, but she didn't. I breathed a sigh of relief. Before I could even properly investigate my surroundings, there was a gentle tap on the door.

An old woman entered. Her face was deeply lined and it surprised me to think of such an old woman working in a place like this. She made a movement with her hands to indicate I should undress.

"Okay," I said awkwardly and started to take my clothes off. I stopped at my bra and panties.

"All. All," she said impatiently.

When I was naked, she led me through a door into a tiled room with a huge Japanese style wooden tub. She sat me on a wooden bench and proceeded to strip every last hair on my body by rubbing a sticky brown mixture over every inch of my skin. She even worked her mixture around my butt hole, which was embarrassing to say the least.

I nearly died of shock when she started pouring icy water that she'd scooped from the wooden tub over my head.

45

"Cold water good for you," she said.

I froze and shivered as I thought of how happy my mother would be when I solved all our problems with the money I made from this club.

To my surprise, I got used to the cold very quickly, and by the time she massaged hot fragrant oil into my body, I was feeling very relaxed and expansive. Draped in a white toweling robe I was taken back to the room where a makeup artist was waiting with her bag of tricks. I sat before the mirror framed with light-bulbs and she worked her magic.

FREYA

I stared at myself in the mirror in shock.

I looked beautiful.

Almost to the point where I didn't recognize myself. The makeup artist had styled my thick brown hair in soft waves cascading down to my shoulders, and painted my lips a dark berry red. But more than that, it was what she had done to my eyes that was really amazing. They looked enormous and the dark brown eyeliner she had used made the gold specks in my hazel eyes glow.

I basically wore nothing except the sheer negligee and a black thong I'd been given to wear. I regretted having cut my waist-length hair before I started my waitressing job. It was too short to cover my nipples.

"Are you ready to join the other girls backstage?" the makeup artist asked.

Stage? Jesus! I took a deep breath, and assured myself once again, that all would be well. I could do this. It would be nothing compared to what awaited Mom if I didn't. I was taken to a large room where there were six other girls and, like me they had all been beautifully made up, were wearing the same type of negligee, and were barefoot.

"Gather round girls," a voice said briskly from behind me, the accent was full-blown aristocratic and I looked around in surprise and saw a silver haired woman. Her sophistication in a velvet skirt suit and a French chignon surpassed even that of my mother at the height of my father's wealth. She, more than anything else that had happened to me, surprised me. I had expected the whole transaction to be suspect and sordid, but thus far, everything and everyone seemed to be dripping in luxury.

She proceeded to address us, "I believe you've all already signed your NDA's, so may I take this opportunity to remind you how serious it is. If you ever reveal or try to sell any information to the media about this club, the things you witness here, or the identities of the people you meet here, the club will bring the full force of the law upon you. Do you understand that?"

Every girl standing in that room, including me, knew she meant every word. We all solemnly nodded.

She nodded. "Good. The reserve price you each set for yourself has also been approved and machinated. If you are having second thoughts and want to make any changes then you can do so within the next ten minutes, otherwise it will be the minimum amount that must be reached before a sale can be achieved."

As she said this, my heart began to pound just a bit harder with worry at the reserve price I had set. I looked around me and wondered what the other girls had set. There were two white girls, one black, one who looked like she might be of Indian descent, but I couldn't be sure, one Oriental, and one who looked like she might be mixed race. But they had all been made up to look beautiful.

Was my price perhaps too high?

The woman ran her gaze across the lot of us, all seven girls in total. "I hope all of you are fully aware of what you have signed up for. Tonight, is a *one*-night affair. After tonight, you will never have to meet your patron again. But tonight …" Her voice slowed, full of intent and coldness. "*Understand* that you are selling your bodies. This night alone, you are not the owners of them."

The room went completely silent as she continued to look us all in the eye, the pause, the perfect effect for her warning to sink in.

A small voice spoke up, "How far can they go?" It was the mixed-race girl.

"They can go as far as they want," she responded. "With the exception of violence of any sort, unless of course it is mutually agreed. Condoms will be provided to protect you all, and I want to strongly advise that you make good use of them. After tonight, none of the patrons have any obligation whatsoever towards you and neither will we."

"What about anal sex? Do we have to submit to that?" another girl asked.

"I'm afraid so. If you are unhappy with the idea, now is the time to leave."

The girl hung her head.

The woman watched us all intently again, as if to drive her point home that tonight we would be nothing more than the playthings of the rich and the famous. "Any more questions?" she asked.

No one had any.

"Good luck," she said, and allowed herself a small, tight smile before she took her leave.

I could feel and hear all the other girls exhale and relax. Music had been lightly playing in the background, but I was so focused on the woman I hadn't even heard it.

One of the girls smiled shyly at me. The girl who had asked about anal sex had gone beyond to the curtain that led to the stage. She came back.

"What can you see?" the black girl asked.

"Nothing. The whole place is full of mirrors. All the men must be hidden in cubicles behind one-way mirrors."

The Indian girl's eyes caught mine watching her so she came over to stand next to me.

"Sorry," I apologized. "It was rude to stare. I'm just nervous."

"Don't worry about it. I'm Indian. I get stared at by all my relatives all the time for being unmarried at my age," she replied.

"Why? How old are you? You look the youngest amongst all of us."

"I'm pretty certain I'm not," she replied. "I'm twenty-four, about to be twenty-five soon. My spring chicken years are coming to an end, well after tonight, they'll definitely be gone forever."

Her spring chicken analogy made me break out into a grin.

"How old are you?" she asked.

"I'll be twenty-two in two months."

"See," she said with a shake of her dark curls. "I bet my auction money I'm the oldest here."

I liked her. She reminded me of Ella. "Well, you certainly don't look it."

"How did you find out about this place?" she asked curiously.

"Through a friend." I returned the question back to her, "You?"

"I was at a party with some friends and someone they knew joined us. He got really drunk and told us he once worked as a bartender here and about the auction. I was sick and tired of living at home and listening to my parents telling me I was becoming an old maid, so I decided to make some money and set off on a trip round the world ... on my own."

"Wow, talk about taking your future into your own hands."

She grinned showing not even a bit of the nervousness I was feeling. "That's me, Anub Singh at your service. What about you? Why are you here?"

"Nothing as glamorous as your reason. I need the mon—" I started to respond, just as there was the sound of someone clapping. We looked to see another woman had come in. She was tall and elegant. There was something about her I instantly didn't like. Unlike the others, she was not wearing a name tag, so I assumed she had higher authority.

"The auction is about to start. When your name is called, you will walk on to the middle of the stage where you will get completely naked."

I froze on the spot, just as murmurings across the room broke out. All those hidden eyes were going to see me naked! I didn't even know when I spoke, "We're going to be completely naked on stage?"

Her response was simple and slightly patronizing, "Of course. How else will our patrons know what they're paying for?"

"I'm so screwed," Anub whispered to me. "My boobs are tiny compared to everyone else."

Mine were a full, decent size that especially stood out against my slim figure, but that was the least of my problems. I was going to stand naked before strangers that I couldn't even see? I turned my face away and stared at nothing.

The woman's voice was all I heard from then on.

"You will go out towards the stage when your name is called, take off your clothes and stand in the middle of the star painted on the floor. Do not speak, just stand with your legs shoulder-width apart. When you're asked to turn around, do so. And just a tip, put a little heart into all your poses. In my experience, the more exciting and eager you appear, the more you will be able to command. Now, as I call your name, please go towards the hallway and wait your turn there. Anub?" she called.

"Oh oh ... here we go," Anub said and went forward.

The woman looked her over, then nodded. "You're first."

Anub walked over to the hallway.

"Theresa?" the woman called.

"Here," the pretty black girl said.

"You're next after Anub."

"Valerie."

The Chinese girl stepped up.

My heart was pounding.

"You'll go after her."

"Eugene? You're next."

"Freya?"

I opened my mouth but it wouldn't work.

"Freya? Freya?"

I raised my hand and the women in the room turned to look at me.

The matron, with a frown on her face asked, 'Are you alright?"

I nodded.

"You're next."

FREYA

The moment the microphone beyond was tapped to signify the start of the auction, the entire waiting room quieted down to an almost scary silence.

There was a brief welcome by the auctioneer and then Anub was called out ... We couldn't hear it all, but it was easy enough to follow her, as the voice asked her to bend forward, turn, show her profile, lie back and ... oh god ... open her legs. Then, we heard the auctioneer begin the bidding. Her reserve price was twenty-thousand. It went up in increments of five thousand, then slowed down to two thousand, down to a thousand and finally to five hundred. We did not hear the final price. Only the auctioneer saying *sold* to telephone Bidder Number 21.

Minutes later, Anub returned, her face glowing. It was clear she was happy with her price. Instantly, she found my eyes.

The other girls watched her curiously especially at the smile on her face.

"I got fifteen thousand more than I thought I would."

My eyes popped open. She fetched £35,000. Up till that moment, a part of me had believed it all to be a scam. "They're actually going to pay the money into your account?"

"First thing tomorrow morning. After ..." Her smile faltered a bit. "... After tonight."

"Was it nerve-wracking?" I asked.

"A bit," she reiterated.

I leaned in. "Did you see any of their faces?"

"No, they're all hidden behind mirrors. When they make a bid, the button underneath their mirror flashes."

The next girl's name was called.

"Good luck," Anub said, and skipped off with one of the employees of the club.

I felt my stomach churn, like I had to rush to the toilet maybe. I placed my hand on my belly and took deep breaths. I didn't need to go to the toilet. I hadn't eaten since lunch. I told myself everything would be okay. I could hear the auctioneer talking up the price, but I had stopped listening. Only when one of the girls in front of me gasped and another squealed that my attention was brought back to the room.

"Oh, my God. She got £92,000!" the girl in front informed me.

My heart stopped. "What? What was her reserve price?"

"40,000," she replied. "Both her and her friend made the same reserve amount."

I turned to them, both girls of Oriental heritage. They were attractive, but in my opinion, not as much as Anub. Perhaps their buyer had a taste for Chinese beauties. Had I done myself a disservice by setting my reserve price so low that the men will think I was not worth much either?

At the worry in my gaze, the girl asked, "Why, how much did you set?"

"15,000," I responded.

She frowned at me. "Why so low?"

"To be honest I kinda didn't expect anyone to pay so much for so little. I've been waiting for the other shoe to drop. I can't even believe that someone actually got £90,000."

"Maybe you can quickly change your reserve price. Speak to one of the staff. After all, it's not your turn for some time yet."

"No need. The woman before said it would be impossible once the show started." I sighed. "Even if I can command £15,000 it would be a great help."

She looked genuinely amused. "What do you mean if you can command that much? Have you looked at yourself in the mirror?"

The third girl returned to the room then, so we turned, expecting to see nothing but smiles, but instead, she was in tears and trembling violently.

The rest of the room quickly went over to console her.

I tried my best to listen in on her lament but she was speaking in Chinese.

"What happened?" the black girl asked.

Her friend looked up at us, mournfully. "No one wanted to meet her reserve price."

A gasp of dismay went around the room. After the rush of thinking, we could make up to 90,000 - all of us who had not yet gone on stage - realized that we could actually leave with nothing.

"80,000 was kind of a stretch though ..." the girl next to me said in a lowered voice.

"But her friend made it and got twelve thousand more," I said.

"I guess, it's all a matter of luck. Regardless, £80,000 is still a stretch. Plus, anyone who has that much money for a night must not be right in the head."

"Freya?"

My throat dried up and my vision actually blurred.

"Freya?" The assistant called looking around. "Where the bloody hell are you? You're next."

With the potential of rejection - and now, I had to show my naked body to a roomful of strangers, no doubt kinky, decrepit bastards - I wanted to disappear into nothing, but I couldn't move.

"Freya, you're on. Can you hurry up please?"

I walked out of the hallway and onto the stage.

When I arrived, I found a white star in the center of the small black stage. The many mirrors glinted in the gloom. To give myself some time, I pretended to be in search of the exact middle of the star. Then I disrobed and pulled down my thong. The aristocratic woman's warning came to mind, and I knew I should undress it in a seductive way to make sure I reached my reserve price, but I couldn't get my body to work properly. It was as though my entire body had frozen solid and all my movements were awkward and heavy.

"Turn to the side," the voice instructed.

I turned.

"Face the back."

I faced the back.

"Lie on the bench, please."

My heart was racing when I lay down on the cold wood that seemed more like an altar than a table.

"Legs," the auctioneer commanded.

I closed my eyes tightly and opened my legs. Part of me felt as if I was dreaming. This couldn't be real. I was not lying on a table while strange men looked between my legs.

"Stand up."

I stood.

"The auction will begin now."

My head remained down even as the auction started, and I couldn't lift it up. It felt as heavy as lead so I gave up, shut my eyes, and managed to stop myself from running off the stage.

"Starting at fifteen thousand," the auctioneer bellowed.

I dug my nails into my palms.

"I have twenty thousand!" he called out.

Hearing this, I began to breathe easier. Even if that was where it ended, it would be alright. Twenty thousand was better than returning with nothing. The relief was short-lived because I was suddenly overcome with guilt. What the hell was I doing? I had come this far and subjected myself to this humiliation, if I put more effort into it I could make more for myself and my mother. If I was already going to go through this nightmare, then why not go all the way to obtain as much as I could? I unfisted my hands slowly, so that I could attempt to do some sort of pose, or at least spin around slowly, but just then, the next increment was announced.

"I see thirty thousand," the auctioneer called.

"Forty-thousand."

I blinked in shock. Unlike the other girls whose value from what I had heard backstage, had skyrocketed in increments of five, and then twenty thousand, it was obvious I wasn't putting in as much effort to invite the same kind of fortune to myself.

"Fifty thousand."

I froze on the spot. At first, I was sure that I had heard incorrectly but then the announcer bellowed again.

"Do I hear sixty?"

This time my head shot up in shock.

"Seventy thousand pounds!" he called and my heart began to race. *Was this real?*

"Eighty thousand!"

I focused on steadying my breathing.

"Ninety thousand pounds! Do I hear a hundred?"

This had to be a dream. It was all going to stop any moment now.

"A hundred thousand," the announcer called.

I wobbled on my feet ever so slightly.

Light murmurs began to break out backstage as I moved my eyes across the mirrors in the hopeless search of whomever was driving this bid.

I saw a flash of light, and the announcer bellowed. "One hundred and ten thousand."

Another flash went up in the opposite corner of the room.

"One hundred and fifty thousand pounds," the announcer roared, and fear gripped me.

What was going on? It couldn't be my body? Was this person insane?

"One hundred and eighty thousand pounds!" he bellowed out.

My hand came to my mouth in shock.

A stunning silence erupted across the room, and soon the announcer began his final call.

"One hundred and eighty thousand," he repeated. "Going once ... Going twice—"

"Two hundred thousand," the other person flashed back.

"One million pounds!" someone roared from behind one of

the mirrors. That person hadn't even been in the running all this while. He had come from nowhere with his crazy offer.

The announcer found his voice, "Uh ... One million pounds?" When there was no take back, he went on. "Going once ..." His voice sounded like a warning to which ever idiot had just blurted out that amount.

"Going twice," he called out once more.

Silence.

"Sold to Buyer Twenty-five for one million pounds!" he crowed triumphantly.

FREYA

The auctioneer's voice was still ringing in my ears as I pulled on my negligee and got off the stage. I trembled with shock and incredulity. Was it real? Did someone actually buy me for one million pounds?

The woman I had instinctively distrusted came up to me. She was unsmiling. "Come. I will take you to your buyer." Without waiting for my reply, she began to walk away.

Every other girl had been allowed to return to the dressing room, but I ... I was being requested immediately. Breathing normally, was now a foregone luxury.

"W-where are we going?" I finally found my voice enough to ask as I ran along to keep up with her long, almost angry strides. Why she was mad at me was beyond me.

She glanced back with a bitter smile. "Your buyer wants you now. Apparently, he can't wait. He must have really liked you." Her eyes ran down my nearly naked body.

I didn't miss the puzzled raise of her brows. I didn't blame her. Something had to have gone wrong somewhere, for somebody to be willing to pay that kind of money for one night with a virgin. Sure, virgins weren't growing on trees and I'm incredibly and unbelievably grateful, but one million?

I spotted a man awaiting us at the end of the corridor, and my chest tightened at the sight of him in a dark suit. Was he the buyer? But he didn't have the look of anyone important. And he looked nearly as young as me. Unless he was the heir to some conglomerate? Only heirs could waste this much money without batting an eye.

I could barely hear anything beyond the drumming of my heart in my ears when I arrived, close enough to see his face.

The woman with me, said, "Here she is." Without another word, she turned around and left.

I turned to look at her departing back.

"Freya?" the man called, politely.

I turned. "Are you the one who bought me?" I asked, even though, I already knew it could not be him. The woman would not have dared behave in such a rude way if he was the buyer.

"No, I am not. My boss did."

"Your boss? Who is he?"

"Freya, I am sure that you've been explicitly warned about asking questions beyond those that concern your safety and overall well being. Please keep to the terms of your contract."

My mouth shut closed then.

"Come with me," he said.

~

I don't know what I had expected. A room with satin and blood red accents perhaps. Instead, I was ushered into a cozy, well decorated space with the real fire going in a marble fireplace. There were upholstered cream armchairs, a big bed with a velvet throw, and a sheepskin rug similar to the one that my mother used to have in her dressing room in our old life. The walls were hung with modern art in silver and black frames.

"Please wait here," he said to me. "Do you need anything?"

"No," I responded.

As he turned around to leave, I wanted to ask him what his name was, but what was the point? After tonight, I never wanted anything to do with him, or his boss again, whomever it was going to be. I did however have one question. "When will he be here?"

"He might be a little while," he responded. "Maybe take a nap? I'll turn down the lights," he said, as he left the room.

I was alone with just shadows for company. I ignored the huge white bed, with its thick fur comforter across its foot, and headed straight for the armchair. There was a massive vase of fresh flowers on the coffee table next to it. The chair smelled faintly of expensive cigars, and brought reminders of my father in his study to me. It saddened me even more.

The minutes ticked by and I gazed so long at the fire I lost myself in the orange flames.

I might have even dozed off for a little while, but was jerked awake by some noise or some instinct for self-preservation. I sat up, just as I heard footsteps approaching. I didn't know what to do.

Before I could make up my mind, the door handle turned with a click. I dared not turn around. I made no sound.

He stood at the doorway for a moment.

I wanted to call out, but my throat was locked and my body was frozen.

He didn't come to me, but headed over towards the bed.

I heard the soft thud of his outerwear hit the bed. I listened to the small clink of what I guessed must be his watch dropping on the bedside table.

I heard him sit on the bed and then I heard nothing else. The room was lit only by the dancing flames. I had since decided it was enough light. I did not particularly need to see what he looked like. I could guess.

Needing for this to end as quickly as possible, even though I suspected that was a forlorn hope, I rose to my feet and turned around. "Hello," I said, my voice quite cold.

He didn't respond. As I watched, he started taking off his cufflinks. He did it quickly, expertly, then he began on the buttons of his white dress shirt. In one smooth movement, he had shrugged off his shirt.

I was ready to look away, but at the sight of the rippling of muscles across smooth olive skin, I stopped.

What?

I was expecting saggy, liver-spotted skin and layers of fat ... not this Greek God.

What was going on?

He flung his shirt away and rose to his feet.

Without even realizing it, I took three steps backwards. He turned to face me then and my eyes were widened in the dark, needing to see his face. He had to be hideous, perhaps scarred and beyond ugly, for him to have to buy a woman.

His face however ...

Was a dream.

FREYA

He pushed his hair away from his face and his amber eyes sparkled like a wolf's in the orange illumination of the room.

I couldn't believe my eyes and for a moment, I was sure that I was hallucinating.

"Brent?"

"Freya," came his mocking response.

My heart fell into my stomach. As I gazed at him, stupefied with shock, a thousand questions flooded into my head. When I broke our gaze to clear my head, the first question finally slipped out, "You bought me?"

His extraordinary eyes narrowed at my words. "I paid for a night with you."

None of this made any sense but at the same time, it was somehow as clear as day. "Is this a joke?" Needing to sit down, I just lowered myself to the floor and folded my legs underneath me. He was bloody handsome ... had always been. I hadn't seen him in about a decade ... not since I was an eleven-year-old busybody.

The last time I'd laid eyes on him he had an 18th century marble figurine raised in the air, ready to bring it down on the head of his younger brother whom he had in a deathly neck grip. Everything about him had been menacing then ... as it was now. Nothing had changed.

My voice was eerily quiet as I spoke, "Did you know it was me?"

"Of course."

I shook my head in awe. "Did you buy me because of what happened ten years ago?"

I watched his eyes darken with quiet rage. "Get up," he said to me. "Let's get this over with."

I don't know why, but it surprised me and even hurt just a bit that he was going to go through with it. In a tiny corner of my heart I must have hoped he had purchased me to protect me. "Will I be getting the one million then?"

He cocked his head. "If you keep your side of the bargain."

"Bargain?" I whispered.

"You sound bitter. Is it not enough?"

I was bitter, incredibly so. I wanted to smash the vase of flowers on top of his arrogant head. "No," I responded, lifting my chin. "It is not." In this moment, I felt beyond crippled by shame. I couldn't believe that from all the people in the world, he was the one present at what would be the lowest moment of my life. "How about doubling it? Make it two million."

He watched me and then folded his arms across his chest. "How are you going to explain to the world where you got two million pounds from, overnight?"

My temper went out of control. "Exactly!" I cried. "Why would you buy me for so much money?"

He narrowed his eyes, "So your problem is that I overpaid for you."

"Why did you even buy me in the first place?" I yelled at him and couldn't believe it when tears filled my eyes. "And what the hell are you doing here? Is this what you do? Buying virgins? Is this what you spend your money on?" Rising to my feet, I wiped the tears off my face and turned around to walk out of the room. Just before I arrived at the door however, his words made me stop.

"You don't need the million?"

I stilled, as it hit me then what I was walking away from. I'd been prepared to go through with it all, to do what was needed to be done with some grotesque, probably corpulent man, old enough to be my grandfather, but not him. Not with him. To think that he had already seen me fully naked and with my legs open wrung my heart dry.

I turned to glance at him. "I just found out what the great Lord of Leighton spends his spare change on. I think this bit of info will probably fetch me more than what I need."

"Where's the proof?" he asked.

I froze once again. *Where's the proof?* That had been the question, and the first words I had asked him ten years earlier.

He began to walk towards me.

Immediately, I backed away until I found my back against the door.

"Don't you need the money? Isn't that why you came to this club?"

I met his eyes with a glare. Turmoil brewed in the pit of my stomach, making me feel feverish. "Why do you do this? Why do you buy girls?"

"I don't buy girls," he answered.

My eyebrows furrowed. "You don't buy girls?"

"I don't. I only took part in the auction because I saw you on stage. It was quite the surprise." He smiled. "I'm afraid I couldn't resist."

"Then what were you even doing here in the first place?"

He paused and I waited for him to cook up a lie.

"This is my club," he said simply.

"You're the reclusive billionaire?" I gasped.

He was now only a short distance away from me. The light from the fire licked the side of his face, making him appear dangerously beautiful. "What's it going to be? Are you going to let me fuck you or not?"

The way he said the word, throaty and full of lust, sent a jolt of pleasure to the pit of my stomach. I stared at him, enthralled by the effortless way he could mesmerize me. I had expected to be revolted tonight and look at where I was instead …

"You really want to do this?" I breathed because I didn't quite believe he wanted to go through with this.

"Yes, I *really* want to," he murmured softly.

FREYA

"Let's get this over with then," I said, and the nonchalance in my tone when I was so close to imploding impressed even me. Holding the light gown, I pulled it over my head and flung it away. My breasts were now on full display.

He stared hungrily at the full mounds. "You've truly grown up," he commented more to himself than me. "Turn around," he commanded in that deep, warm voice.

I did as I was instructed, fully aware my exposed ass was only covered with a black lacy thong. I felt his warmth as he reached me, and shut my eyes to contain it all when his hand slithered around my waist.

No one had ever touched me so intimately before. Given the setting, obviously romance wasn't part of the agenda, but the way his warm hand moved across my skin, then flattened on my stomach to press my frame to his ... My eyes fluttered *shut*. His touch burned like a brand, and hot molten desire began to pool between my legs.

I could feel his hardness through our clothes, and it quickened my breath dangerously. He towered considerably above me, so he had to lean down to bury his face in my neck as though he were breathing me in, his hand moving up from my stomach. When it arrived at my breasts, his hands covered both swollen, heavy, mounds.

As he fondled me, my entire being began to ache ... for him ... for more.

I needed more ... I needed him to hold me, but I didn't want to show any of this. I tried to keep still, but before I realized it, my head tipped back as he traced warm, hair curling kisses along my neck and shoulders. I tingled all over from the sheer anticipation of his lips on mine, but it never came.

His hands began to slip away from my breasts, downward. My eyes snapped open. Angling my head, I found his gaze and the world seemed to completely stop in that moment. Our chests rose and fell. He waited ... without breaking the gaze for me to say what burned on the tip of my tongue

"Kiss me," I whispered.

He turned his head away from me and his response was brief, but commanding, "No."

Before I could stop it, his hands slipped down and grabbed my already soaked thong. The pleasure that shot through my body at the seize was borderline painful ... but it wasn't enough to mask the sting of his rejection. I didn't want to feel that way about the arrogant brute, but the possessiveness and domination with which his hands travelled down to my sex took over my body and spirited my breath away. He began to circle his finger around the swollen bud, in slow precise motions at first, and then in rapid strokes.

I writhed uncontrollably against him.

One of my hands tangled in my own hair to somehow keep my mind intact, while the other made feeble attempts to release his hold. My moan was breathless and when he went even lower, past the ineffective barrier of my thong to slip a finger inside of me, I lost control of myself. Like an animal, my feet left the floor as I started to raise myself higher as he pushed into me. He dipped his finger in and out with maddening slowness. I wanted to scream.

"Relax," he whispered. "I need you to be very wet to take me inside you."

Soon, he had increased it to two fingers, which felt like heaven, and made me want to have more. *"Brent,"* I gasped, my writhing bringing my butt unabashedly against his hardness. I started to quicken at the build-up of ecstasy tearing through me, but just when my eyes were about to roll into my head, he pulled his hand away. My eyes flew open in disappointment. I spun around, barely able to catch my breath. "Why did you stop?"

"I haven't stopped. I'm just getting you slick and ready. Would you like a drink?"

I shook my head silently and watched as he walked away to the tray of liquor on the mantle. I watched him pour the golden liquid into a crystal tumbler, then head over to one of the armchairs I had fallen asleep on.

"Come here," he said.

When a few seconds passed and I hadn't moved, he turned to me.

I did not want to be seated. I wanted him to finish what he

had started so we could both get this sorry affair over with and move on. In fact, I felt quite embarrassed at the way I had so shamelessly lost control of myself.

"Come here," he repeated, but there was a slight edge to his voice.

I was forced to head over to the fireplace. I stood before him, frowning. "Brent, you don't need all night, do you? Just take what you want so we can go our separate ways."

As he sipped from the tumbler, he lifted his gaze to mine and watched me. Eventually, he spoke, "I paid for the entire night, not an event. Taking your virginity is only the start, so *sit*."

With a sinking feeling in my stomach, I lowered myself onto the chair, and pretended to be very interested in the flames. I could tell that he was watching me, and my body throbbed against my will with excitement.

His hand shot out and touched my thigh.

I turned towards him. It was a mistake. The fire seemed to light up his hair and eyes and it all made him look so deliciously dark and tousled. I wanted him and despised him at the same time for torturing me.

We have all night.

His eyes glowed as he simply looked at me.

For a few moments, there was only the sound of the fire crackling. Then ...

"Take off your thong," he ordered. "Hook your legs over the arms of the chair and open up wide for me."

75

FREYA

I was sure I hadn't heard him right, but it was clear from the deathly seriousness in his eyes that I had. I quaked and opened my mouth to refuse outright, but he beat me to it.

"I'm going to remind you one more time that I'm paying for this night. If you no longer wish to continue, then you are free to leave right now … with nothing but what you came with. Otherwise, I will not tolerate your disobedience any longer."

I held his gaze, and once again, I was taken back to the steel-hearted man I had perceived him as years ago. I knew he meant every word. I had already come this far, and had been immensely lucky that I wasn't sleeping with some old frog. I squared my shoulders. I would do everything I had to do to get the money, but while I was doing it, I was determined to wring as much pleasure as I possibly could from this night with him.

I took off the thong then I lifted both my legs and let them hang over the arms of the chair. His gaze focused between my thighs on my exposed sex and my clit throbbed with wild excitement.

"Touch yourself," he instructed, taking his shoes and socks off.

My eyes widened. Surely, he was not going to make me masturbate in front of him.

"Do it like there's no one else here, but you," he said to me. "Show me how you've kept yourself sane for this long without being fucked."

I could feel my cheeks burning a bright red, but I ignored it and shut my eyes.

His next command was an aggravated rasp, *"Keep your eyes on me!"*

My eyelids fluttered open and met his unflinching gaze. In them, I saw raw, primal lust blazing like an out-of-control forest fire. Purposely, I kept my strokes slow and sensual. I wasn't just pleasuring myself I wanted to titillate him. I wanted to see how much I could affect him. The delicious coaxing made my hips take on a life of their own and writhe in response. My toes curled, my thighs clenched, and my breathing quickened until short spurts of air were all I could take. But I never took my eyes off him.

"Uh," I moaned, as if I was some porn star and not an inexperienced virgin.

His fists clenched so hard the knuckles gleamed white in the dancing light. I lifted my palm and smacked it hard on my painfully sensitive flesh ... just before my finger slipped into my opening.

"Fuck," he grunted, and sat up straighter on the chair. His control was slipping.

I pushed my finger in and out of me as if I was challenging him. Taunting him. To come get it. The whole scene was turning me on in a way that I could not explain. But then I felt my climax start to build. I forgot about him, my movements frantic as I chased my release. I did what I had never done before: I joined three of my fingers and rammed them in a deliberately vulgar assault on my soaking wet pussy.

I wanted him to see. I wanted him to be shocked. The need had been building for years.

I gave my clit another hard smack, and my back arched off the chair as a trickle of pure lust oozed down from my opening. Almost incoherent with excitement, I saw Brent jump out of his chair and in moments, he was on me. Flinging my hand aside, he covered my cleft with his mouth in a brutal suck.

My cry was wild, torn from somewhere deep inside me, as waves of pleasure locked my body into a stiff arc. As though he expected me to fight him off, he threw a hand across my stomach to keep me in place. With a hard lick, he lapped up the juices pouring out of me. From the base to the top, and back to the base. Then he sucked on my swollen clit like a starving beast. It was like nothing I could have imagined.

"Brent," I cried, my whole body shivering violently. I had touched myself countless times, but never once had it felt like this. I was seizing, my vision and mind losing coherence. Nothing existed beyond the ecstasy ramming through me.

His tongue dug into me and my hands clawed ferociously into his thick hair. Swinging my legs off the arms of the chair, I locked them against the sides of his head, entrapping him.

Undaunted, he dug even further into my sex, his hands grabbing my hips to hold me in place.

"*Fuck ... fuck*. Fuck." I crumbled, my entire frame twisting with sensation. Another climax was on its way. With both of my legs on the floor, I pushed us both forwards and we collapsed on the ground, my pussy on his face.

Shamelessly, I began to ride his mouth, wetting his flesh with the drenched lips of my sex. He caught up in a heartbeat, and I could have sworn I heard a feral chuckle from him, but I was too far gone to properly register anything other than the ephemeral pleasure I was chasing.

With my hands on the ground for balance, I rode his tongue, like an unthinking beast, and when his teeth bit down on my clit without warning, I exploded on him.

"*F-uuuc-kkkkk,*" I screamed, my entire body jutting forward and landing on the rug. I felt my fingers grabbing the fur of the rug as my eyes rolled back into my head. Even then, I couldn't stop writhing my hips against him, wringing every ounce of pleasure I could out of his sarcastic aristocratic lips.

As the moments ticked by, I tried to contain the sweet tremors that were still rocking through me. I regained some semblance of reality and my heart found its way back to a semi-normal rhythm. As my brain restarted functionality, I realized that my ass was jutting out and completely exposed to his gaze. I started to rise but once again, Brent's hand came for me. Locking my hips in place with an iron grip, he spread me further apart and began to lick me clean. It was all too much too soon. I found myself struggling once again to breathe.

"Brent," I gasped, but he was relentless as he lapped up every trace of my explosion up my thighs and between the crevices of my sex, even my ass. It was beyond invasive and I almost couldn't believe what was happening.

I could feel myself start responding to him again, so I tried to scramble away from him, but his strong grip wouldn't let me move even an inch away. I had no choice but to submit to his tongue. Only when he was finished and I was once again utterly turned on, did he move his way upwards. When he was aligned with my body, he lifted me off the floor and put me on top of his body.

I was a tangled mess of naked limbs, but before I could even manage to find some sort of balance, his mouth and hands were on my breasts, kneading the swollen mounds and sucking my engorged nipples.

His suction tightened every single muscle inside of me until I was almost painfully taut and dripping all over again. All I could do to ease the insatiable ache was to ride my sex against the hard ridges of his torso.

"You're driving me out of my fucking mind," he rasped.

For some crazy reason, my heart swelled with intense emotion at his words, but I didn't allow the primitive elation to show on my face. His hands moved away from my breasts and began to unbuckle his belt. I could feel the hardened swell of his cock, straining against the material.

His lips stretched out into a wolfish grin, the pearly perfect whites stealing my breath away. He was so damned handsome. I felt enraptured by his beauty as I stared down at him, my eyes inspecting the curve of his brows, the rise of his strong nose and the sensuous swell of his soft lips. I could hardly believe that just a moment ago they were eating me out. I'd have given anything to slip my tongue into his mouth.

"Why won't you kiss me?" I asked, almost angry at the deprivation.

Instead of replying, he stared back at me, quietly as though he was trying to see something. He slipped his hand into his pocket breaking the moment between us and brought out a condom. He put it on the ground and roughly pushed his pants and underwear down his hips just enough to set his dick free.

I felt it spring free against my back, rock hard, thick, strong and vital. He tore open the condom packet and expertly rolled it on to his massive cock. Of course, I'd seen a man's cock in porn movies, but seeing it in the flesh, one as huge as his thrilled me.

I wanted my mouth on him, so I lowered my lips to his neck. Placing hard almost brutal kisses on his skin, I nipped and sucked my way up his heated flesh and along the line of his jaw. I moved to his face, and we both knew what I was going for. He allowed me, but as soon as my mouth reached the corners of his, he caught my bottom lip between his teeth.

"Ow." I winced as I tried to drag the delicate flesh away. He smacked me hard on my bare ass once, then again, the spanks shooting pain as well as a sweet tinge of pleasure through my body. He did it again and again until my ass felt like it was on fire and I couldn't take it anymore.

"Stop!" I said, grabbing his arm.

"Don't try that again," he said.

I started to pull away but he smacked me one more time and commanded, "Lock your hands around my neck."

I did as I was told. With me clinging onto his neck, he rose. As soon as he was upright, I swung my legs around his hips, my sex coming in contact with the hot, flat flesh of his stomach. He began to shuffle his pants down his legs. As soon as the material had pooled around his feet, he kicked them aside and began to walk with me towards the bed.

He laid me on the heavenly soft bed, before he positioned himself on top of me. My hips started to gyrate against his hardness as my hands went in a desperate search of his cock and took a fierce hold of the impossibly thick and lengthy monster.

I felt a sudden excitement tinged with slight fear as I moved my grip up and down the impressive length. I lifted my eyes up to meet his piercing ones. He nuzzled his nose against mine savoring the feel of my hands up and down his shaft as I gently fisted him, sizing him up with concern. "Brent."

"Hmmm," was his intoxicated response.

"Will …will I be able to take all of this?"

His eyes fluttered open to gaze deeply into mine. We were so close I could see the beautiful golden flecks in his irises.

His response was a very low chuckle.

I frowned at his reaction to my extremely real and serious concern.

It was then he leaned down to whisper into my ear, his hot breath an entire aphrodisiac on its own, "You're going to take it," he said, "even if you won't be able to walk for a week."

My frown deepened at that statement, but it made him laugh, the deep sound smooth and enthralling.

"You'd better be joking," I said warningly.

"I won't hurt you," he murmured. "I'll never hurt you, little Freya."

BRENT

I had laid her on the bed with her hair fanned out around her face, a pillow under her delectable ass, and her legs open wide enough to offer the perfect view of what I had bought. I looked down at her, her young ripe breasts, her naked pussy leaking honey.

It was so hot to watch her drip for me. My balls ached for release.

Hell, she was absolutely perfect. And she was all mine. Bought and paid for. I still couldn't get over the fact that such a beauty could remain untouched at her age. A strange thought flashed into my head. Of her after tonight. With another man. It filled me with uncontrollable fury, which I couldn't understand. She was only here for my pleasure.

Nothing more than that.

I ran my finger possessively along the inside of her thigh, and her legs fell wide open for me, exposing more of herself. Her little virgin pussy already looked swollen and a bit abused, but there was a lot more she was going to have to submit to before the night was over.

"Do you want me to fuck you?"

She licked her lips. "Yes."

God, how I wanted her tongue in my mouth, but I let my eyes wander away, back to her eager cunt. Tonight, was supposed to be only about sex. I was here to put to bed an old fantasy. Hopefully, it would never again keep me awake at night.

I lowered my head, sucked her clit into my mouth, and tasted her sweet heat. A small whine escaped her lips. That was all it took to nearly make me lose control. Animalistic need coursed through my veins as I hungrily licked the nectar running down her slit.

I lifted my head. "Now spread your pussy lips apart."

With her fingers she pulled the puffy lips apart, making her small, pink opening gape. It was so sweet I couldn't resist poking my tongue into it. Then I raised myself and I brought my sheathed cock towards her entrance and let it lie flat against her slit. Slowly, I moved it back and forth. Not penetrating, but simply rubbing her clit. Back and forth until she started to wriggle her hips with aching need.

"I want you inside," she begged, her fingers still holding her pussy lips open for me.

Some part of me wished I could always see her open like this, ready and begging for my cock to take her. It was a stupid thought. This was a one-time thing. I was going to mark her, then let her go.

I dipped my cock into her. No more than an inch though.

H er hands curled around my shaft. "Oh, that feels so good. I want more."

I wanted her fiercely, but I didn't want to hurt her too much. I was over twice her size and my dick was bigger than most men. She was small and there was no getting away from the fact that it was going to hurt. Her tongue came out to lick her lips.

"Take your hands away," I ordered.

She obeyed and I pushed myself where no man had gone. I took the thing I had dreamed of for years. My cock was inside her warm cunt, and I could tell by the shocked gasp that exited her mouth, her eyes widened with pain, and the way her walls gripped my shaft so fucking tightly that I had stretched her to capacity.

"Are you okay?"

She nodded.

"Perfect. So perfect," I whispered in her ear as the scent of her hair filled my nostrils.

She wrapped her arms around my neck and held onto me.

"Ready?" I asked.

"Yes, Brent," she whispered.

Slowly, I pull out of her, and thrust back in again, more firmly this time. I had to grit my teeth to keep from exploding. I kept up the rhythm of slowly pulling out and thrusting back into her tightness, until she was able to take all of my cock.

I wrapped my arms around her back and held her to me as I rutted into her and listened to her shouts of pleasure. I gripped her ass cheeks and held her hips even higher so there was not a tiny inch inside that I had not touched. All of it belonged to me. I had waited all this time for this.

As I kept thrusting into her, I felt her legs cling to me tighter and her pussy pulse on my dick.

"Yes, yes, yes," she muttered.

Her words are cut off as screams of pleasure are torn from her throat. Her face flushed as I rode her hard towards the edge of the abyss.

"Wow, that was amazing," she gasped, as the echoes of our release fade away.

My cock twitched inside her. I was still hard. I felt proud I had taken her cherry. Moving my mouth to her nipple, I sucked one of the soft pink buds in my mouth. She moaned with pleasure. Giving it a little teeth, I gripped her ass and pulled her hips aggressively up my hot dick, all the way to the fucking root.

"Are we going to do it again, Brent?" she asked, her eyes wide.

"Freya, I'm going to fuck you until you can't walk," I growled.

"I want that too," she whined.

FREYA

It took me quite the while to return back to earth, but even after I did, even after my brain restarted and my heartbeat settled, I remained on top of Brent. I was no longer a virgin. Brent had taken it. Actually, Brent had bought it. And it was the most amazing feeling in the whole world. Everything I'd heard was untrue. With the right man, it was heaven. He was still inside of me, and neither of us wanted to pull apart, at least that was what I hoped.

My head was on his chest, feeling its gentle rise and fall, and the rhythm of his heartbeat, a melody I didn't want to break away from. His warmth seeped into me, and when he suddenly moved to wrap his hand around me, his nose softly nuzzled the crook of my neck, and my breathing became labored all over again.

We only had this for tonight, so there would be no holding back. A separation, especially after the profound experience we'd just shared seemed unfathomable. I wanted him to touch me again, continuously until the sun rose.

He began to move. For a few moments, I tried to ignore his intention to separate from me, but he curled his hands around my ribs, lifted me bodily, and pulled out of me. I gasped at the loss of our warm, wet, joining, but he deposited me on the bed next to him.

I shut my eyes to hide the emotions inside me.

After disposing of the used condom, I felt him settle in the space beside me. I waited for him to immediately rise and get out of the bed. When a few minutes passed and he didn't move, I began to feel a bit of warmth flood into my chest again. Perhaps he would be here until the morning.

"How do you feel?" his quiet voice filtered over.

"I'm fine. I am perfectly fine."

"Good," he said, "because we have a long night ahead of us."

"Have you not had enough?"

"Have you?" he countered.

I was immensely sore but we only had tonight. Nothing could hold me back. I shook my head. And he reached for me again. I felt my body open up to him like a flower. I screamed his name three more times before my eyelids shut.

It felt as if I had closed them only a few minutes before morning arrived. I felt him move beside me, then his warmth was gone. I opened my eyes to the vivid reminder of all that had happened the previous evening. It all still seemed like a distant dream.

For a while, I considered pretending to be asleep. My chest tightening with apprehension when I heard him moving around the room quietly. I thought that he would wake me up, at least say goodbye, but instead I heard his footsteps heading towards the door.

I instantly shot upright.

True enough, he was heading towards the door, fully dressed.

"Brent," I called out, my tone sounded strangely lost and small.

Stopping, he turned around to glance at me. He didn't say anything, just waited.

I hated him for not saying a word, for not caring, for treating me like a whore. I knew I couldn't say what was in my chest, my heart, my belly, my skin, my mouth, my sex. I couldn't tell him I didn't want him to leave. Ever.

He quirked an eyebrow. How distant he had become. Last night, he had worshipped my body, now he was the mysterious, secretive billionaire again.

"How are you going to send the funds?" I asked, putting as much nonchalance as I could muster into my question.

"The club will wire it to your bank account," he responded. "You've already provided the information, I believe."

I glared at him.

He turned fully to face me. "What is it?" he asked. "You're doubtful you'll receive it?"

"No, but how am I supposed to explain one million pounds in my account?" I asked sullenly. "To anybody?" I hated talking to him about money, when all I wanted to do was have him inside me again. I wish I had never fallen asleep. I wish I had let him have me one more time.

He shrugged his shoulders without looking up. "A gift sounds reasonable enough."

"A gift of one million?"

"Why not? You picked up a rich boyfriend. I don't see what the problem is."

"Don't send it yet," I said. "I'll think about how to receive it, and get back to you."

"alright," he agreed easily and turned away from me again.

I couldn't let him go. "You will send it, then," I asked, my fingers plucking at the delicate embroidery on the sheet. "Won't you?"

He smiled sarcastically. "Don't you trust me, Freya?"

Knowing that I was parting with him for good, made me very, very sad. "I don't know you."

He sighed. "Should we draft a quick contract of goodwill, then?"

I nodded.

He placed a quick call, and a few minutes later, there was a knock on the door. It was his assistant. After speaking to him, he returned with a pen and a blank sheet of paper. He sat down for a little while to scribble on it, and when he was done, came over to my side to hand over the agreement.

I saw his signature across one bottom of the page, and the next line drawn to put mine.

I took it from him and signed.

He took a picture of it, and then handed the paper over to

GEORGIA LE CARRE

me. "Take care," he said to me, and made his way out of the room.

I rose to my feet refusing to let myself feel anything. This was, after all, what I had signed up for. I'd receive more money than I could ever have dreamed of. And I had been luckier than most. No one knew, but I had held this man in my mind for the longest time. I had absolutely nothing to complain about.

FREYA

I didn't want to go home smelling of Brent so I decided to go to Maddie's place. I arrived at her home a few minutes past eight, certain that she would have left for her job at the physiotherapist's clinic, but just as I inserted her spare key, the door was jerked open from inside the house. My hand flew to my chest in shock.

"You're back!" she exclaimed, her eyes filled with a mixture of curiosity and worry. Without preamble, she pulled me into her living room. "Are you alright?"

"Yes, I'm perfectly fine."

A few minutes later, I was settled on her sofa with a hot mug of tea clasped in my cold hands.

"What happened?" she asked, unable to hold back any longer. "Are you alright?"

"Stop it, Maddie, I'm fine. Quit looking so worried. I just did what a lot of girls are now doing when they are teenagers."

"Okay," she said, taking a deep breath.

I eyed her over my mug. "Why aren't you at work?"

"I took the day off, in case you needed me. I didn't know what state you'd be in."

That touched me. "Oh."

"So it was really okay?" she asked again. "I don't know how to believe that. It must have been traumatic."

"It wasn't actually."

"Are you lying to me?"

"I'm not," I responded immediately, "I got lucky."

Her eyes widened. "What do you mean?"

I thought for a moment what aspect of my great fortune I should share with her first.

"How much did you make?" she asked curiously.

"The other girl's got between thirty thousand and a hundred and ten."

"And you?" she asked, "you set your reserve at fifteen-thousand, right?"

"Yeah."

"Come on, what did you get?"

I raised the mug to my lips. "One million," I mumbled.

She laughed. "I don't think I heard you right, because it sounded like you said one million."

I put the cup down, and arranged myself. "You didn't hear wrong. I got one million."

Her jaw dropped. "One million what? Pounds?"

I nodded.

She unfolded her legs from underneath her and sat upright. "Is this all a scam?"

I shook my head and reached forward to grab my drink.

"How can it not be a scam?" she exploded. "What mad maniac pays one million pounds for one night with a girl?"

I abandoned the drink. "Brent Lucan."

At first, the name did not register with her. "I mean. You haven't got the money yet. So maybe they have no intention of payin—" She stopped suddenly. "Did you just say Brent Lucan?"

I nodded.

She shot out of the sofa and started pacing the floor "Are you serious?"

I nodded again.

"*That* Brent Lucan?"

"*That* Brent Lucan," I confirmed.

"The Duke of Leighton?"

"Well technically, his father is the Duke, he's just a lord now until his dad passes—"

"Whatever," she cut me off. "What the hell was he doing there? He buys virgins?" She leaned away in wonder. "Wow, just wow. On the surface, he seems so regal, but behind closed doors, this is what he's into?"

"He claims he doesn't usually buy virgins."

Her face screwed up in distaste at the blatant lie. "Really?"

"Yeah," I responded.

"So what was he doing there?"

"He owns the club."

She stopped pacing, and looked thoughtful. "And so ... Did he buy you to save you ... Did you still have to sleep with him?"

"Why would he save me?" I hissed, remembering the moment I had hoped he had done it because he wanted to protect me. "For a moment ... I thought he did it because of our families, but he didn't."

"You slept with him?"

"He paid a lot of money for it, didn't he?" I mumbled.

"Wow. Wow. Wow. Have you told Ella yet?"

"I sent her a text, but I think she's still sleeping."

We both remained silent like that for a little while, both lost in our thoughts.

Eventually she asked. "But why you? Did he do it to spite you? Because of what happened years ago?"

"I asked him the same question."

"And?"

I shrugged my shoulders. "No response. I think, he still resents me for it."

"Well, if that was the case, he wouldn't have paid so much money … unless his plan is not to give it to you. Has the money been sent to you? Have you checked your phone for any alerts?"

"I told him not to send it."

"What?" she shrieked. "Why?"

"How am I going to explain one million pounds in my account? I'll be flagged down for money laundering or something."

"Who's asking you to explain? It was a gift. They'll just call both parties to confirm it."

"That was the same thing he said, and it made sense but it wasn't what I wanted." I didn't want her to read into what I truly wanted, so I rose to my feet with my mug in hand. "And what about Mom? I don't want her finding out I sold my virginity at an auction."

She came after me. "Freya, why are you dragging this? Call him right now and tell him to send the money. Get this mess over with."

I focused on making myself another mug of tea while she watched me, surprised at how calm I was. "Freya!" she called, and when I still didn't respond she realized that something was off.

"Freya what's wrong … did that bastard hurt you?"

I shook my head and poured the hot water into my mug. My mother would have had a heart attack if she knew I was not properly brewing my tea in a teapot, but she was not here to witness my transgression so ...

"Then what's the problem?"

I stirred the mix until my mouth could open. "I want to see him again."

FREYA

I pretended to be nonchalant and let Maddie watch me with open-mouthed shock until I couldn't take it any longer. "You're going to catch some flies if you don't close your mouth," I said. Taking my mug with me, I returned to the living room.

She followed me.

I sat down on the couch and looked up at her.

She had closed her mouth and appeared to be working my words out in her brain. "Are you planning on having a relationship with him?" she demanded.

I responded as honestly as I could, "I don't know what I can have with him. I have this … this … connection with him. It's strange, weird and bizarre, but it's there…alive and beating like a heart. I know he doesn't feel the same. This morning he was going to walk out without even saying goodbye, but I couldn't bear the thought. My body actually wanted me to run to him, fall at his feet and beg him not to leave. Of course, my head didn't let me do anything so ridiculous so it came up with the next best option. If I had not done this, who knows if I'd ever see him again?"

"Wow," she said. "Freya, you're one insanely lucky girl. I was expecting some kinky old bastard to buy you, instead you ended up in bed with basically the only guy you've ever even shown an interest in."

My head snapped up then. "What?"

"And don't you dare try to deny you've been lusting after Brent Lucan for years! You shut up and sit down whenever he comes on TV. Should I remind you of how many magazines you have of him?"

"Okay, now you're just lying. He isn't even on magazines much."

"True, but every one he has been on, you own. It's actually beyond lucky. It's incredible. I can't believe he's the one you slept with. He's all you wanted. Wait till Ella hears this new … development."

"For fuck's sake, Maddie."

"Oh wow, you're cursing with the f word now," she crowed, and began cackling like an old witch. "You've tasted the forbidden fruit and become an adult."

"I'm going to bed," I said, and rose to my feet.

A few minutes later, I collapsed on her bed.

She jumped right in beside me.

"Maddie, I'm really tired," I said, hiding my face in her pillow.

"Just tell me one thing before you sleep. Was he good in bed?"

I sighed. I knew she wasn't going to leave till I did, so I gave her a response. "Yeah, he was good."

"Just good? No details?"

"When I wake up."

"Okay, just tell me this. Was he big?"

I felt myself flush. "Yes."

"Oh, my God. You lucky bitch you. How big?"

"I didn't take out my tape measure, okay?"

"alright. Ella is going to be so upset, though. You not only scored on the 'good first time', you found a man with a donkey cock. Even I'm jealous." She grinned to show she didn't mean it. "Go to sleep, then. I'll make you something to eat for when you get up." She shut the door.

I clenched my eyes shut, to try and stop the scenes from my night with Brent Lucan from flooding into my head, but no such luck. My head was full of the sound of our labored breathing as his cock thrust in and out of me … the sensation of my hands in his silky hair, the taste of his skin in my mouth.

I tossed and turned until I fell asleep from sheer exhaustion.

The sound of my cellphone jarred me awake. I dragged my eyelids open and saw Maddie trying to leave the room quietly.

"What is it?" I asked, groggy with sleep.

"Uh." She turned around. "I didn't want to wake you. You got a text."

"Oh?"

"It's from Barclays bank," she answered.

My heart caught in my throat. Without realizing it, I pulled the covers just a little higher. I suddenly felt cold.

"It was alerting you to a deposit. He sent the money, Freya."

A few seconds ticked by before I could nod in response. I felt empty and numb. "Thanks," I said, and shut my eyes.

She didn't leave. A little while passed before she spoke again, "Do you want dinner? I've made chicken casserole."

I knew she wasn't going to leave me alone so with a nod, I rose to my feet and followed her out. I sat at her tiny dining table by the corner while she served up two plates of her famous broccoli rice chicken casserole. We began to eat quietly as I tried to sort out the terrible pain in my chest.

He had cleanly cut off all contact between us. There would never be a reason to get in touch with him again. I didn't want to care, or feel anything, but the fork clattered from my hand as I turned to Maddie. I spoke before I could stop myself, "He didn't want to kiss me. What does that mean?"

Maddie raised her gaze to mine, but didn't say anything. She looked a bit sad.

I picked my fork back up again and pushed my food around. "Perhaps he ..."

"Perhaps he what?" she encouraged.

"I don't know." I picked up my phone on the table and unlocked it.

A few seconds later Ella was on the line. "Tell me everything," she responded, her mouth full.

"Ella, what does it mean when a guy doesn't kiss you?" My voice lowered. "I mean ... when he sleeps with you."

She sounded confused. "What are you saying?"

"Nothing," I muttered. In fact, I already knew what it meant. It meant he didn't want to.

"You mean while they're both having sex?"

"Yeah."

She burst out laughing.

"What's so funny?"

"I never heard of a man that didn't want to kiss a woman. It usually only happens with prostitutes. Kissing is deeply personal, and when they're fucking someone random for money, they don't do it. That way they can continue believing they haven't given anything important away. I guess it keeps them sane."

I lifted my gaze very calmly to Maddie.

She watched me with worried eyes.

Ella went on, "I suppose in a man's case, it could be he's just chasing the release, nothing else. Maybe that is what guys do when they are hate fucking."

"What the hell is that?"

103

"You know when you hate someone's guts, but you want to fuck them at the same time. Why are you asking by the way?" She stopped, and went quiet.

"Woah! Freya, did you ... did some guy not want to kiss you?"

"Hmm ..."

She went silent again. "How much did you get?"

"One million," I answered, the enormity of the amount hitting me all over again.

She choked on whatever she was stuffing her face with. When the coughing episode passed, she rasped into the phone, "Are you joking?"

"I'm not, and it's all thanks to you, babe." I handed the phone to Maddie, then I rose and returned to bed.

FREYA

That evening, I returned to work as though absolutely nothing had happened. However, a lot of things were now different.

For one, I didn't need to be there any longer, but I remained. I served customers with a smile, cleaned the floor with a mop when a child threw his food on it, put up with a drunken customer who pinched my bottom as I passed by his table. All the while thinking how life can change in a day... I was no longer the girl I'd been just a mere night ago.

Throughout my life, I had felt an emptiness I could not explain, like something was missing. Then it had meant nothing, but not anymore. Not after last night. Now I knew exactly what the craving was for. Until my body had joined with his, I had not known that I was just one piece. Another piece fitted perfectly with my piece and only when the two pieces were together was I whole and complete.

What scared me the most was that I almost couldn't picture him any longer. I knew what he looked like, but perhaps I had thought of him too much, or perhaps not enough. Every time I brought him to mind, the distinctiveness of his features seemed to fade farther and farther into the distance.

All I could feel were his fingers, gliding like feathers down my arms, the burn of his kisses across my skin, the feel of him inside of me. I recalled what it was like to be so completely filled, the walls of my sex, convulsing around his cock. I throbbed with arousal at the recollection of how my sex had sheathed him like a second skin.

I clenched my thighs at the memory. My underwear was already drenched, my breathing faster, and my stomach tight with the need to *fuck* him just one more time. To drive my hips up and down his impossibly thick cock, to have his arms on my waist, and my gaze lost in his lust-filled hazel ones.

Smash!

Someone blew their horn on the street outside and I jumped, my heart nearly popping out of my chest. It was followed by more deafening crashes, and I looked to see the tray of glasses that I had been standing next to was on the floor in what seemed like a thousand pieces. I lifted my head then to the other waitress, Melanie's confused gaze.

"What's wrong?" she asked. "Why did you jump like that?"

Flustered, I said the only thing I could, "I'm sorry. I'll pay for it all."

She frowned. "No need. That's fifty-quid's worth of glasses there. Go get the broom and dustpan and clean it up quickly before the boss sees it," she said, walking away towards the kitchen

If I continued like this I was going to lose it. Last night had to remain the only thing that it could ever be with Brent. A distant memory that had no business recurring in an endless loop inside my head.

"Freya, fucking get it together," I muttered under my breath as I went to get the broom and dustpan.

"I was supposed to be heading home but I ended up taking the bus to your house instead," I said into the phone to Maddie. Somehow, her little apartment had become our hideout.

"Are you on your way here now?" she asked.

"Nah, I jumped out at the next stop. I'm on my way home. Haven't seen Mom since yesterday morning. Just a second." I pulled the phone away from me ear. After attaching my ear piece, I slipped the phone into my pocket and headed over to a recently vacated seat on the bus. In the background, I could hear Ella asking who it was.

"I'm here too." Ella's voice screamed from the distance, when Maddie told her it was me.

"Why did you take it off speaker?" Ella complained. "Put it back on."

Maddie snapped. "It's not on speaker!"

"Then why can't I hear her?" Ella whined.

"Because she's not freaking saying anything."

"Hi, Ella," I greeted.

"Why are you not at work? Don't you have a shift tonight?"

"I got fired."

She burst out laughing.

"I told him I needed another night off and he went off on me."

"Life is funny," she said. "If this had happened a night ago, you would have been devastated."

"Perks of being a millionaire."

"What an understatement."

"Have you decided how you're going to hide your overnight wealth from your mother?" Ella asked.

"I thought about it all day, and the best I can come up with is some sudden internship at a big shot company. Then I can appear flush without actually showing her how much I have."

"No intern is paid enough to fund a mortgage and pay off their university fees. She'll still be worried when there's no longer any need to be. Why don't you just tell her the truth, plus she knows Lord Lucan ... perhaps she won't be too upset."

"You must be joking," I said. "My mom has her shallow ways but in this instance, I think she might actually kill me. It'll break her heart that I had to do it."

Maddie sighed. "If only Brent Lucan wasn't such a douche, he would have helped you out a bit. Is there no way you can reach him?"

I sighed. "Even if I could, I wouldn't. I couldn't get him out of my mind all day."

"In a bad way or ..."

"I don't know, but I thought I would never care much for sex."

"But ..."

"No, you don't understand. That man has a hold on me. I do things I would never do when I am around him. I'm still shocked at who I was last night."

"Uh, oh. Tell us more."

"That's enough detail for you," I said primly.

"I don't know," Ella said. "If it were me, I would seek him out and fuck him until I got him out of my system. I would just turn up at his office."

"And you think you would be let in?"

"Probably not, but maybe I should try it—"

"Shut that thought down, right now!" I shot back, my voice louder than I intended. It shocked me to know how much it hurt me to even think of him with beautiful sexy, Ella.

"Chill, babe. I was only joking."

"I'm sorry. I'm just stressed and so confused. I don't know what to do. I'm trying to picture his face ... but I can't."

"What does that even mean? You can't remember what he looks like?"

"No, not that. I ... oh ... forget it. I think I need to get it all straight in my head. I'll be better in a few days."

"In situations like this the best thing to do is to rip the bandage off in one go. Force yourself to snap out of it!" she said.

"For once, I have to agree with Maddie," Ella shouted in the background.

"Right. I'm at my stop. I'll call you both later."

"Bye," they both shouted.

FREYA

When I arrived home, my mother was waiting for me in our small living room, settled on the couch in front of the television. "You're back early," she said, and started to rise. "Why didn't you tell me? I would have made you something?"

"I'm fine, I ate at the restaurant."

"Oh, you had a shift this evening. How come you're back so early, then?"

"I was fired."

Only after the words left my mouth did I realize how I sounded.

It took her a few more moments to process what I had just said. "They fired you? Why?"

"I'm a lousy waitress, Mom," I replied as I headed into the kitchen and pulled the refrigerator open. I pulled out a can of Coke. "How's the store?"

"We're doing great," she thrilled. "We had a huge sale yesterday, and I'm pretty certain I'll be able to handle the mortgage arrears. Sorry for making you worry the other day."

I didn't believe a word of her report.

She looked nervous. As she leaned over the couch to get a good view of me, her smile slipped and her eyes were shifty.

I took a sip of cold Coke and made my voice sound light and casual. "I am searching for internships for my third year. I will make sure to get a paid one so that I can help out a little more."

She frowned at the piece of news. "An internship? Have you done interviews?"

"Not yet," I responded and turned towards the sink so she couldn't see my face. I couldn't remember the last time I lied to her. It didn't feel good, but I was doing it for her.

She went quiet for so long it made me think she knew I was lying. Then she spoke and her voice was trembling and I knew she had been too choked to speak. "I'll get all of our problems sorted out," she promised. "Don't worry about it."

"I trust you, Mom," I said softly, and was pleased at the smile it gave her.

She shifted on the couch. "Oh, Freya, do you remember the charity fundraiser that's usually held at Eaton every winter? I took you along to one a few years back."

"I do," I responded. "Terribly dull."

"Oh," she uttered softly.

Then my suspicion was confirmed. "Are you going to attend it this year?" I asked.

"Yes, I think I will."

"Oh, Mom, you can't do that."

"I was able to get myself an invite. I need to attend for the sake of the business. I want that crowd's patronage, so I need to socialize with them and win some of them over."

I was so taken aback. "Mom, that was your circle a year ago, but it's not anymore. They will all be there, all those people who turned their backs on us, and they all remember."

"I don't care," she said. "I did nothing wrong." She repositioned herself on the couch.

I left the kitchen and came over to her. "Most of the women that will be there you were acquainted with for years. Will you be okay, trying to get them to buy clothes from you?"

"I'm not asking for handouts, Freya, I'm promoting my business, and there's nothing to be ashamed of. Don't worry, I'll be immaculately dressed and no one will look down on me. They're going to ask me where my outfit is from, and I'll use that to draw them in. I've been opened half a year now and not gone very far, so I'm going to do whatever it takes to move ahead, for the both of us. Making business acquaintances are what these events are truly for. And that's what I'm going to do."

"That usually applies to their husbands, Mom. They get introduced to Dukes and oil magnates, while their women stand pretty on their arms and talk about their latest diamond purchase."

My mother pressed her lips together. "Freya, you don't have to come with me."

"It's not about that!" My voice rose. "I don't want anyone to look down on you, in any way. I won't take it."

She sighed then. "My mind is made up, Freya. I need to, at least try, for myself."

"Oh, Mom," I whispered, truly sad for her that she could not see what her friends were all about.

FREYA

THREE WEEKS LATER

The fundraiser was just as I remembered it.

Extravagant, highfalutin, and the last place on earth I wanted to be. No doubt, a handful of the attendees had some interest in the cause the event was promoting, and what they would eventually be donating to. The rest of the room however was filled with millionaire and billionaire hyenas looking to either show off their ill-gotten gains, or secure access to new territories.

The women were dressed in elaborate gowns and the men in tailored tuxedos. None however, could in my eyes, compare to the sheer elegance of my mother.

The velvet cobalt blue wrap dress was especially made for her, I was sure. Flipped thickly over her neck line in a perfect V, showing just a bit of cleavage and hanging off the shoulders, covering the tops of her long creamy arms. The electric fabric hugged her hips and extended to the floor in a soft, beautiful, train. Her hair was bobbed perfectly away from her face and matching sapphire stone earrings dangled from her lobes.

I, on the other hand, had put in little effort, only for her. My dress was a halter neck, mid length in black - a perfect reflection of my mood - while my hair had just been blow-dried and let loose.

We both walked in and like the rest of the guests we were shown to a spiraling flight of stairs that was intended to announce one's arrival. I could feel the room turn quiet as we stood at the head of the grand stairs. Surely, not everyone knew us and our history, but for those who did, we were most unwelcome.

I turned to look at my mother.

Her chin was high and there was a sophisticated smile playing on her lips. She wasn't going to let them decide how she felt.

I forced myself to relax. Since she believed this would help her, I had come ready to protect her. We were shown to our seats which just as I had expected, a table near the kitchen door and filled with unknown nobodies. I didn't mind that at all.

Mom however took a quick sip of water and got to her feet.

"Mom." I rose, feeling quite sick with worry.

At my hand on her arm, she turned and gave me a smile.

"Do you want me to come with you?" I asked.

"I'll be fine. We're not completely ostracized. I'll say hello to those who'll allow it and make some new friends."

I couldn't sit down, so I grabbed my clutch and kept my arm in hers. "Let's go," I said to her and we glided across the hall.

The center of the room was filled with sumptuous bouquets of snow white tulips and roses. Ignoring the many eyes watching us surreptitiously, I escorted my mom to wherever she was taking us.

She stopped to pick up two champagne flutes for us. As soon as I took my glass from her, she began to socialize. She was speaking to an aged but elegant couple I didn't recognize. The woman seemed to be asking her about her dress. My mom was smiling as she slipped her boutique card into the woman's hand.

Then she was off, ever the perfect socialite.

I remained her shadow. I tried not to drink too much champagne, but I was halfway through the third one before I realized I was already feeling a little light-headed.

When another couple she had been talking to moved along, she looked around for me.

I returned to her side and she held up a business card, her eyes sparkling with success. Although it made me happy that she was doing what she wanted, I wished that I could tell her she did not have to.

Next week I intended to drop the first news of internship money.

"Mrs. Evelyn Anderson?" someone called out.

Mom and I turned to see another elegant couple.

"I haven't seen you in ages," the woman said somewhat politely to her.

My mom instantly responded gracefully, their conversation full of smiles and small chatter.

Before Mom could introduce me, I gently slipped away, and once again retreated into the shadows. Perhaps none of this would be so bad after all.

A tray of finger food was passing by so I quickly stepped forward to grab something, but when I saw the Mallory twins approaching, I quickly turned away and retreated back to the shadows, but I was too late.

Eliza allowed her mouth to fall open at my presence while her sister, Elise's grin was filled with sick amusement.

"Freya! What are you doing here?" Elise asked brightly.

We had both grown up together in circles such as these. It was impossible not to become somewhat acquainted with the daughters of the big shot chairman of investment companies while my father had been in the same field, but thankfully, our paths never crossed in schools or anything beyond these kinds of social gatherings.

Perhaps it was the alcohol, or perhaps I didn't give a damn about much anymore, and especially not these two, but I slipped the smoked salmon on dill pikelets into my mouth and walked away without a word.

Searching for my mom, I saw she had moved on to a different set of acquaintances, this time a smaller group, and judging from her smiles I suspected she was doing okay. I left the hall and went in search of the bathroom.

A grandiose center arrangement of flowers had been placed in the Ladies. All of these touches of extravagance used to once be so familiar to me that I had thought little of it, but now it seemed so wasteful.

A few people came and went from the bathroom and I went into a corner stall. A loud group came in just as I was about to rise, so I sat back down for a little while longer, so that they would reapply their lipsticks or whatever business they had and be on their way. I had no desire to make small talk with anyone.

"Did you see Evelyn Anderson?" one began.

I instantly froze.

"I almost fell over when I did," came the response. "I had to hold onto my husband. We quickly walked away before she could spot us and come over for a meet and greet."

"What a shameless hussy," another puffed. "How could she still show her face in such a place after what her husband did?"

"What did he do?" someone else asked.

I rose to my feet.

"He was charged with massive fraud. He was the founder of this virtual reality company that claimed to have some over the top technology. My husband said he applied this to some game set specifically in Italy or Spain, I forget which, and it attracted millions in investment. Turns out it was all an exaggerated lie. The technology did exist but he stole it from some kid, but something must have gone wrong. The boy just disappeared one day and till today, his whereabouts are unknown, but he had put some malware into it so it couldn't be used. So everything eventually crumbled. What a coward though! He should be sitting in prison after defrauding his associates and investors, but he couldn't even own up to his crimes and accept the shame. The coward killed himself."

It felt as though someone had stabbed a knife into my heart. I held my hand to my chest. That was not what had happened. He had been sold the technology and then the boy had disappeared. He had been the one defrauded. *I* wanted to scream at them, but their words continued to wash over me.

"She has some kind of clothes shop now and she's going around begging everybody to buy something from her," another woman spoke up.

"What a brazen hussy. I almost told my husband to get someone from the committee to kick her out. I can't believe she was invited here," another voice spat spitefully.

"I saw that she brought her daughter along. Perhaps she's trying to find a husband for her. Good luck with that. No one here will touch her with a bargepole. She's toxic forever."

"But I heard that her husband was framed, and that was why he couldn't take the shame—"

"He wasn't framed!" came the argument from the first voice. "My husband was in charge of the investigation then and had direct access to all the facts."

"She shouldn't even be allowed here then."

"She tried to speak to my husband and me about her new boutique. When we showed her no interest, she had no choice but to move on. That's what we should all do. We should boycott her."

"I'll see how long I can stand her and then I'll get someone to kick her out," said a woman.

I thought I recognized her voice. Her husband used to do business with my father. She was always on the committee of Charity events.

Someone added something else that I couldn't catch, but no doubt spiteful and cruel, and they all laughed. It was followed by clicks of their heels as they headed out of the Ladies. Like a pack they came in, and like a pack they left.

Tears rolled down from my eyes at the memory of the father I had so loved, and of the last moment I had seen him, lifeless and hanging from the ceiling of our magnificent home back in Mayfair.

I rose to my feet then and pushed the door open. I wanted to run to my mother, and to quickly drag her with me out of here, but as I caught a glimpse of myself in the mirror, I loathed what I saw.

A spineless scurrying victim, indeed akin to the very rat they had ascribed us to.

My father had indeed been framed and no one in this room had any right to condemn us. We would be staying till the end no matter what. I went towards the mirror and after washing my hands, tidied my makeup and walked out into the party. But as I passed by the hallway leading to a small but glorious city garden, I couldn't help wandering out there. Just for a few minutes. Then I would rejoin the jackals, hyenas and cold-blooded crocodiles.

I was so numb I didn't realize my legs were trembling, but as I was walking down the short flight of stone steps my knees wobbled, my footing slipped, and I began to fall, my arms flailing out uselessly as I tried to grab something and caught only empty air. I would have tumbled down the short flight of steps and turned the nightmare evening into a complete disaster.

If not ...

For the strong arm that came around my waist to pull me up. Shutting my eyes with relief, I accepted the support and tried to regain my footing.

"Thank you," I breathed. Then something clicked inside me and my heart jumped. That aftershave. The strength of the hand. I glanced back to see the all too familiar hazel eyes of Brent Lucan. I wanted to move away, but he held me tightly in place. I tried to loosen his steel hold around my waist, but he refused to let go.

FREYA

"Why are you crying?"

"Let me go. Don't you know I'm toxic?" I muttered.

He frowned. "You're not toxic."

"Well, you should go back in there and tell all those fine folks that."

"Are you alright?"

"Let me go!" I repeated through clenched teeth, but to my shock, he scooped me into his arms.

"Brent!" I yelled in shock.

"I don't trust you on these stairs. I'll let you go at the base." He did as he promised and looked down at me curiously. He had on a long dark coat and a simple black tuxedo. His torso filled out the rich material, his dark hair slicked away from his face. He looked like he had stepped out of a James Bond movie.

I felt my heart start beating too fast.

"Why are you so upset?" he asked.

I wondered if he also knew. "Do you know about my father?"

He didn't miss a heartbeat. "What aspect are you asking about?"

"About the … reason he … he … took his own life."

"Yes, I know."

I didn't know how to feel. I shouldn't have cared but I did. I looked away and brushed my hair over my shoulder. "And what is your opinion about it?" I demanded. "Do you also think he was a fraud?"

"Why does what I think matter?"

"I just want to know," I insisted.

His eyes glittered. "Tune out the world, Freya. These gossips are nothing. Focus on yourself alone. You have enough money now to pay all your debts and concentrate on your education. You have your whole life ahead of you and if you play your cards right, you could have a wonderful life."

I stared at him wordlessly. "So you were helping me that night when you offered so much money for me?"

"No. Don't fool yourself. I'm not your hero. I was being selfish and making damn sure nobody else got you." His voice was harsh. It was clear he didn't want me to feel grateful to him or read more into his actions than he had intended.

I licked my lips nervously.

His eyes dropped to my mouth, and a strange expression

passed in his eyes. "Enjoy the rest of the evening," he said before suddenly turning around and walking away.

I stared at him, numb but for my drumming heart. His gait was enthralling. I couldn't understand how he pulled it off, but even in his evening wear, he had a lethal and effortless animal grace to him. Like a panther sitting on a warm rock and calmly observing the world as it churned in turmoil, while he watched with pity from his own ordered powerful domain.

"Brent," I called out, before I could stop myself.

He turned and glanced back at me.

I walked up to him. "I want to *feel* good again."

He glanced briefly around the courtyard, and then slipped his hands into the pocket of his coat. "Go on," he encouraged.

I gaped at him, furious that he wanted me to completely lay out my request. "Don't you understand what I mean?"

"No," he responded quietly. "I don't make assumptions."

I took a deep breath then. "I want you," I whispered hoarsely. "You have a few minutes to spare, don't you? I don't care where."

He watched me intently, his eyes darkening with primal lust.

In response, my chest swelled with a throbbing warmth that took my breath away.

He fished out his phone from his pocket and lifted it to his ear. "Bring the car back to where you just dropped me off," he said into it.

I went with him, my heart pounding loudly. What the hell

was happening to me? Was I under some kind of spell? As we walked past the garden pathway and towards the driveway, I started to consider that perhaps I was being too impetuous. Perhaps a quick phone call to Maddie right now would snap some sense back into me before it was too late.

Then Brent's midnight blue Rolls pulled up and the moment was gone.

FREYA

He held the door open for me, the fire in his gaze was a promise of what was to come.

I wanted to *feel*. I needed to wash away the hurt that was throbbing in my heart, and nothing else could do it but Brent, inside me, fucking me, taking me away to a place where there was no need to think.

"Is a hotel okay with yo—"

"No, the car is fine," I responded, not wanting to make anything whatsoever out of this. "We'll make it quick. Somewhere secluded." As the words left my mouth, it amazed me that I felt no shame whatsoever. Perhaps it was because we both knew that he was the only one I had ever been intimate with, so there was little risk of me coming off as promiscuous. I had a feeling he would have rejected the offer otherwise as he didn't seem like the kind to respond to just any call for a quick roll in the hay, but then maybe I was wrong about that too.

"Michael, find a secluded spot to park in, away from the lot," he instructed.

A few minutes later, Michael exited the car.

I was left staring at the massive but naked silhouette of the tree beyond the windshield, the rhythm of our breathing now the only sound in the car besides the steady hum of the running engine.

Brent's deep voice finally broke the silence, "What is this going to cost me?"

For a moment, I felt struck.

It took me a few more seconds to see that he meant absolutely nothing by the question. I realized by the frankness in his gaze that it wouldn't mean a thing to him if I said nothing or something. He didn't know me and I wanted to keep it that way.

"What are you willing to pay this time around?" I asked as I rose up from my side to position myself astride him.

"How much do you want?"

"Double," I said softly, as if I was really serious.

"That's a pretty expensive fuck."

I leaned forward, trailed his jawline with the tip of my nose, and breathed in his heady scent. Surrounded by his scent and warmth, I breathed him in and committed every little nuance to memory. This was just what I needed. I felt the knots inside my stomach slowly begin to unravel. I recalled then, like a splash of cold water that he had refused to kiss me even during our first time at the club.

"Why didn't you want to kiss me?" I asked, holding his gaze boldly.

He didn't retreat from the question. "I didn't want to give you too much head space."

"But fucking is okay?"

"Fucking is easier."

"So ... I'm just a body to you?"

"I think we both know the answer to that."

I waited to see if he would explain himself a bit more, but he just watched me intently with those glowing eyes of his. So, I closed my eyes and settled into the warmth of his body, letting it surround me like a shield; a shield from the ills of life outside the interior of this car. Slowly, he began to stroke his fingers lightly down my arm until my eyes fluttered open.

He shifted, and the movement rubbed my already wet underwear against his hardened crotch. He pulled at the delicate ribbons behind my neck that were holding up my dress. They unraveled and my dress fell apart exposing my breasts. They felt swollen and heavy. I pushed my chest out and he inhaled sharply.

His mouth latched on to my breast. I moaned as my arms cradled his head to my chest and my fingers dug into his hair. The rhythmic pull of his mouth on my nipples echoed the throb of my sex. I ground myself restlessly against his cock, seeking some kind of relief.

Waves of red hot lust rocked through me. It felt as if my bones were melting.

"I want to see you naked," he growled.

Quickly, I pulled the dress over my head. Before I could take my lacy thong off, he ripped it off me. I felt the sting of the rip and was glad that he was so eager to see me naked he could not wait for me to take it off myself. He flung away the destroyed strip of fabric and pushed me back so I was leaning against the partition that separated the front from the back of the car.

"Spread your thighs and show me your pussy," he ordered harshly.

Immediately, I opened my legs wide and exposed my wet, eager sex to his gaze.

"Look at you. You're soaking wet," he said huskily, as he inserted a thick finger into me.

I gasped and closed my eyes.

"Look at what I'm doing to you," he commanded.

There was something so erotic about a man leisurely and unhurriedly finger fucking a woman. I was so wet my pussy made sucking sounds as his fingers moved in and out of my puffy folds. He was calm and controlled, but I was not. My hips writhed and twisted uncontrollably as I tried to ride his palm.

All the while, he watched the total and absolute control he had over my naked body. As if I was his toy. He could have done anything, asked me to do anything and I would have done it.

I begged him to enter me, but he sucked hard on my nipples, and forced me to climax on his fingers. My chest was heaving and my breath was coming fast when I began to work with urgency on the buttons of his crisp dress shirt.

The longing to taste any part of him that I could have access to beyond his lips was strong so I could only work a few buttons before my mouth was on his smooth chest. I kissed my way across the ridges of his toned torso, my tongue tasting and relishing the heat and taste of his flawless skin. I felt his breath become harsh at the graze of my teeth on his nipple. I pulled at the small bud.

In seconds, his fly was undone and his hard cock had sprung free. "Now get your mouth on my dick."

I wanted to kiss him, needed to taste him fully, but he had restricted the act so I was only too happy to get on my knees and take his silky-smooth cock into my mouth. I sucked the thick hard shaft eagerly, swallowing more than I thought possible. The warm wet heat of my mouth made him drop his head back and groan.

His hands slid down to cup my breasts and pinch my nipples. "Fuck. I'm not going to be able to last." With a groan, he pushed a button to the left of me and brought out a condom packet. I didn't stop sucking. I sucked as if my life depended on it until he pulled me off his cock. I watched as he rolled the rubber over his huge throbbing length. Cupping my ass, he lifted me up and positioned me over his shaft.

My heart skipped several beats at the thought of that thick shaft inside me again. I grabbed it to fist from root to tip and stroked the head across the lips of my sex. Shutting my eyes, I positioned his thickly veined, hot cock at my opening, and let him impale me.

Oh, the sensation.

"Don't move," he rasped, as he too savored how greedily my walls gripped him.

I couldn't, however, remain still for too long. My hips began to buck, as wonderful tingles of pleasure shot through my veins and set me on fire. The moment his hands splayed on either side of my hips, I took it as my approval to set off. I rose along that thick tower slowly, and paused when the mushroom was all that was left inside me. I knew how it would feel when it was buried to the hilt inside me.

"Fuck," he groaned against my neck, when I slammed my ass back down on his groin.

I lifted myself and did it again. And again. And again …

The world outside ceased to exist. There was only this. Us. Our bodies, his hard cock, my wet cunt. Being with him was an escape like no other. I never wanted to break apart, or to return to the real world. Never. If I could just be here in this moment and time forever … It would be enough. It would be euphoria.

He shifted at that moment and I instantly turned my face away, terrified of revealing any bit of the raw emotions he had wrenched out of me. But to my surprise he suddenly caught my hand and locked me in place, his breathing ragged, and his eyes clenched shut.

He also did not want me to see into his soul.

Before I even understood what I was doing, I leaned forward and pressed my lips on his. I expected him to recoil from me. Instead, he grabbed my body and pressing me against his body, he began to kiss me back. It was no ordinary kiss though. He kissed like a man who had been starving for me. His tongue entering my mouth, hooking my own tongue and taking it back into his mouth. Once inside his mouth, he sucked it hard.

The kiss went on and on. Until I was breathless. Until my head was spinning. Suddenly, he pulled away. We stared at each other. Both of us shocked. His eyes were so dilated they were almost black. He was still inside me, but something had changed. I felt him pull away from me in some invisible way.

I had done the thing he had asked me not to do—I had kissed him.

He watched, without a word as I pulled myself off him. I threw my dress over my head and tied the ribbon with shaking hands.

He watched as I pushed my dress down and pulled at the door handle to scramble out of the car. For a split second, I thought he would call me back … even expected it, but I escaped from the car without any trouble. The moment I landed on my feet, I hurried away from the parking lot.

FREYA

I wanted to go straight home, especially as I saw the taxis passing by, but I didn't want to leave my mother alone. Anyway, I had to go back. I left my phone at our table. Even so, I dreaded returning to the Ladies to clean myself up. I knew I must look a state. It would just be fresh ammunition for those gossipy bitches.

Closing my eyes, I looked up to the vast night sky and allowed myself to feel. The waves of passion were still coursing softly through my body, almost making me forget how cold I was beginning to get. I couldn't believe I had kissed him. I thought about the kiss. No man had ever kissed me like that. I touched my lips and they were swollen. I thought about the expression in his eyes. He seemed shell-shocked, but he also seemed to be angry. I bit my lip. The way I left was childish. He didn't even come, but I panicked and ran off like an idiot.

There was nothing he could do about it, except decide never to see me ever again anyway.

What else was new? I was the toxic creature no man would touch with a bargepole, after all.

After stopping by the thankfully empty bathroom for some damage control, I headed back into the hall to see that most of the guests were already seated. I saw my mother waving to me to come take my seat, so I hurried over to the table.

A few minutes later, she was rearranging my bangs and I was brushing her off just as the announcer started to mention some of the big names present. My gaze wandered idly around the room. I wondered if he would come back to the party. I looked at the coveted tables in the front that would no doubt have been reserved for him

Just then, I saw him come in, alone, his coat off, his superbly cut suit, showing his body in all its glory. I couldn't take my eyes off him. He was shown to his seat, and slipped into it with a nod before turning his attention to the stage.

I tasted my lips to recall our kiss. It was the perfect punctuation to the explosion that was the session we'd just had together. *But was it a full stop, or a comma?*

Shaking my head to clear it, I decided not to care. It was just what it was. I'd needed to feel better, and now I did. Pulling my eyes away, I picked up the flute of champagne that had just been filled by a passing waiter, and began to sip slowly, doing my absolute best not to allow my eyes to go over in his direction, but more times than not, it did just that, and I didn't stop myself. Who knew when I would see him again?

"They're really going all out with these donations, aren't they," my mom leaned over to whisper. "How can someone just drop five million a go for a cause he probably doesn't care about?"

GEORGIA LE CARRE

"That's what dad used to do," I reminded her.

She wrinkled her nose at me. "Your father cared."

"No, he didn't, Mom. He did it for the same reason all these men are doing it. He wanted to be recognized as a great philanthropist."

"I refuse to believe that," Mom said, pulling away.

My mind went to what the women in the bathroom had said and once again, my heart began to ache. I felt my chest constrict with sorrow, so I dropped my head and tried to get myself back together.

Thankfully, dinner was announced. The waiters came around and I occupied myself with my phone while my mother made conversation with the people at our table. On a whim, I sent a text to Maddie.

I kissed him.

But her response did not come. She must be away from her phone. Bored, I picked at my food, the salty duck confit, and the near perfect gratin of potato, the delicious lime soufflé.

Brent looked quite occupied on his table with all the people around him, desperate to catch his attention and pull him into conversations.

As I watched him, I wondered just how much of me he recalled. He hadn't even turned around to search if I was present in the room.

You shouldn't care, my mind reminded me, and I nodded in agreement. Maddie's response came.

What the hell are you talking about?

136

I filled her in on what had happened and all I got was radio silence, even though the message had been clearly read. Eventually, her reply came back.

Can I call you?

I replied. *Yes, but I won't speak.*

A few seconds later, I answered her call and was greeted with a long-suffering sigh. "What the hell are you doing?"

Don't overreact, I wanted to say, but I held my tongue.

"Wasn't it meant to be just one night? You're both supposed to go your separate ways."

"We have," I muttered.

"Then why did you go to him again?"

"I didn't—" I began.

My mother had begun to frown at me.

With a smile at her, I excused myself. Holding the phone to my ear, I spoke as quietly as I could, "I didn't go to him."

"Who initiated it then?"

Spotting a waiter passing by, I sighed and went after him. "Maddie, you didn't call me just to scold me, did you? I was hurt about my dad. I overheard some bitches discussing him and he made me feel better. There's nothing else to it."

"Then what about the kiss?"

I shrugged my shoulders. "I just wanted to know what it would feel like. He definitely won't contact me after this, so you can relax?"

"So why did you even bother telling me then?"

Her sullenness made me smile. "I don't know. Maybe I was just bored."

Just then, I noticed a man coming up to me, a smile plastered on his face. At first, I ignored him, but I realized our eyes were locked and his smile wasn't faltering. I had absolutely no idea who he was, so I turned around to check if there was someone behind me.

There wasn't.

"Let me call you back," I said into the phone.

FREYA

The man was tall and well built, but his choice of the evening's attire was quite garish; a blood red velvet blazer and a silk dress shirt, open down to his chest. When he arrived in front of me, he got straight to the point. "May I have this dance?"

I blinked with astonishment. Men didn't come up to ask strangers to dance at these kinds of events. Besides, I thought everyone knew I was toxic. I recovered my equilibrium pretty fast. Smiling, I gave him the only answer I could, "No, thank you."

Ignoring my refusal, he made to reach for my hand so I quickly pulled away. The last thing I needed was more gossip at my expense.

"Oh, I do apologize. I've just been watching you for a while now, and I'm eager to have a little chat with you. Just one dance?" he pleaded.

I didn't want to be rude, especially given that the caliber of the event we were at did not encourage scenes. Regardless, I truly did not want to dance. "I don't want to dance," I repeated politely. "However, if there is something I can help you with I'll be happy to?"

His grin brightened even further, and although he seemed harmless, it still made me feel slightly paranoid that I was the butt of some joke.

"Don't you remember me?" he asked, showing me his palms.

My eyes narrowed. "No. I'm sorry, should I?"

"No?" He shook his head. "It's been a few years but I recognized you instantly. I'm Liam Lucan. We met in the kitchen of my father's manor house almost a decade ago. I believe you might have even saved me from certain death at my brother's hands."

My eyes widened. He was Brent's brother! God, I had absolutely no recollection of him. I could remember every detail of Brent's face from that day, but Liam's was a complete blur. I felt myself soften just a bit towards him. "I'm sorry, but you must have grown up a lot because I don't remember you at all."

"That's alright," he said, and held out his hand. "A dance?"

I looked at the hand and sighed inwardly. I guess one dance won't hurt. I could do with a friend in this hostile place. I was about to take his hand, when my phone rang. "Excuse me," I said and pulled it out to glance at the number. There was no ID. Under normal circumstances, I might have ignored it, but not right now. It was the perfect excuse to escape.

"Hello?" I answered, and at first, there was no response.

"Hello? Who is this?"

There was a lot of background noise, but when he spoke, I knew exactly who it was.

"Don't," Brent's commanding voice came through, "do it. Stay away from him."

I froze, taken aback that first of all he knew or had even bothered to store my number, and secondly, that he knew what was going on. I looked in the direction of his table. but couldn't get a clear line of vision with all the people moving around. "Why?" I asked into the receiver.

The next sound that followed was a rude beep. He had hung up.

I pulled the phone from my ear and turned back to look at his brother. I was going to step away, but a sudden surge of anger filled my heart. I didn't even want to dance with him, but Brent's tone pushed me in the opposite way. Based on what I recalled hearing between the two of them that day I had interrupted their savage argument, I had no business stepping in, but I needed to know what exactly Liam wanted to say to me, or perhaps, I just needed to piss Brent Lucan off.

Putting my phone away, I accepted Liam's hand, and was pulled onto the dance floor.

It was mighty uncomfortable being in such close proximity with him, especially since I was now aware of Brent's disapproval, but I sucked it up, ignored the sick feeling at the pit of my stomach and focused on not stumbling to the quick waltz. He danced expertly, but years of previous training came in handy, and soon I was able to take my overactive mind away from the dance moves to the strange man in front of me. I tried hard to, but I just could not detect any physical resemblance between him and Brent. Where Brent's nose was high and aristocratic, his was narrowed and almost girl-ish. His eyes were close set and a bit shifty, and his dirty blond hair was not quite the best complement to his pale skin.

"What did you want to talk to me about?" I asked.

He smiled at me and raised his hand to spin me around, which I found slightly irritating because I knew he had done that to avoid answering me. Refusing to ask the question again, I went on with the dance, stiffly enveloped inside the circle of his arm.

He laughed at whatever look was on my face. "You really hate dancing, don't you?"

I didn't bother to correct him that it had more to do with my partner, and overall circumstance, than the activity itself. "Yeah, I'll be done after this song," I said.

"Your wish is my command," he replied.

I exhaled like a bull. I'd never disliked someone instantly in my life and worse, I didn't even know why. Perhaps it was because of Brent. I submitted to the dance and not until it ended did he say another word.

"Thank you, Freya, for the dance," he said with a deep bow. "And thank you for saving me from Brent years ago. I'm so sorry that I couldn't do the same for you and your family. I truly apologize."

The hell?

"What do you—" I started to ask, but he was already walking away, and I was left in the middle of the dance floor, with a very stupid look on my face.

FREYA

"**B**rent didn't cut in at any point?" Maddie asked a few hours later on the phone.

"No, he bloody didn't," I fumed. "In fact, I didn't see him again. I think he left."

"Wow," she breathed the words out. "But what could his brother have meant by 'sorry I couldn't do the same for you?' Perhaps it was just a thoughtless comment."

"Perhaps," I replied, "but something keeps bothering me. I know these people, and that dance wasn't for nothing. Also, when he said that line, all the dazzle from his face disappeared. He acted like we were in a life and death game and he was giving me an important clue."

"That gives me the chills. By the way, do you remember what you heard when you walked in on them years ago? What was the argument about?"

I turned around on my pillow and lowered my voice so my mother wouldn't hear me from the living room. "Ten years ago and I was eleven, so I could have got the wrong end of the stick, but I think Liam Lucan was accusing Brent of trying to kill his mother."

Maddie went very quiet. "Whoa! Brent Lucan a killer? No way. That's not even funny."

"I'm not joking," I replied.

"Aren't they blood related?"

"No. Brent's father married Liam's mother after Brent's mother died," I replied. "But that's a whole other bitter situation. Anyway, Brent had a marble figurine held high over Liam's head and his neck gripped in his hand. If he had smashed it on him, he would surely have killed him. I got scared and ran in. I threatened Brent that I would expose him if he did it."

"That was impressively brave for an eleven-year old child!"

"Not really. I'd never met his brother, but I knew Brent. I had seen him at a friend's birthday party where he had been rude to me so I was annoyed with him, but I think I also secretly liked him and I didn't know what to do with it. I guess in my childish mind, I thought I would have one over him, but as Brent walked out of the room he stopped in front of me and told me I was going to pay for what I'd just done. His face was so black and thunderous I felt my blood freeze over."

"My God, Freya! And you still slept with him?"

"Um ... the first time, or the second time?"

"What the hell is wrong with you?" she yelled into the phone. "The man sounds like a right psycho. Stay away from him! And his brother."

"What about the money?" I asked. "Should I give it back?"

"No. Don't you dare! I'll never speak to you again if you do that. You earned that fair and square." With the sense of drama worthy of a Kardashian, she hung up on me.

I couldn't help my amusement. It was short-lived however. As I pulled the covers to my chin, and gazed at the ceiling, I knew something without doubt though.

Something was very wrong. And I intended to get to the bottom of it.

FREYA

A	uditing in Context, taught by Steve Barron, was one of the few classes I could usually sit through. The overweight, but still bikeresque instructor with silver white hair, cowboy boots, and distressed jeans held in place by a skull belt was usually visually entertaining enough to encourage a full attendance to what might otherwise be an extremely dull course.

Today was a first for me, as not only was I on time, but I was not in the midst of a constant battle with sleep because of abject exhaustion. I was however, distracted. Very distracted. My financial woes were now a thing of the past, but next in line was my worry about Brent and Liam and how I figured in that mess.

I was taking notes, but when I looked down at them, I saw they had stopped being legible quite a while ago. I threw my pen down in annoyance and exhaled noisily.

Stacy, my Jamaican classmate turned to me with amused eyes. "Today's class is not that bad."

Knowing our position by the corner would be an appropriate shield, I rested my cheek on my palm and turned towards her. "Do you think people constantly seek out troubles for themselves? Like when one is solved they move on to creating the next?"

She laughed softly.

"You laugh, but I'm dead serious," I said.

"Are you talking about yourself? What 'next trouble' are you spinning?" she whispered back.

I shook my head to end the conversation and turned back to my notes. Yeah, my new trouble is called *Pining over a man who seems to have difficulty recalling your existence.*

Forty-five minutes later, we were done with the class and we were separated into groups for our next project.

I found mine forming a small cluster of eight at the back of the auditorium. I was glad to find a familiar face in Abel Norman. We had once worked together on another project last year. He was tall, but so lanky that he always seemed as though he was leaning over, constantly on the verge of being snapped in two.

"What happened to your hair?" I asked as I walked up to him. "It was neon pink."

"Yeah, changed it three weeks ago," he said, his smile awkward. "Why are you talking to me?"

"What do you mean?"

"We've passed by each other multiple times and you've looked right through me."

I shook my head. "Oh, I definitely did not see you. I would have said hello, otherwise."

"We've literally been in the others line of vision and you just walked past."

"I'm really sorry I did that," I apologized. "For the past year, I've been working two jobs plus classes, so I was more like a zombie than a human being."

For a moment, he looked as though he wanted to prolong the beef, but then he shrugged and called a truce with his boyish grin. "We're heading out to Blue boat for a pint and maybe to discuss the project. Come along."

"Where's Blue boat?"

"It's the Pendle residence pub close to the library. You don't know it?"

My smile was apologetic. "Maybe it's because I Live off campus."

"You've been here almost two years now."

I smiled. "Stop making me feel like I've missed out on everything."

"You probably have," he said. "But not tonight. Wanna go?"

There were three other girls on our team, all of whom Abel was acquainted with, so I was introduced, and we were all on our way. It was only a fifteen-minute walk then I was seated with a glass of wine before me. The others teased me about being fancy, but I couldn't stomach beer. Since I could afford wine now, all was well.

"I heard you're bloody rich," a man's voice bellowed.

My heart seized, and I turned around to see one of the boys from another team had come over. I could also see that he was just a bit tipsy as he tried to pull out a chair several times, but missed the handle. I didn't want him to sit down, but fear fluttered in my chest at the possibility that someone had spotted me that night at the club and knew what I had received.

"What do you mean?" I asked cautiously.

"Your father," he said with a wet mouth.

Relief surged through my body as I rose to my feet and took my drink along with me. Unfortunately, in my rush to put distance between the idiot and myself I bumped into another student and spilled my blood red wine on the front of his rusty corduroy jacket. My eyes were agape with horror as I watched the liquid soak into his outfit.

"I'm so sorry," I apologized, horrified. "Can I get some napkins please?" I called out to the bartender, but he was too busy. I found some serviettes on a table and brought it to him. He took the serviettes from me and smiled. "It's alright," he said, taking his jacket off. "Now I have a reason to force you to have a drink with me."

I hesitated.

"I may or may not have allowed that to purposely happen."

I laughed. "You do know you're not helping your case at all."

He laughed too. "What can I say? I'm a moron."

"Nah," I refuted and took a seat. He was a nice guy giving out good vibes and I felt comfortable with him. If Brent was straight whiskey, this guy was a glass of fresh wholesome milk.

We got to talking about how I chucked all the fun by living off campus and missed out on probably the most exciting time of my life. There was time to make up for it now that I'd met him, he told me with a grin. To avoid his eyes, I looked up to the bar's muted television and Brent Lucan being reported on television.

Time stopped.

I couldn't hear what the caster was saying, but I didn't need to. It looked like he had once again been spotted with Judi Mirren at some posh restaurant in Pimlico. It was nothing new as their relationship had constantly been the talk of the town over the last two years, and made to continuously blaze since neither of them had ever denied or confirmed any of the relationship rumors that constantly besieged them.

I'd always been able to ignore it, as it had nothing to do with me, but not now. Technically, it still had absolutely nothing to do with me, but I couldn't look away. I watched, the taste in my mouth going completely sour as he and the actress exited the restaurant together. He pulled open the door to a black SUV for her and then went over to the driver's seat to buckle himself in. They zoomed off, but not before the cameras caught Brent's irritated expression through the windscreen.

I quickly took my hand away from my glass of wine before I cracked the stem in two. The hurt that twisted my insides numbed me to all else, especially the boy by my side who was carrying on with his monologue without noticing how utterly devastated I felt. Suddenly, the lively chatter of the bar and the excitement of my teammates a short distance away made me feel like I was an outsider who didn't belong. I drained the glass, excused myself from the boy's presence and went up to the bar for a refill.

The joy was completely gone from me as I fought the tears that wanted to well up in my eyes when I faced the truth: I could never have him. Two more glasses later, I headed over to the bathroom. I had no need for the visit except to hover over the delete button against Brent's number. I wanted to press it. I swear, I did. I tried to rouse all kinds of fury at him. He was rude, arrogant, brutish and cold and ... I glared at the number.

I should hate him. He was no good for me.

It was as if from outside myself that I watched myself begin to draft a message. It was angry and of what it said, I wasn't even sure. I should have called Maddie first for her opinion. Or even Ella. I should at least have read it again and made sure I hadn't just completely humiliated myself, but without giving myself any time to change my mind, I hit send.

I turned around to stare at myself in the mirror. I sensed I had just made a mistake that I would soon regret, but I did not care. I pulled out my hairbrush, brushed my hair, re-applied my lip gloss, and walked out of the Ladies.

He would receive it, but probably ignore it.

That was alright. I'd said my piece, whatever it was.

Even before I could get to the bar, my phone began to ring. I jumped. Then I hit the connect button and pressed my phone to my ear.

"Where are you?" he rasped.

"Campus bar," I replied. "Blue Boats."

He ended the call and I stared at the phone in shock. Rude man. That was not the response I had expected and 'Campus bar, Blue Boats' wasn't enough information to get him anywhere, *if* he was truly coming to me. I looked towards the bar's entrance and wondered if he would be able to find me. Did he even know what University I attended?

I took my seat, my heart beating like crazy, until I received my next text. I opened it with my heart in my mouth.

Outside.

FREYA

I wanted to rise but I couldn't seem to move. I remained where I was and listened to my teammates discuss our project without hearing a single word they were saying. Very soon another text came.

You have two minutes. Then I'm out of here.

I immediately scrambled to my feet, making my team mates all stop talking and stare at me in surprise. Grabbing my backpack, I apologized for my sudden exit, walked out of the bar and into the parking lot.

I saw the same black SUV I had seen on television earlier, with its engine running. I arrived at the window and the door was pushed open. I refused to look at him as I got in and even after I did, I leaned back and looked straight ahead.

He didn't look at me either and as unreasonable as it was, considering I wouldn't look at him, the fact of him not looking at me made my blood boil. I took a deep breath and my nostrils filled with his now familiar scent of musk and luxurious spices making me remember his naked body on top of me. It didn't help either that I felt as though the world was spinning round me.

Perhaps I was more intoxicated than I had judged.

"What was the text you sent to me about?" he asked.

I shut my eyes at the way his voice rolled down my skin. Jesus, I felt a bit sick. Beads of sweat gathered on my forehead and I was sure it was the car. I rolled down the glass just a little for some of the wintry air to filter through.

"Fuck. How much have you drunk?"

"None of your business," I croaked.

"Do you need to be sick?"

I shook my head. All I needed was the chill of the evening air. "I feel better now."

"What did my brother say to you last night?"

I braced myself and turned towards him. To my surprise, he had on a pair of dark rimmed reading glasses and as I stared at him, I felt my bones begin to melt. His sex appeal in that moment was beyond the usual primal lure. He seemed so sophisticated. So different. Almost as if he existed on a different world from the one in which I lived in.

My eyes roved over him hungrily.

He had on a thick cream turtleneck jumper and black jeans with his dark hair tousled away from his face.

I tore my gaze from him and looked away with a heavy heart. No one looked like Brent Lucan ... or could even come close. He was so vital, so special. So unforgettable. Unreplaceable.

I wished then, it had been some random stranger who had bought me that night. I'd always considered myself to be quite level-headed and sane, but in the presence of this man, I was slowly but surely losing my mind.

"I asked you a question, Freya." He sounded impatient.

"He said that he was sorry for not protecting me from you, the way I did for him years ago." I turned my head and looked at him.

Brent didn't blink, just continued staring at me.

I wondered what he was seeing or searching for, then I didn't want to know. "What did he mean by that?"

"How would I know? Why didn't you ask him what he meant?"

Asshole. I looked away, certain now of what he was seeing. A silly girl doing what she could to get his attention. I hated myself in that moment and worse, I hated him for turning what should have only been a momentary nightmare into a phase of addiction that had rendered me frighteningly brainless. I jerked the door handle suddenly, the door opened, and cold air rushed in. I don't even know what I was thinking of. I definitely had no intention of hurting myself or falling out, but Brent's reaction was shockingly fast and violent. In a heartbeat, his hand reached over to yank the door shut.

From his side, he pressed the control down and sealed me inside the car.

I turned to him in surprise.

"I'm not done talking to you," he said, his eyes watching me intently.

I hated how small my voice sounded but I couldn't help it. "Let me go."

"Why did you send me that text?" he asked.

I bit my lip and looked at my hands clasped tightly in my lap.

When I didn't respond, he went on, "Didn't we agree that we wouldn't see each other again? Or do you need to feel *good* again?"

"Well, what if I do?" I responded.

He leaned back into his chair, his arms folded across his chest. "What for, this time around?"

"Why do you want to know? It's not like you care."

Without a word, he grabbed the seat belt's strap and locked me in place.

My brain moved at a very slow pace with all the alcohol sloshing around in it and I felt almost confused by the barricade. "Brent," I called.

He started the engine and zoomed us both into the night.

I know I should have insisted he let me out, but instead I settled in and waited to see where he was taking me. About half an hour later, we arrived at the gate of a residential compound in Chelsea.

He parked the car in the driveway and immediately one of his staff came over to take his keys from him. I watched as he circled the car and then jerked my door open none too gently. He unbuckled my seat belt.

"Where are we?" I asked.

"You're intoxicated," he said to me. "Sleep it away and you'll be on your way tomorrow." With that, he turned around and walked into the house.

For a few minutes, I remained in the car deep in thought. Hmmm ... He should have driven me home if my intoxication was his concern. Why had he then, brought me to his home?

FREYA

B rent's townhouse was brighter and even bigger than I'd expected. Somehow, I had expected his taste to be dark and sinister, but instead it was an extremely tasteful palette of cream and brown with subtle silver accents. No doubt the creation of some talented interior designer.

There was no one to welcome me at the door and certainly no Brent to explain to me what I was supposed to do in a house of this magnitude. With little interest in sightseeing, I headed up the stairs, nearly breaking my neck in the process as my foot caught on the runner carpet. I managed to catch the banister, and gave myself a good talking to before I went up the marble grand staircase.

"You won't get rid of me that easily, Brent Lucan," I muttered as I reached the top step. I was faced with lots of doors. Undaunted, I boldly opened them all. Behind them, were lavishly decorated bedrooms that I supposed he expected me to just choose from while I held my peace till the next morning. I however, had no intention of doing that. Perhaps it was the alcohol still running wild in my system, or perhaps it was the fact that I had more than halfway lost my mind.

I told myself I wasn't staying, but just before I left, I wanted to speak to him. Give him a piece of my mind. How dare he bring me here, then abandon me like this? Who did he think he was? Bluebeard? Arrogant sod.

I opened another door and found what had to be the master bedroom. It was larger than all the other rooms and his jacket was carelessly strewn across the bed. Even in my state, I could hear the running shower. I marched towards the bathroom.

For a second, I hesitated.

What would Maddie do? Or even Ella?

Then intoxication prevailed and I walked boldly into the steamy marble room. He was behind the frosted glass of a massive shower stall. It seemed as if he was leaning his head against the wall as the water cascaded down his head, completely still, as if deep in thought.

With a shaky breath, I walked over to the glass stall and knocked softly on it. "I want to go home," I said to him. "My battery's dead. Call me a taxi please."

He remained still for a few more moments before he straightened and finger combed his hair away from his face.

I grabbed the handle of the stall and slid the door open. I was determined to keep my eyes solely on his face, but with the cascade of water rolling down the ridges of his torso, my gaze eventually followed all those lovely droplets to his groin to see that his cock was already rock hard at a ninety-degree angle to his body.

I took a step back unconsciously and dragged my gaze back to his.

He shifted away from the cascade and stood fully naked in front of me.

I felt my legs begin to dissolve under me. It must be a delayed effect of the alcohol. "Why did you bring me here?" I demanded loftily.

"You keep asking that," he said, his tone aloof. "Is there an answer that you would prefer?" He wasn't going to let me in. He wasn't going to let me know what exactly was going through his head.

I took a deep breath and thought about what I truly wanted to say to him, without restraints. I had a lot I wanted to say to him. A lot. "I'm surprised you were able to come at my request. You seemed to be quite busy with Judi Mirren." The moment I spoke, I felt disappointment and disgust with myself. Never had I sounded or felt so petty.

His eyes narrowed. "Is that why you're acting out?"

"I'm not acting out. You know what. You deserve to be left alone. Maybe you can call Judi Mirren around to take care of that massive erection you've got going on." I turned around and ran away, almost stumbling in my haste to get away.

I got as far as jerking open the door to his bedroom. Then all hell broke loose. The door was slammed closed. Before my mind could even begin to process what was going on, my arms were caught, I was spun around, and pushed against the door. With a hand beside my head to cage me in place, Brent stood close to me, his face glowering in a mixture of exasperation and something else.

His gloriously wet and naked body was only mere inches from mine.

My gaze slid down to his fully aroused dick, poking tauntingly at me. Bulging veins ran down the thick, heavy length, and every part of me began to ache in response. In that moment, I wanted to feel him more than anything else in the world. I wanted to hold his cock in my hands, and to slip that beautiful pink tip into my mouth, to take him deep into my throat while I fisted him so hard that he exploded in my throat, with my name and my name only on his lips, and on his mind.

I squirmed against the door, the folds between my legs now soaked, swollen, pulsing with the need to receive him. I lifted my gaze back up to his face and I could see that he knew exactly what I was thinking and how I was feeling. There was no denying my crazed attraction to this man. All I wanted was to be in his arms. He didn't have to love me, all I needed was for him to fuck me until I was out of my own mind. I slipped my coat off. My jumper followed, and I was left standing in my bra and jeans.

He came at me, and plunged his tongue into my mouth.

I moaned at the taste of him. There was no teasing quality or gentleness to his kiss. It was passionate, possessive, and raw. He pulled my lips into his mouth and sucked them with a fervency that made me feel as if I was drowning in a vortex of pure pleasure.

With his naked body against me, he locked his hand around my waist and pulled me tight against him as though he couldn't bear even an inch of space between us. I clung to his neck and savored the assault of his wet velvety tongue as I sucked wildly on it. He deepened the kiss, tightening his hold around me until my toes were lifted off the floor and I was no longer standing on solid ground.

Like a man dying of thirst in a desert who finds a cool fountain, he was insatiable. Our wild kiss continued. Completely unguarded and ruthless in its chase of the desperate need to be one with the other beyond even what was physically possible.

I felt as though I was drinking up all that he was, his essence, his thoughts, his ideas, his emotions, his feelings, his pain, his sweetness, his beauty, his horror, and in that moment, I felt as if I was him and he was me. I felt as if I was breathing through his mouth. Our limbs became so tangled so tightly pressed together, I didn't know where I stopped and he began.

All I did was *feel*: the rough, possessive caress of his hands as they roamed down my back and grabbed my ass, digging into me as he pressed me urgently into his groin. My hands moved from his neck, my nails raking his back as I moved my hands down to squeeze his perfect ass.

He put me back down on the floor so he could unbutton my jeans and drag them down my hips. With a roar, he ripped my little black thong off. Before I could brace myself, his hand was tightly cupped around my sex. Two fingers entered me and my pussy received him with feverish excitement. To my shock, he lifted his palm up and suddenly my feet left the floor. I whimpered at his brute strength, but there was no pause for recovery. My jeans were sliding on their own down to my ankles. A sweet fire started blazing through me as he held my body pinned against the wall and plunged his fingers in and out of me, furiously, while his thumb played with my clit.

"Brent," I cried. I had a vague awareness of him, pulling my jeans off my legs, and then hooking one hand around my knees to pull my leg up all the way to his chest for better access. I writhed and jerked in response, as my mind went completely blank. All I could do was chase the release he was driving me to, my entire body was tensed and rippling with pleasure.

I was so close to the edge when he pulled his fingers out of me. I jumped in panic but a second later, he was on his knees, my leg over his shoulder and his tongue digging into me. The scream caught in my throat as my body shuddered and exploded and I came all over him. He lapped up the juices shooting out of me, sucked feverishly on the delicate folds of my sex, and held onto my hips as I jerked violently in the aftermath. When he had licked me clean he rose to his feet, I collapsed on him, out of breath and incoherent.

He kissed me then and as I tasted myself on him, tears rolled down my eyes.

"Is this the kiss you wanted?" he asked harshly.

I threw my arms around him, refusing to let go. "I don't want you to kiss anyone else," I said and my words shamed me, but I couldn't take them back or pretend I hadn't said them. They were the truth. I pulled away to gaze into his eyes and saw him watching me intently. I could never read him and that drove me mad with frustration.

"Brent," I called, worry slithering down my spine.

"Okay."

I was struck dumb for a few seconds. "Okay, you won't kiss anyone else?"

"Yeah."

I tried hard but couldn't find a trace of sarcasm or mockery in his tone. He was dead serious. Then I had to go and ask, "What about Judi?"

"Judi and I were lovers a long time ago. We're just friends now."

"So you don't mind being seen with her in public, but not with me? It's because I'm toxic, isn't it?"

"You are toxic, but not for the reason you think."

I looked into his eyes. "Tell me the reason, then?"

"You're toxic the way heroin is. You come into my life and you take over, until there is nothing else but your body, your smell, your mouth, your taste, your sweet cunt, your voice, your silly ideas about me, the childish games you play with my idiot brother. I can't say no to you. The more I try to walk away, the more I want you. I can't get you out of my mind, Freya. Do you understand now?"

"What are you going to do?" I whispered, staring at him with wide eyes.

A few minutes later, I was hanging from his hips in the bathroom, our bodies slick with the heat from the shower, and the air swirling with the scent of our joining.

Now that I had permission *and* free reign, I couldn't stop kissing him again and again until he whirled me around and with my palms pressed against the wet tiles, he slammed into me, his heavy balls slamming against the curve of my ass. I sobbed while he panted with the fiery intensity of his lust.

"Fuck! Fuck," he cursed.

The sounds of his wild curses made my blood quicken with delight. There was no doubt that I was driving him just as crazy as he was me, and the sensation of power consumed me. This position drove him so deep inside of me, deeper than he'd ever been, and the walls of my pussy milked him ravenously, extracting every ounce of pleasure from him.

When he exploded inside of me, my whole body froze with the sheer force of his release. It occurred to me that we had not used a condom, but instead of being dismayed, the thought of his hot seed spurting deep into me made new ripples of pleasure crash through my body. His cry was animalistic, a growl, perhaps a mating call. Barely able to catch my breath, I grabbed his ass and pulled him towards me.

It took quite a while for us to return to some semblance of normality, and when we did, he tried to pull out of me, but I held on tight. "I don't think I can walk on my own," I whispered.

His soft chuckle close to my ears made me tremble. It was the first time I'd heard him sound so relaxed. Slipping his hands under my knees and neck, he carried me out of the bathroom towards the bedroom. He settled me on the bed and stood over me. "We didn't use a condo—"

"It's okay, I'll take care of it in the morning," I said quickly.

He nodded. "We should have showered."

He was right, we were a sticky delicious mess of sex, and

sweat, but there was no other state that I would have preferred in the whole world. "We're not done," I said to him, exhausted from that explosive climax, but still holding onto my dreams of giving back to him just as he had to me. "I want to take you in my mouth," I said, "and drive you mad."

His laughter once again in my ear was nothing but music, the sweetest kind. "You've already driven me mad."

"You'll teach me, won't you?" I asked.

"You don't need teaching, Freya. You were a born seductress."

"Really?" I whispered. With joy filling my heart, I began to lightly trace a tightly bunched, gleaming muscle in his thigh. As I watched, his cock began to stir. I looked up at his face.

He was staring down at my naked body. "You'll be the death of me, Freya," he groaned as he bent his head and captured my mouth in an all-encompassing kiss.

And it began all over again.

FREYA

I awoke the exact same way we had fallen asleep with Brent's hand around my waist. I looked down and the duvet was tangled around his hips.

I didn't want to move, but it hurt a little as he had been there I was certain all night, I looked up at his full head of hair and moved my hand to touch it.

I couldn't believe that I'd been this intimate with someone. My chest was bared with his impossibly warm, strong body glued to mine, but it was incredible how comfortable I felt. I looked out of the massive sliding windows at the view of the lustrous back garden beyond. It was snowing. Thank God, I sent my mom a text last night to tell her I wouldn't be coming home. I knew she would automatically assume I was going to spend the night with Maddie or Ella.

He stirred then and my heart seized, as I waited for him to come awake.

He lifted his head from the pillow and looked at me.

My mouth felt dry with nervousness. Would he be the same as he was yesterday or would he be cold and arrogant in the cold light of the morning?

When he noted my presence and our position, he rose without a word to sit on the edge of the bed, his back to me.

"It's snowing outside," I said.

I watched his smooth, tanned back, refusing to believe that he would withdraw from me after the night we had just had together.

He turned to look at me. Despite his tousled hair and the dark shadow of stubble, the regality of the man couldn't be dented.

"Is this how it's going to be?" I asked, trying my hardest to keep the hurt from my voice.

"There is a lot you don't understand," he said softly.

"Then explain it to me."

"I can't."

"If you're not ashamed to be seen with me, what is it?"

"It's complicated."

"Is it because of the sex club? Are you into kinky things?"

His lips quirked with amusement. "No, it's not the sex club. I am into kinky things, but nothing that cannot be shared and enjoyed with you."

I stared at him. "Then why do you have the sex club? What's it for other than for selling virgins?"

"Blue Butterfly is where people go for extreme sexual pleasure."

"What is that?" I asked curiously.

"Extreme pleasure can only be derived by special techniques, ancient secrets. I found out about them while I was living in Tibet. I met a very old monk who told me about these forgotten techniques. He said human sexuality had devolved to such an extent that we are now using sex to sell detergent and toothpaste and watching porn so full of violence it was toxic to the soul. He asked me if I would go back to England and start such a club, and he would send me the old women who knew the techniques to work in it. The techniques belonged to the people and needed to be relearned by humanity. One day I'll take you there and let you experience them."

I frowned. "Then why is it a club only for billionaires?"

"Because it is special and must be seen and treated as special before it can grow. Would you put your fifteen-thousand pound Louis Vuitton dress into the wash with your waitress uniform? Slowly, over a very long time the techniques will spread to the rest of the population."

"How did you know I was working as a waitress?"

"There's very little I don't know about you, Freya," he said very quietly, his eyes were suddenly shrouded. Then he stood, filling the room with his deliciously naked presence. When he spoke, I felt myself shudder ever so slightly.

"I'm running late for a meeting so I'll get someone to drive you home. I'll arrange a pill for you to take before you leave." With that, he walked away and shut the door behind him.

Wow! He didn't even trust me to get my own morning after pill!

≈

L ater that morning I was sitting in class deep in thought about the forgotten techniques taught in the Blue Butterfly when someone suddenly squatted by my side.

"Hey."

I looked down to see the nice guy I had spilled my red wine on yesterday evening. He was smiling at me and there was a twinkle in his eyes.

"Hey," I responded, wishing that I could be attracted to him instead of crazy about Brent.

"You disappeared last night," he complained, good naturedly.

I smiled. "Something urgent came up."

The class was restarting from the fifteen-minute break so he gave me a charming smile and rose to his feet. "See you around."

I nodded in agreement, and marveled at how detached I felt from my entire class. They all felt like complete strangers to me. This entire past year since my father passed away I had barely noticed anyone. I'd been too focused on my grief or on how to chip away at the mountain of debt his departure had left us. Now I had money, but the current headache was how to explain its existence to my mother.

Picking up my phone, I pulled up Brent's number. I had since calmed down from the sting of his less than loving departure that morning and chalked it up to the nature of our agreement.

I wanted to send him the message, the way a lover would, but I wondered if that would be too clingy. I put the phone away and tried to concentrate on the lecture, but five seconds later I had the phone back in my hand.

Can you talk? I need to ask you something.

I pressed the *send* button before I could think it through, just like I had done the previous night, and waited for the rewards or disaster of my action to arrive.

A painful hour passed, then the class came to an end. My teammates came by, so we could all attend our project planning meeting.

We headed downstairs to the lobby of the building and sat around a table to begin. I kept my phone away so I could concentrate, but I didn't have the heart to mute it. In case he answered. The moment it began to ring half-an-hour later, I jumped up and hurried over to the wall where it was charging.

The incoming number was unknown, but it wasn't Brent. It wasn't the one that he had used to contact me previously, anyway. I hesitated for a moment and then quickly picked it up. Perhaps it was another number of his. "Hello?" I answered, supporting the phone with both hands to keep it still. I hated how nervous I felt.

I waited for his voice, but it didn't come, instead someone unfamiliar responded.

"Who is this?" I asked.

"Hello, Freya. It's Liam Lucan. Can we talk?"

FREYA

Three hours later, I was seated in a glamorous cafe in West London.

Liam Lucan had said there was something very important I needed to know and that it could not wait. At first, I was reluctant to go, because I remembered Brent telling me he didn't want to be with me because of the childish game I had played with his brother when I had danced with him to make Brent jealous, but then Liam said the magic words.

"It's about your father, Freya."

I was sitting by the window facing the street, so the moment he arrived, I saw him. He got out of a burnt orange Mclaren, and took his time to acknowledge the cat whistles and buzz his vehicle garnered by some teenage boys who had hurried over from the bus stand to come and admire his car.

He found me easily, and took his seat with a smile.

I could barely work up one in response. My nerves were frayed as nothing about any of this felt right, especially as

Brent had warned me away from him, but I needed to hear what he had to say.

"Hello, Freya," he greeted formally. "Thanks for meeting me."

I nodded and waited as he placed a quick order for organic chrysanthemum tea. He was dressed more simply today, but no less opulent in a gray sweater and a charcoal thick coat. The skinny white pants that completed the look was sufficient enough to remind me of my unease of him.

"What do you want to talk to me about?" I asked, needing this meeting to come to an end as quickly as was possible.

He regarded me plainly. "To be honest, I didn't know how to take this up with you when we first met at the banquet, but in light of what I have found out since then, I think you will definitely want to know about this."

"What are you talking about?" I had a sick feeling in my stomach.

"I found out that you have quite an *interesting* physical relationship with my brother."

My heart slammed in my chest. "Excuse me?"

"I don't mean to offend you," he continued smoothly, "and it's none of my business, but I am quite certain that you wouldn't be doing that if you knew what he has done to your family."

I leaned back into the chair. I couldn't believe what I was hearing, but maybe I just didn't want to hear what he had to say because I knew it would hurt me. I hardened my heart, turned my gaze towards the window, and allowed him to continue.

"I'll keep this brief. I'm sure you're already aware that Brent remains close to the actress, Judi Mirren. They are not lovers, so the question is … why doesn't he break off with her the way he does with all the other women he beds?"

My ears perked up at the mention of her name and the acknowledgment that they were not lovers. I knew that no matter what he said from here onwards, no matter how bad it sounded it was going to contain some element of truth that was going to severely affect me.

"Judi's father, Rolland Mirren, was the owner of a venture capitalist firm. When he passed away five years ago, the company was of course, passed on to his only child, Judi. She has no interest in business affairs, so to the world it has seemed thus far as though she passed on its operations to the current CEO, Bradman Murray. This is not true. In the five years since her father has passed away, the company has jumped from being worth 150 million pounds to 450 million pounds. No mere CEO, especially one who has already been there since the company's inception could pull this off. So, I looked into it and just as I had suspected, it has a silent chairman. Her father passed the company to her, but must have handed its operations over to the only person he could trust to run it, Brent."

His tea arrived then and he leaned back into his chair, taking his time to leisurely sip from the glass teacup.

I turned a hard gaze to him. "Why the hell would he give his company to Brent? Is that because he is in a relationship with Judi?"

"He's not in a relationship with Judi," he corrected with a frown. "At least not that I know of. You know this, or else I doubt you'd be sleeping with him. Based on the premise of how you both reconnected, you don't seem to be the promiscuous kind."

My heart stopped. I glared at him, and he raised his hands up in the air, amused. "I'm sorry, I didn't mean to mention that."

Furious, and unable to take anymore, I rose to my feet.

"Don't leave," he said. "I'm not done."

"I am," I replied, and rose to pick up my backpack.

"Brent killed your father," he stated flatly.

My legs collapsed under me and I fell back heavily into the chair.

His voice quieted down as he went on. "I'm sure you know of the investment company that was the reason behind your father's downfall. After the software malfunctioned and they lost their investment, they painted your father as the thief who stole someone else's work. They stripped him of everything. Judi Mirren's company is called Gray Stallion's Capital, and they were the ones that created and fueled the entire case. And at the helm of it all was Brent."

Silence.

I lowered my gaze and when I saw that my hands were trembling I hid them from sight. "Is this a joke?" I somehow found my voice.

"It is not," he answered, "and I have all the proof you need."

I shut my eyes as my vision clouded up with tears. "Why are you telling me this?"

He was straight to the point. "Because I owe you for saving me all those years ago."

My head snapped to him then and I didn't care that he saw the tears in my eyes. "What?"

"Freya, the technology's original owner, David Styles, went missing. No traces of him have been found but I have been able to retrieve the backpack he had with him that day, and inside it was his phone. All the emails sent between him and your father prove that their relationship was a genuine one, and that he had no hand in getting rid of David is more than enough to clear his name and bring the truth to light. This way, you get to clear your father's name."

"So you're saying that you're doing this to help me?"

From the corner of my eyes, I saw him lean back into the chair and fold his arms across his chest. "You didn't let me finish. And I get to see Brent squirm like the worm he is. You don't know, but he tried to get David to sell to him directly, but the boy was loyal to your father and refused. Whether Brent truly went the other way and dealt with him, I am not certain, and this is one of the things that I want you to find out about."

"You want me to help you find things out?"

"Yes. Brent is no ordinary person. For anyone else, the circumstantial proof I have would have been enough to send them to prison. Not Brent. We have to have concrete proof and the ability to shake him up even a little, otherwise we would all end up wasting our time. Please don't think that you will be able to fight him on your own, especially not with that measly amount that he gave to you. It will dry up before you know it and you will be dragged into even more debt. This is not a battle that you can win on your own."

"And besides your deep gratitude to me for saving your life, you're willing to so graciously assist me because ...?"

I watched his lips stretch into a blindingly fake smile. "Because, in addition to your own inquiries, I have some of my own that I would like you to help me find out."

"Why? Why am I the one that has to find out stuff for you?"

"Because we have something in common. We both want to avenge the wrong done to someone we love and you seem to be the best person for the job so far. From what I have seen, it looks like he feels some guilt towards you. Which could be why he allowed your initial physical ... well, shall we just call it ... contact to happen, and why he paid so much."

I held on to my temper with difficulty. Supercilious asshole. I wanted to kick him in the groin.

Undaunted he went on, "Since there is still a physical relationship between you, I would hazard a guess that he is beginning to grow somewhat ... attached to you. We can exploit that weakness. By getting closer to him, perhaps he will drop his guard around you and you can find out all that we need to know."

"And what exactly do you need?"

All semblance of amusement left his face then as he leaned forward. "I need to find out if he has, or is making any plans to hurt either myself or my mother."

My eyes widened at his response. I did not expect that.

"A few weeks ago, he came to my father's birthday dinner and threatened my mother and I. My dear brother has many hateful flaws, but failing to keeping his word is not one of them. He meant every word and now I know that there is a gun pointed at me at all times. I just need to know what type of gun it is and where exactly he has it stationed, so that I can protect my family."

"Why the hell would he want to kill you?"

"I am sure to an extent you must have overheard the argument between us a decade ago. It's all related to that. I'm not allowed to tell you anymore so consider this your first assignment. If you're able to weaken him enough to get him to tell you the history of our family, then I will know for certain you are someone worthy of investing in. If you can't do that, then you are just a woman who warms his cold bed."

I gasped at the image his words produced.

"I should be going. Good luck and keep in touch."

He emptied his cup of tea, and I watched as he exited the restaurant.

FREYA

I sat in bed alone that night, completely bewildered.

I didn't know what to believe. Maybe I was being a sappy idiot, but I couldn't bring myself to believe that Brent had anything to do with my father's death. Even the idea made me shake with dread. He was everything to me and I just couldn't imagine giving him up now.

No, I'd rather trust Brent than Liam any day, and yet Liam had been convincing. As detestable as he was, I knew there was some truth in what he was saying. The problem was which part was true and which part was the lie?

I considered calling Maddie, but I knew she would immediately talk me out of everything, especially out of ever having anything to do with the Lucan family again. I also needed to talk to my mother and get her take on Liam's accusation, but it bothered me that it would reopen barely healed wounds, and force my relationship with Brent out in the open.

I remained on my bed in the dark, my arms around my knees and my head swirling endlessly with a maddening blend of dread and confusion. A message beeped its arrival on my phone, I looked down to see it was Brent's long awaited response to my message earlier in the day.

I was occupied. What do you need to ask?

I stared at the message, a couple of questions already coming to mind. Did you orchestrate the entire downfall of my father and family? was at the top of the list and the second sadly, which hurt just a bit more ... was why you purchased me and at such a ridiculous amount?

I dropped my head in my palms and rocked my body slowly. In the end, I couldn't take it any longer. I picked up the phone and called Maddie. After I explained it all to her, she went into the longest silence I had ever heard. It went on for so long, I literally had to keep asking her if she was still connected.

"I am. Just give me a minute. I'm thinking." The silence went on again until, eventually she spoke, "Can you forget about everything?"

I sighed. It was just as I had expected.

"Can you forget about it all? About Brent, about his brother and what he told you and about the club? Can you forget about all of this and just move on with *your* life? Your father is past, Freya. You need to start thinking of your future. And your mother's. How is helping this guy going to help either you or your mother?"

I answered as best as I could, "I don't know if I can forget everything and just move on as if nothing happened."

"If you go forward with this, you will dig yourself even deeper into whatever mess is going on between the both of them. To be perfectly honest, I really don't like the sound of what Liam is suggesting. He wants you to get involved in something that actually sounds dangerous."

"But what about what he said about my father?"

"He might have been lying. Even if he produces all the evidence he claims to have right now, how will you be able to prove its authenticity?"

"And what if he's telling the truth?"

"If he is, then do you want to open that can of worms? Are you willing to fight until the last with him to bring Brent down? And what retribution does Liam get from all of this? From what you mentioned about the past, Brent seemed to have a good reason behind his suspicion of his mother's death having something to do with his stepbrother. Perhaps he has never been able to do anything about it because he doesn't have the evidence. It doesn't make his suspicion untrue."

"He told Liam that he is going to kill both him and his mother, Maddie."

"You believe that?"

"I don't know. I'm just so confused."

"Even if that were true, it is none of your business. Right now, as we speak thousands if not hundreds of thousands of people are plotting the murder of someone. Are you going to become the champion for all of them?"

"Well, it is my business."

"Perhaps it was a bluff, or perhaps he was just trying to smoke them out in some way. You can't get involved, Freya, in any of this. If you want to find out more about your father, then do it on your own. Have nothing to do with the Lucans, starting from here onwards."

I said nothing.

"Excuse me. Did you hear what I said?"

"Yeah. Let me think about it, okay?"

"Okay. You do know that it is Ella's birthday tomorrow, right?"

Shit, I'd forgotten. "Yeah, yeah, of course. It's on me. Let's go somewhere nice and celebrate."

"Yay. You'll come over to mine."

"Okay."

"Goodnight then. Remember, you have your whole life ahead of you. Don't let either of the Lucan brothers manipulate you into playing their twisted games."

"Goodnight, Maddie. Thanks for being a real friend."

FREYA

Last year was the only year we had not gone out to celebrate Ella's birthday. The tradition had been abandoned in light of my family's tragedy.

When we were younger, it had involved the three of us sneaking out to cheap and discounted pub crawls, but this time around, I intended to sink some of my money on my two best friends. They had been with me through thick and thin and this would be one of the best ways of saying thank you. I decided I would take them to Black Fire. I didn't usually like going there, the drinks were expensive, and it was usually filled with cocaine-snorting Middle-eastern playboys, but Ella loved it there, so that was where we were going.

We went out shopping courtesy of me, then we got ready in Maddie's place and I hired a limo to take us to Soho. We drank champagne while they blew me kisses and threw comments about having their millionaire friend back. It was a members only club and since my father used to be a big spender there, Dom Perignon all night, all the staff knew me by name, so I called ahead and booked a table for us.

However, this would be my last splurge before I sat down and figured out our finances. Something I should have already done, but I'd been too distracted by Brent. And if I were honest, it was something I wasn't looking forward to. Having money in the bank again felt so good and I had a feeling all of our debts were going to wipe out fifty to seventy percent of what I had. Depending on what was left, I planned on paying off as much of Maddie's mortgage as I could and giving Ella some cash.

When we arrived at Black Fire, the bouncers allowed us to beat the queue and go right in. In no time, we were shown to our table close to the dancefloor. When my father used to come here, he would go straight to the VIP section, but I wasn't planning on buying champagne all night, so I did not ask for a table there. We ordered our drinks and went to the dance floor. It was already heaving with people. They were playing an old eighties song that my father loved and suddenly, I felt sad again.

I tried to pretend to my mother, Maddie and Ella that everything was fine, but my heart was broken. Brent had made three calls and left nineteen messages for me, but I had not opened them yet, even though I was dying to. I wanted to give myself a bit of time to think of what I needed to do. Everything had happened so fast, I felt almost paralyzed. I just needed a bit of time and distance to see the woods for the trees. If I acted now, in the heat of the moment, I might make a very big mistake.

Even though my heart said otherwise, my head knew: Brent was not for me. No matter which way you cut it, he was wrong. Even if he had not cheated my father and smeared his name, he was still too addictive. When he was around, I couldn't do anything. I hungered for him. Even now, huge chunks of my days were spent trying to get him out of my mind.

I finished my drink and yelled near Ella's ear over the loud music, "Refill!"

She nodded.

I headed over to our table and sat down. Sipping my vodka and cranberry, I looked around and spotted quite a number of couples grinding against each other amongst the crowds, and my mind couldn't help but wander again to Brent. If he were here now, what would it be like?

I realized I wanted to dance, but only with Brent Lucan. As I stroked the wedge of lime on the rim, I shut my eyes and wondered how it would feel to be completely in his arms in such a place. I never danced with guys in clubs because being groped by strangers was not particularly thrilling, so all I'd had was the dream that someday, I'd be able to have every-thing with the right man.

Right now, that lover had a name, but I was banned from even thinking of it.

"Hey!" Maddie screamed as she arrived. She was still danc-ing. She stopped dancing and looked at me. "You're having fun, aren't you?"

I gave a brilliant smile and lifted my glass. "Of course. Are you?"

She nodded vigorously, her neon pink eyeshadow sparkling on her eyelids. She ordered a refill of her cocktail and settled in beside me. We watched Ella let loose with complete strangers, yeah, they were Middle Eastern playboys, but for a moment, I envied how carefree she was. I was too reserved to let myself go like that. The only man who had made me behave like that was …

"You okay?" Maddie screamed.

"Of course," I yelled back.

"Just checking."

"You ask me that everyday." I wish she didn't keep asking, as it just took my mind back to places I didn't want it to go.

"I can't help it. You've grown quieter, Freya."

"I'm fine," I insisted, and got up. "Just going to the Ladies."

"Want me to come with you?" she asked hopefully.

"Nah, just guard my drink for me. I'll be back in a sec." I grinned at her to take the sting of my refusal. The moment I exited the dance floor and into the hallway, I immediately spotted the long queue ahead waiting for the bathroom.

Someone suddenly cut in front of me, forcing me to a stop. It was one of the staff, with a tray in his hands. "Hey, I know your Dad. I was really sorry to hear what happened. Not only was he a great tipper and great fun, he was also a nice guy."

I swallowed hard. After all the bad things people had said about my dad, it was wonderful to hear someone say something nice.

"Listen, are you trying to get to the toilet?"

I was so choked up I couldn't speak, so I just nodded.

"If you don't want to queue up for an hour, you can just use the VIP bathroom back there. Come on, I'll let you in."

I followed him past the red ropes, then he disappeared and I made my way to the VIP bathroom. I walked in to an empty, clean bathroom. I couldn't have been happier. In no time, I was done and in front of the mirror washing my hands when someone walked in. I glanced up then expecting to see a woman, instead Brent Lucan made his entrance and the breath was knocked out of me.

FREYA

For the longest time, I just stared at him and he did the same until I recovered enough to turn off the faucet. I wished I was strong enough to not even acknowledge his presence, but my hands were shaking and my eyes kept darting to his reflection. I tried to hide my trembling hands by wiping them as slowly as I could and then gluing them to my sides since all I had on was a strapless, black leather cropped top and a matching skirt.

I didn't dare meet his eyes. My heart was pounding so loudly that I was sure he could hear it in the deathly quiet space. I got my mouth to work, but my voice sounded strange. "What are you doing here?"

"Looking for you. Why else would I be in this dump?"

"But how did you know I would be here? Did you follow us?"

"No, I asked my secretary to call your mother and pretend to be one of your friends," he admitted.

"That's devious," I whispered, my brain blank. He went to all that trouble to find me.

His mouth twisted. "Hardly."

"Why?"

"You disappeared," he said simply.

I couldn't tell him here. I needed time. "I tried to contact you, but you didn't respond ... in time."

"And so you decided not to bother again?" he asked softly.

In his eyes, I saw the restrained anger. I wanted to feel nothing. I wanted to walk away and have this conversation another day, when I was not dressed in a small leather dress, or trapped in a club's toilet, but my skin was prickling with the awareness of his presence. The room was suddenly too small, too hot, too suffocating. I needed to leave, so I moved forward, but stopped a considerable distance away from him.

"I need to leave," I stated as coldly as I could.

"Why didn't you respond to me, Freya?"

"It doesn't matter," I replied.

"Are you toying with me on purpose?" he asked, his eyes flashing.

As I watched him, I finally realized what was going on. He had been affected by my absence! My eyes widened in surprise at the idea.

He turned away in exasperation, or perhaps it was to hide his vulnerability.

"I didn't expect you to care whether I disappeared or not."

His reaction was instant and explosive. He came for me like a wild animal. I took several steps backwards, my eyes fixated on him, my pulse racing crazily. My back hit the sink counter and he was upon me, his face so close to mine I could see the beautiful streaks of gold in his eyes.

His familiar scent filled my nostrils and swirled around me like an aphrodisiac. I lowered my gaze and put out a hand to keep him away. It landed on his chest—it was useless, and we both knew it. I was already losing my ability to stand. If not for the counter behind me, I would surely have landed in a pool at his feet. My bones had already started melting.

His voice was deathly cold as he spoke, "You didn't expect me to care?"

I opened my mouth to speak and his tongue found its way in.

That first contact ... completely did me in.

The shot of pleasure to my groin instantly knocked out my knees. His arm shot around my waist to hold me up. His tongue hooked mine and sucked it into his mouth. Heat filled me. I felt feverish with all the emotions he was wreaking through my entire body. My sex was throbbing and pulsing at the return of its master. It was already soaked and ready with unashamed need for him.

The voice of reason at the back of my mind was silent. I was panting.

He pulled away from me suddenly.

We stared at each other. Our ragged breathing was deafening in the cold, empty space.

"Why did you cut me off?"

"I don't owe you anything."

"No, Freya," he responded. "You owe me. You taunted me into a relationship with you and then you just disappeared without any warning. Am I supposed to just let that go and move on?"

I was taken aback. Liam had mentioned this. Brent Lucan did not let things go. Liam had also said, Brent Lucan was unforgiving and ruthless, and if you ever hurt him, he was sure to hurt you back multiple times over. "Why do you sound like the victim here?"

His eyebrows rose with incredulity. "Do you believe yourself to be a victim?"

"Why do you even want me?" I asked. "There are so many other women around that you could have."

"Why did you ask me to make you feel good at the charity event? There were so many other men who could have made you feel better."

Suddenly I couldn't take it anymore. I couldn't stand that he could be so calm and guiltless, and have absolutely no qualms about sleeping with the daughter of the man he had probably ruined. I couldn't hold my tongue any longer. Somewhere at the back of my mind I also suspected that Brent feared no one, or thing, and thus would never sink low enough to lie. Perhaps I was wrong. I would soon find out. "Don't you feel any guilt?"

He frowned. "About what?"

It was so hard to breathe. It felt as though time had stopped and yet again, everything was about to change. "About my father and about my family."

His eyes narrowed. "Why would I feel guilt?"

I wanted him to assume I knew much more than I did to trick him into giving up information. I treaded carefully. Making my accusation general. His response could mean nothing, or everything. "You put us in quite a mess," I said. "We're struggling like this because of you. How can you have no qualms whatsoever about sleeping with me after what you did to him? I lost my father because of you."

With a bored sigh, he folded his arms across his chest. "Freya, if you truly knew what happened to your father you wouldn't be asking me these questions or making these unfounded accusations."

It felt as though the bubble around me shattered. "What?"

"Who told you that I was responsible for your father's death?"

I panicked as I thought of what to say, it felt like I was about to be shut down. "Are you saying that you aren't?" My nails dug into my hands with anxiety as I waited on his response.

"Why would I be? He wasn't murdered, he took his own life."

My blood began to boil. "Didn't you contribute to it? Aren't you the one who accused him and his entire company of fraud and possibly of murder?" My voice had become a screech, but I couldn't stop. All the pain, sorrow and confusion I had kept inside me came flooding out. "I loved my father. He was strong and ambitious and he loved my mother. He would never have taken his life if you had not destroyed him. And now we are like pariahs in our community. Everywhere we go, we are whispered about and mocked. I had to watch my mother crawl around on the floor begging for a bit more time to pay her bills. That's what you've done to my family. Do you understand, Brent? I LOVED my father!" I shouted. Tears were now pouring out of my eyes. I didn't attempt to hide or wipe them away. I let him see how ugly my pain was.

His eyes grew shrouded.

"Aren't you going to answer me?" I demanded furiously.

"What answer do you want from me?" he asked. "And would you believe it?"

"Are you fucking responsible for my father's death or not?" I hurled at him.

"I am not." Then he turned around and walked out of the bathroom.

All the fight went out of me as I slumped back against the sink.

FREYA

I returned home in the early hours of the morning to see my mother asleep at the dining table, her face resting on her arm, her reading glasses pushed into her cheek. Spread on the small glass table were sheets of papers. I went over to her and as gently as I could, removed her glasses.

She jumped awake. "Oh, Freya," she whispered, looking up at me with a slightly disorientated expression.

I took in her sunken eyes, the red mark left by her glasses on her cheek and her scrunched up messy hair, then I pulled out the chair beside her and sat down. "What's wrong, Mom?"

"Nothing is wrong. I just fell asleep. I must have been tired. Did you have a good time tonight?" She patted her hair and began to gather the papers.

"I'm not a child anymore. Tell me."

"I know you're not a child, Freya."

"Then what is it? You don't want me to be worried?"

"Well ..."

"You can't shoulder all of this alone."

"I won't," she said. "Not anymore. I'm going to see your aunt Bethany and ask her to lend us some money."

I reared back. "No, Mom. You can't do that. You cut off all contact with her years ago because she used to treat you like shit. She'll make you grovel for the money."

"I know," she replied, lifting her chin. "But it's either that or we lose our home."

"What?"

"I'm sorry honey, but I need to raise sixty thousand pounds by the day after tomorrow, or we're going to be kicked out of here by the Bailiffs."

My heart seized, realizing it was worse than I thought. "Sixty thousand pounds. Mom? How long has this been going on?"

"I just thought I'd deal with it later. I didn't realize it was already a court matter. The court sent the order two weeks ago. I hoped I'd be able to gather enough before tomorrow, but ..." She bit her lip, "I barely have eight thousand."

My jaw dropped. While I've been mooning over Brent, my mother has had this axe hanging over her head. I had the money in the bank. I just needed to find a way to tell my mom about it. "Mom, Aunt Bethany is not going to lend you sixty thousand pounds."

"If Bethany refuses me, we still have some of your father's associates. Perhaps they'll be able to chip in a little bit for us. Your father did a lot for them while he was alive. They owe us some help." She patted my hand. "Don't worry honey. I'll handle it."

She got up to walk away and the ache in my heart constricted my throat. "Mom?" I cried.

"Yes, darling"

"Don't go anywhere!" I said, rising to my feet. "I'll get you the money tomorrow."

She looked at me blankly. "How?"

"I already have it."

She sat down heavily. "You have that amount of money? Where did you get sixty thousand pounds from?"

I swallowed, and allowed the words to just flow out, "I got a job."

"That pays you sixty thousand pounds?"

"Uh." I couldn't look her in the eyes. "It's over a period. My course's work placement begins in January so I asked them for a large advance, you know to help out. It's more like a student loan. I have to pay it back, of course." I knew I had started babbling so I snapped my mouth shut.

"And they're willing to grant you the sixty thousand pounds?"

I didn't blame her for her skepticism. I sounded like I was out of my mind. "It's a chartered firm my professor recommended to me. He knows the partners personally so when I made the request today after explaining my situation, he promised to vouch for me. They've agreed to grant it to me to be repaid in installments at later dates."

For the longest time, she was quiet, but Mom was never knowledgeable about finances, so I prayed with all of my heart that she would buy into it.

Then she leaned forward and hugged me tightly. For a while, we just held each other in silence then I felt my coat become damp with her tears. And that was the moment I knew for sure that I had done the right thing to sell my virginity at the club. No matter what happened between me and Brent—I had done right by my mother.

FREYA

Five hours later, I was going mad with frustration as I sat in the customer service section of Barclays Bank pondering on what to do next. Over the last one-and-a-half hours I had been passed between departments in a bid to figure out why the hell my account had suddenly been frozen. Until now, no clear explanation had been given to me except some vague statements about investigations, standard procedures at sudden and unexpected transactions, and suspicions of those monies being linked to money laundering activities.

I had tried my best to avoid any involvement with Brent, I eventually had to pick up the phone to dial his number. I listened to it ring and prayed with all of my heart that he would respond.

He did.

"Brent," I said swallowing my anxiety, "Barclays says that your bank will have to send a swift message confirming that the money you deposited is legal. Please contact them to get this sorted out."

"Okay," he said calmly, and ended the call.

A few minutes later, his call came through to relay disheartening news. "They can only do that if Barclays instigates a request. Hand the phone over to the staff in charge."

I shot to my feet and went in search of help.

Brent got his call escalated to a manager. Her response was simple. She had no authority to intervene in the standard protocol put in place. I could hear Brent losing his temper. He asked her if that was the same procedure they used when they laundered the money of the drug cartels. She went stiff and doubled down on her insistence that there was nothing she could do. She was just a cog in the machinery. She infuriated him so much he cut the line. Red-faced she turned to me and said she would make enquiries and try to hurry the process along for me.

"I don't have time. I need the money today or else I'm going to lose my home."

"I apologize," came her lifeless, uncaring response. "We are instructed by the government to flag down and thoroughly investigate any suspicions of fraudulent activity in our customer's accounts. Once the investigation is over, your account may be restored if no issues arise, however if otherwise, other stringent resolutions will follow."

I wanted to tear her skin off her body, but I managed to calm myself and walk out of the bank. Once I was on the bus, I shut my eyes and tried to figure out what to do. First, I called my mother to ensure that she had heeded my warning.

"Did you get the money, Freya?" she asked eagerly.

I hated to disappoint her. "Er ... no, but I will."

"Oh, never mind. It was a long shot, anyway."

"Mom, you didn't go asking anyone for money, did you?"

Her sigh was heavy and it terrified me that she might have. "Mom!"

"Well, I made a few calls. I've set up some meetings for tomorrow."

"Mom!" I cried.

"Freya, don't be so upset. We wi—"

"Mom, I don't care what happens. You're not going to see those people. I don't want you to beg from anyone. So what if we lose our home? We'll use the eight thousand we have now to get a temporary place, then once my money comes in, we'll buy ourselves a small place, okay?"

"It's grandma's home," she said to me. "We can't let them take it away. It's your inheritance."

I tried hard to keep my voice bright and happy. "It's okay, Mom. It's okay. We'll manage."

"Come home now," she said to me. "We need to talk about this."

"I'm already on the bus and on my way."

"I love you, Freya."

"I love you too, Mom," I said and my voice broke. Once we had been so rich and look at us now. I had money I couldn't touch and we were about to be kicked out of our home.

My mother and I began to pack up almost as soon as I got home. We didn't say a word to each other beyond the practical comments of where what should go and the surprise of just how much stuff we had. Maddie had said we could stay at her apartment until we found a place and she would go stay with Ella.

I burst into tears when they came around to tell me that. We had a group hug and bawled our eyes out. Afterwards, they helped too. Everything was in boxes when an envelope was pushed through the door. It bore the mark of the bailiffs, and I opened it with shaking hands.

And … stared at it in shock.

"What is it?" Ella asked at the look on my face.

I couldn't speak.

"Honey," my mom called.

Maddie snatched the letter out of my hand. "Let me see that," she said taking over.

"What's going on?" my mother asked, her voice thin with worry.

Maddie looked up from the letter. "The arrears for the loan against the apartment has been paid. The bailiffs have been called off."

My mother crumpled into a heap on the floor.

I hurried over to her. "Mom?"

"How? By whom?" she whispered.

"They don't say," Maddie said.

"Yay!" Ella screamed.

"Well, I went to your uncle Leslie yesterday, but he wasn't very welcoming. Was he the one? But then ... I didn't even get the chance to mention the amount before I was shut down. How did he know where to go or how much to pay?"

Both Maddie and Ella looked at me with knowing expressions.

I looked away, and the sickening feeling returned to my stomach. I excused myself and escaped to my room. There, I thought long and hard, and eventually picked up my phone. I dialed Brent's number multiple times but could not reach him.

Both Ella and Maddie came into my room.

"You want to go to him, don't you?" Ella asked.

I nodded dumbly.

"Just go," Ella said softly. "We'll sort everything out with your Mom."

"What if he had something to do with my Dad's death,?" I whispered.

"He is innocent until proven guilty. No matter what, he just saved your ass for you, Freya. Go say thank you."

I grabbed my coat and ran out of the apartment after telling my mother some yarn about having to meet a fellow student.

FREYA

It was already late evening and devastatingly cold when I took the train to Brent's home in Chelsea. To my surprise, I didn't even have to ring the bell before I was immediately let in through the gates.

When I arrived at the door, a thin man in acid washed jeans introduced himself as Brent's PA. His name was Michael and he seemed to know exactly who I was. "Let me take you to him. He's in his study," he said. After a brief knock, he opened the door.

I walked in to meet Brent seated behind a heavy oak desk. He was on the phone. He indicated with his palm that I should take a seat opposite him.

I just stood close to the door and looked around me so I wouldn't have to look at him and his devastating beauty. The space was lavishly endowed with wall to ceiling bookshelves, an antique fireplace and mantle, leather furnishes.

I tried my best to keep my nerves, and the memories of the

last time I had been in the house at bay. Soon, he was done with his call and I was forced to look at him.

He was wearing a sky-blue sweater that hugged his broad shoulders and the warmth from the room and fire, gave his skin the sheen of warm milk. I wanted nothing more than to run my fingers through his hair, have his beautiful mouth on my breasts, and his hard cock inside of me. Would every man I tried to love from now on, always fall short of him? *Jesus! Love?* Where did that come from? I must be losing my mind.

He was watching me quietly.

I cleared my throat. "Oh … uh," I began. "Did you … Did you pay the arrears outstanding on my mother's apartment?"

"I did," he responded.

I wasn't touched … I was just speechless. "Why?"

He shrugged. "I hate it when banks bully their most vulnerable customers."

I had never been so confused. "Why are you doing this?" I asked. "Are you trying to guilt me into sleeping with you?"

He grinned suddenly. "Freya, I don't need to guilt you into anything. With or without the money, I could have you any time I wanted to."

At my widened gaze, he cocked his head. "Is that not true?"

"You speak as if I have no say in the matter," I retorted annoyed.

He looked genuinely amused as he rose to his feet.

I staggered backwards a few steps before I caught myself. I was not afraid of him.

He began to circle the desk and the air was suddenly charged with danger and tension.

I started to feel like a prey. "Brent," I called.

He smiled. "You're already out of breath."

"Don't touch me," I cried, but I wanted nothing more in that moment than to kiss him. I almost couldn't believe that those lips had been on the most intimate parts of my body.

"Oh, don't worry, I won't," he said, stopping just a couple of feet away from me.

My heart fell into my stomach with disappointment, especially since the scent of him was filling my nostrils. That scent … of tobacco and musk. I was certain it would forever haunt me. I couldn't stop my eyes from drifting down to the expertly tailored dark slacks.

He laughed, and I hurriedly dragged my gaze back to his.

"I won't touch you," he said, "until we have an agreement in place."

"Agreement?"

His lips spread to reveal his perfect teeth, in what would have seemed to the casual onlooker that he was smiling, but I could tell from his eyes there was not an amused bone in his body. "You see I have a very vivid memory. I can't stop thinking of how sweet your cunt tastes or those little mewing kitten sounds you make when I run my tongue along your slit. It blows my mind and has made the past few weeks excruciatingly difficult for me. I'm constantly distracted at work … and it really pisses me off when I can't concentrate on the job at hand. I can tell just by looking at you now that it is the same for you. So how about you and me stay together for a month. The goal is to get you out of my system and me out of yours."

I couldn't believe what he was saying and my heart was beating ferociously.

"I didn't kill your father," he continued. "And if that's what's holding you back, and if it was indeed Liam who put such a crazy idea into your head, then you can go back and tell him that I'm especially angry now. His death was meant to be slow, but now, tell him to expect the worst in a few weeks. Let that drive him crazy just as you're doing to me right now."

"Brent!" I gasped, shocked out of my mind. "You can't say things like that."

"Why the fuck not?" he asked, his brows furrowing into a deep frown as he slipped his hands into his pocket. "Do you think I'm joking? Liam knows me. He knows I mean every word I say. You don't have to believe me, but he will."

"Are you stupid? Do you want to fucking throw your life away? If anything happened to him, you're going to be ruined."

His smile was mocking. "You'd have to prove that I was responsible first."

I felt my belly clench with fear for him. What was this feud between them? Whatever it was, Liam was not worth it. "I'll stop you," I said, "so for Pete's sake stop whatever the hell you're doing."

"Okay," he said, and turned around to return to his seat.

I felt like I was being toyed with. "I'm not joking, Brent."

He narrowed his gaze at me. "Why do you even care? You did the same thing a decade ago."

"I don't believe that you truly wanted to go through with it. You were just furious. You needed someone to make you stop."

He was genuinely amused. "You think I didn't go through with it because you stopped me? I stopped because I didn't know how to get away with it."

"And now you do?"

"It's been ten years. What do you think?"

I felt something very cold run down my spine. "Hearing you speak like this, it truly makes me wonder if perhaps Liam was telling the truth about what you did to my father."

"Freya, if I killed your father I'd let you know that I did. I'm not a scurrying rat like Liam is." He replaced his glasses back over his eyes. "You can see yourself out."

I watched him as he returned to his laptop, his gaze moving between it and the other three giant screens before him. I hated how he could just cut me off like that and I wanted to hurt him. Really hurt him the way he was hurting me. "Actually, Liam is not such a scurrying rat. I found him quite attractive."

He shot to his feet and I could have sworn that I felt the room slightly shudder. In one swipe of his hand, the laptop flew from the desk and crashed into the book cases on the opposite end of the room.

My hands flew to my mouth in fright as I watched the equipment smash violently against the wood and fall to pieces on the polished hardwood. "Brent," I gasped.

His voice was as cold as ice as he spoke, "You're testing me. I was trying to be polite for old time's sake, but I can see now that I've given you too much power. I want you and I'm going to have you. I've settled your immediate debt, but that's not the end of it. In less than forty-eight hours, the Bailiffs will be back at your door."

"What the hell are you talking about?"

"You didn't know, did you?" he asked, with a mocking smile.

"Know what?"

"Your mother took a second loan against the property."

My heart sank. He knew what I didn't and was reveling in the power his knowledge gave him over me. "It doesn't matter. I'll pay it myself," I responded tightly.

I watched furiously as he turned his back and walked over to the drinks cabinet. "You want one?" he asked.

"No thanks."

"You look like you could do with one," he said sarcastically and began calmly pouring himself a drink. Then he turned his attention back to me. "I'm afraid paying it yourself is most unlikely since your account is frozen. In my experience of these situations, the bank will be in no hurry to unblock your funds. Especially since they will have already placed those funds into a high interest account. It could take two weeks, but the bailiffs will be at your property tomorrow."

My mind was a firestorm of confusion and anger. Why didn't

Mom tell me about this second loan yesterday when she had the chance?

Suddenly, he came close enough that I could smell his familiar scent. His eyes were intense and intimidating. "You want to keep your property, you fuck me. One month, or until I get you the fuck out of my head. Call me when you're done weighing your options." He stepped over the carnage of metal and glass that used to be a laptop and walked towards the door.

"Brent?" I called, feeling sorry I had infuriated him so much.

Then just before he disappeared from sight, he stopped without turning around. "I know what it's like to lose a parent to idiots, so I'm not one to do that so carelessly to others. Think about that before you go believing every tale that is spun to take advantage of you."

FREYA

When I arrived home, Maddie and Ella were gone and my mother was sitting in front of the TV. There was an empty glass of wine on the coffee table. There was something so sad and forlorn about her that I felt the hair on my arms rise. Just then, she turned to face me and I saw her reddened eyes and knew she had been sobbing her eyes out.

My poor, poor mother. I hurried over to her and immediately held her in my arms. Although she was my mom, I was a head taller than her, so she fit quite snugly in the crook of my shoulder. "Why are you crying?" I asked. "We are out of danger."

She touched my face gently. "I'm sorry, Freya. I've put you in danger by being a *very*, very foolish woman."

"It's okay, Mom. It's settled now. The debt is paid fully."

She dropped her head. "No, it hasn't."

"No?" I asked softly.

She shook her head. "I took another loan and they have been chasing me on that as well."

"I see. Don't worry, Mom. I'm pretty certain my professor will help out."

She peered at me through wet lashes. "Why would he help? He doesn't want you to do anything with him, does he?"

I pretended to laugh. "He's old enough to be my grandad, Mom. It's not like that. He's just a kind man. Anyway, it will just be a loan. I'll pay it all back." I was getting so good at telling lies it surprised me.

She took a deep breath. "Are you sure?"

"Yes, I am sure."

"Oh, Freya." She let out a long sigh. "I've been so frightened this last month. I didn't know what to do. I thought I was going to get a heart attack. I was supposed to be protecting you and I was getting us into deeper and deeper trouble. After what happened to your Dad, I swore to myself that I would take care of you, but look at what I have done."

"Oh, Mom, you have done great. I wouldn't change you for the world," I burst out.

"I'm so tired, Freya," she whispered. "I just want to lay my head down for once and have my heart actually know what it means to rest. Sometimes, I think I can't take it anymore."

I led her head back to my shoulder and tried to keep my own tears at bay, as she sobbed, her shoulders quietly shuddering. Even when my father had died, I hadn't seen her cry this much. It bothered me to no end, but I understood ... I understood that she had never allowed herself to properly grieve. This was her outlet.

I held her even tighter to me until she eventually lifted her face. She brushed my hair softly away from my cheeks and looked into my eyes. "You're so strong. So strong. I'm so proud of you."

I planted a kiss on her cheek and felt my heart break just a little when I noted the wrinkles around her eyes. She had foregone her Botox injections to save money. As if she was a child, I placed another kiss on her nose and she squeezed her eyes shut.

I wiped the tears from my eyes. "I love you, Mom."

"And you're a blessing, Freya."

"Well, you didn't say that when I was sixteen."

"You were a brat, and I'm not taking that back."

Suddenly, my phone rang. I knew it was one of the girls so I gave my mother a quick kiss on the cheek and hurried to my bedroom. I ran the shower and in the lowest tone I could drop my voice to, I gave Maddie a quick update on what had gone on with Brent. There was of course no mention of his proposal but it was not difficult for her to put two and two together.

"So he is responsible for this?" she asked.

"Yup."

"What's the catch this time?"

I hesitated about whether I should tell her about Brent's proposition, as I knew what her reaction would be, but I really needed to talk it out with someone or I would go insane. "A one month relationship with him, purely physical."

"Over my dead body," she said.

I smiled. That is exactly the kind of over-the-top thing I expected from her.

"What the hell does he take you for? Chattel?"

"That's a fancy word," I commented lightly.

She ignored my attempt at jest. "This is not funny. What is wrong with him? Is this legal? Can't he be reported or something? I mean, I used to wonder what kind of guy you'd get involved with when you finally started dating, but never in a million years would I have thought this? How the hell did you find a maniac right off the bat, but he looks so gorgeous and so damn sane—"

"I have an incoming call, Maddie," I said. "I'll call you back."

"I'll be waiting," she warned.

I immediately accepted the waiting call without giving the unknown number a second look. Whoever it was would be better than listening to Maddie continue ranting. I had a feeling she was going to go on for a while.

"Hello," I answered.

"Is this Freya Anderson?" a sultry woman's voice responded.

It could very well be a response from the bank, but this late? "Yeah, who's this?"

"It's Judi Mirren. Uh, do you mind if we speak? I'll be very brief."

"When?"

"Now. I'm outside your apartment."

I frowned. This would be interesting. "Okay." I held the phone as I headed out.

"Where are you going?" my mother called out.

"Uh, I just want to check the mail, I'm expecting something," I answered putting on my Parka. I shook my head at how easily the lies were flowing out of me these days. It just seemed so wrong, but what choice did I really have?

FREYA

A few minutes later, I was in front of the hedge of our small apartment with my phone to my ear.

"Where are you?" I asked.

"Just a bit further down. Oh, I see you. I'm in the white Mercedes."

She flashed her headlights at me and I knew where to go. I disconnected our call and soon, I was sitting beside Judi Mirren in an overheated car.

When she greeted me, I smiled but couldn't meet her eyes. There was something too disturbingly unreal about the moment for me to accept. I didn't know where to look so I just stared straight ahead.

"I've heard a lot about you, Freya," she began.

Her voice ... There was something about it. Breathless, calculated, intended to manipulate. I had never seen her in real life before, or known her beyond her status as an actress, and of course, Brent Lucan's rumored girlfriend. I summoned up the courage and turned to look into her ocean blue eyes. They were mesmerizing. She was eight years older than me, and supremely confident. I didn't understand why I was sitting in her car.

"It would have been lovely for us to meet at a café, but it would have caused quite the stir if I were to be spotted."

"Yeah, it would," I responded, clasping my hands in the dark of the car, impatient for her to get to the real reason why I was here.

"I heard about how you and Brent met," she drawled.

My defenses instantly went up. My hands tightened with nerves as a chilling calm came over me. I wondered who exactly was telling everyone about how I met Brent.

"And I've also heard that you've been spending quite a lot of time with him," she continued.

I turned to her, the smile gone from my face. "That's actually not true and even if it was, why would it matter to you?"

She looked away from me and smiled into the dark. "Because I'm his girlfriend. I've been with him for years and I don't intend to walk away because of a little infatuation with a kid. What are you? Nineteen? You have no idea how to keep a man like him." She turned to face me again, the blue of her eyes almost violet with emotion. "He's taken. He's my man. Do you understand that? I need you to stay away from him. He's not someone to be toyed with."

I couldn't believe what I was hearing. I was being warned off Brent.

"I propose Brighton," she said with a dazzling smile. "It's a lovely bohemian city. Full of people your age. It'll have all that you'll both need. There's not much going for either of you here anyways, well except your university, but I'm sure a transfer can be arranged. I know people who can do that for you."

"Either of you?" I asked. I knew what she meant, but I wanted to hear her say it.

"Well yes, you and your mother. Quite frankly, I don't understand how you both have stayed so long in London when there is so much nasty talk about your family. Please understand, I'm not trying to be rude, I'm just trying to be realistic. You both need a fresh start away from all the drama here and you especially, do not want your mother finding out about how you came in to your ... little ... umm ... nest egg."

There it was. The other shoe had dropped and it smacked me right in the face. "Are you threatening me?"

"It's not a threat," she said. "It's a friendly warning. Going away will tie up everything neatly and grant everyone peace."

I turned to her. "And you have the right to do this because?"

The smile instantly wiped off from her face. The gloves were off.

"Because I have a lot at stake. Brent Lucan is the brains behind my company and distractions like you are going to make things very difficult for everybody. You're just some shiny new toy, so please for the sake of yourself and your mother, go somewhere else and start anew. I'll help you in any way that you need. Money and any kind of support either of you need. I think you'll find I am very generous when I get my way."

"Is Brighton far enough?" I asked, my tone distant and condescending.

"Excuse me?"

"We might as well leave England. Paris seems like quite the place. My mom was raised there. She also had her honeymoon there. Or is that too close? How about a different continent? I've heard South Africa is stunning. Along the coast perhaps."

"You're funny," she said icily.

"No, you are. Either that or you're deluded to think that my life is somehow worth so much less than yours that it can be uprooted and flung to wherever pleases you." I grabbed the handle of her car door to storm out. She tried to stop me, but I got out, slammed the door shut behind me, and returned home, feeling as if my heart would burst with fury.

I couldn't even respond to my mother as she called out to me. Or even my phone when Maddie began to call back. I let the call go unanswered but when she kept calling, I picked it up and spoke as calmly as I could.

"Ella says we should go out for a movie," she said.

"Come on. Let's go!" Ella screamed from the background.

"I'm sorry, count me out, please. I'm tired. I'll call you guys tomorrow, okay?" I didn't need to go to the movies. My life already seemed like one. I ended the call and went in search of my mother.

She was seated in the living room, the television on, but muted. Like she too, was deep in thought. When she noticed me, she smiled and called me over. "You didn't eat. I didn't want to disturb you, so I just left some chicken and potatoes in the oven for you."

"Thanks, Mom." I sat beside her.

"Why did you go outside?" she asked.

"Uh." I quickly put together another lie. "I was returning a call I missed earlier for an internship interview."

"Oh, I thought you found somewhere already?"

"I did, but I'm still reviewing new options."

"Oh," she said innocently, making me feel worse for lying to her.

"How's the store doing?"

A light came on in her eyes. "It's doing much better. I was seriously considering shutting it down, but I then received some contacts from the charity event and since then, fingers crossed, business has begun to flow. I'll give it a little more time to see how things go."

"Give it a lot of time, Mom," I said softly. "This is what you've always wanted to do. Don't let it go."

"When did you get so mature?" she asked in wonder.

"Born this way. I inherited it from my mother," I replied.

She giggled and for a while, we were both at peace with each other. I figured it was as best a time as any now to bring it up. "Mom, do you know Brent Lucan?"

I held my breath as she stilled and then turned to me. "Not really, why are you asking?"

"Uh, someone was talking about him the other day, and I remembered I used to see him when he was younger, when we would go to all those boring social events."

"Ah," she said noncommittally.

But I needed more from her. "He runs his own company now, doesn't he? I even heard that he might be running Judi Mirren's company for her." When she didn't say anything, I went on, "Isn't that the company that was involved in Dad's case?"

She turned to me and I could see that she was already very upset. "How did you find that out?"

"Is it true?"

She sighed. "I don't know the details, your father wouldn't tell me, but I do know that he was very upset with Brent Lucan. It's all water under the bridge now. Let's not talk about him, again," she said. "I don't want to deal with memories from that time anymore."

I should have left it there, but I had just one more question, "Mom, do you believe dad was innocent?"

Her eyes widened with genuine shock. "What on earth do you mean?"

"Nothing. I was just reviewing the reports about the case—"

"Reports are not the truth. How could you even think that about your Dad? He loved you, Freya. No matter what anybody says, that man loved you and I don't want you to go poking around all that now. It's in the past, Freya. Leave it there."

"Mom."

"Please darling, don't talk to me about this again," she said, rising to her feet. "Let's just figure a way to get our finances in order and move on."

Things were changing so quickly in my life. I've had to grow up really fast. I went back to my room and sent Brent a text.

I accept your arrangement.

FREYA

The bailiffs did not turn up and I went back to Uni the next day. Everything had seemingly returned to normal in our life, but for some reason it felt like the calm before the storm. I was edgy, my thoughts constantly swirling around what I would say and do when I met Brent again. Of course, I was excited about being with him again, but aggravated that our time would be on his terms. There was no happy ending to our relationship. I was like an itch to him. He was to scratch it until it was no longer itchy.

Then I would be gone.

When my phone rang and Mom calling came up on the screen it was like that first dark cloud that blew on the sky before a storm. She never called me while I was at school. I quickly excused myself from the circle of conversation with my team and went to huddle in a corner. "Mom?"

"Do you know what's going on?" She sounded agitated and distraught.

"What do you mean?" I asked, going into panic mode.

"I'm outside the boutique right now and I've been locked out. Some men came over and said that my lease had been taken over and the store has been rented to someone else."

"They can't do that!"

"Apparently, the one time they *can* do that is if you fall back on your rent. I don't know why the landlord didn't remind me for the money. He's always done it in the past and I've always immediately paid it whenever he did. I just don't understand. I have the money now, but they've given me a week to get rid of my stuff. I don't know—Hey! What are you doing?" she screamed frantically at someone.

In the background chaos, I could hear a man's voice.

I tried my best to hear what he was saying to her, but his voice didn't carry well. Then she came back on the phone.

"What is it, Mom?"

"I don't know what the hell is going on, Freya?" she cried. "Who is doing this? I know it is not some random person wanting to rent this shop. The shop two doors down is empty. They could have taken that. Someone wants to ruin me."

"They didn't tell you who took over the lease?"

"Of course not. The man said that you're aware of what's happening? What the hell does that mean?"

My stomach swirled and tightened.

"Freya? Is that true? Do you know what's happening?"

"I'm on my way," I said and ended the call.

The moment I found a taxi, I settled in. Then I placed a call to the person I suspected would be behind something like this.

A few moments later, Judi Mirren's silky voice came through the receiver, "Freya," she greeted in high spirits.

Her voice seemed to crack a splitting headache down my skull. "Do you have anything to do with the closure of my mother's store?"

"I thought that I'd help you kick start the decision to leave London. I figured it would help you sell the idea to your mother. If she didn't have anything keeping her here, then it'd be easier for you to —"

"Are you fucking out of your mind?" I screamed. My hands pounded on the seat as I exploded in fury. "How dare you? How fucking ... *dare* you?"

"Are you done?" she asked coolly.

"We're human beings," I said in disbelief. "How the heck can you do this? How can you toy with people this way?"

"Freya, I warned you. You're the one toying with me. I'm happy that I was finally able to get my message across, but this is just the start. I can see your mother right now, and she's quite ... well ... frenzied. I hope you won't cause her heart to completely break by allowing her to come to know of things that she should not. Let me know when you've made your decision." She ended the call then.

For a second I stared at the phone, then I called her back.

"That was fast," she said smugly.

"Judi, you may be a good actress, but you are a bad judge of character. I'm not some bimbo you can push around. I am in a relationship with Brent and guess what? I'm going to make that information public and you're going to no longer exist in Brent's world. This is what you're scared of, isn't it? Go ahead, tell my mother all about my involvement with Brent, and how I came into my nest egg. I don't give a fuck anymore, but what you want of him, I'll ensure that you will never be able to get. Oh, you know what else? Go ahead and keep that shitty shop. I'll use my nest egg to get my mother another one."

She laughed then. "How silly you are. Brent will never claim you as his own, so don't worry about the publicity. I won't expose it either, because the last thing I want is the world knowing how he bought you, but your mother however will find out."

She had called my bluff. Of course, she wasn't going to publicize my relationship. It didn't suit her, but my mother on the other hand would find out. There was nothing to it. I'd have to tell her myself, which might be a relief since I was getting tired of all the lies I'd had to concoct and continue to concoct ever since. I called Mom and told her I was working on it and not to worry, then I made my way to Brent's office.

His office building was a sleek spire of magnificent glass and steel in Bishopsgate. Office workers clad in crisp suits and austere heels clicked their way across the granite flooring to their destinations.

I walked through the glass and chrome rotating doors of the

building. I headed across the expansive lobby to the reception desk manned by three receptionists, two females, and one tall male and quickly demanded to see Brent Lucan. No, I didn't have an appointment. One of the females, her picture-perfect smile not altering in the slightest, asked my name, made a call to inform someone, then, stepped away from the desk and asked me to go with her.

I followed her as she clicked her way across the polished floor. She took me to a private elevator by a small bohemian fountain and tapped a key card to gain access. The glass barricades slid away and the elevator car dinged open. She gestured for me to enter and the door slid shut as she took her leave.

Then I was on my way to the top most floor.

When the doors opened again, his personal assistant, Michael was there to greet me. His smile was curt.

I felt the sting of it too. I also didn't blame him. I looked like a tramp. An angry tramp. I was led through a lavishly decorated hallway with wall fountains and plaques of games, until I arrived before heavy oak doors.

"He's expecting you. Just knock and go in, Miss Anderson," he said to me and turned around to leave.

I didn't knock. I grabbed a hold of the handle and pushed my way into Brent's office. He was sitting at his desk radiating power and confidence.

"Get that dog, Judi off me," I shouted.

He scowled. "What's going on?"

"First she comes around to my home and threatens me with

exposure for selling myself in your club, if I don't leave you alone. And now she's done a deal with my mother's landlord and taken the lease for herself."

"Judi?" he asked.

"Yes!" I yelled, almost hysterical. "Fucking yes, Judi Mirren. Why are you both haunting me? What have I done? Get her off my back and tell her we are fucking. We're fucking for however long it takes her to realize that she can never have you."

The room went silent.

I sounded crazy and it showed in his eyes.

In my fury, I had forgotten he didn't want me for more than a month. Oh, hell. The nightmare just got worse and worse. I was infuriated with myself. This had to count as the lowest point in my life so far, even worse than selling myself. I couldn't bear anymore mocking, rejection or humiliation, I turned around to leave, but as I got to the door, he caught my hand and spun me around.

"Don't go," he said softly. "Let's … fuck for as long as it takes Judi to believe we're together, and that she can never have me."

"Brent," I whispered, as his magic swirled around me again. "Um … we don't have to tell everyone … If you want to keep this quiet."

A small smile tugged at his lips. "I do what I want and I don't care who knows. If you want to sing it to the moon or announce it to the ants."

"You won't be ashamed?"

"No, I won't."

"So you'll sort out my mother's boutique?"

"Of course. Tell your mother to go home and relax. Everything will be fine tomorrow."

"And ... and ... you'll stop her from telling my mother about the auction?"

"Oh yes, I'll make her understand how little benefit there will be to undertaking such a foolhardy exercise."

"Brent, how come so many people know about the auction? I never told anyone but my two best friends."

He frowned. "Yes, how come? Leave it with me."

At that moment, I wanted to cry. It felt so good to have a man to take care of the problem. Ever since my father died, I've had to work two jobs and worry about my mom and the relief was incredible. I didn't even realize tears were running down my cheeks until Brent used his thumbs to wipe them away.

"Don't cry, Freya. Nothing bad will happen to you or your mother while I'm alive. I promise you that."

Too choked up to speak, I just nodded.

"I'll see you at dinner?" he asked.

I sniffled. I didn't think I could face being in a public place with him and the gossip that would follow yet. I felt too raw. "Can we not go out tonight? I'm not ready for ... people."

"Okay," he said. "So how about dinner on a yacht?"

"A yacht? I'm not very good on the sea."

"Don't worry," he responded. "I'll make you forget where you are."

Something deep inside me responded to his words. "Okay."

"Good. I'll get Michael to pick you up about five o'clock?"

I nodded.

He smiled gently. "Now go to your mother."

FREYA

Once I sorted Mom out and sent her home, I went to see Maddie at work. Luckily, she was able to spare a few minutes away from her office so we both sat on a picnic bench to talk.

"I feel like my whole world is upside down," I said.

"Is he going to stop her from speaking to your mother?"

"He said he would."

"Will that be enough to tame her? She sounds insane."

"He seemed pretty confident. He's in charge of her company, so I guess he has power over whatever sick emotions she's nursing over him."

"I don't understand some women," Maddie observed. "Every time I hear things like this, I am sure it's a joke. She's fucking beautiful, successful, and over-privileged, and she still has to resort to threatening another woman to get a man? Disgusting."

There was silence between us for a while.

I knew she was watching me. I lifted my head to meet her gaze.

"Are you truly going to go through with it? Sleep with him, I mean."

"I will," I responded, "just enough to rub it in her face."

"I don't think that's a good idea?"

"Why not?"

"I can think of at least a hundred reasons."

"Well, right now, I can't think of any. It's not as if I'm not crazy attracted to the guy. Since everyone can do whatever the fuck they want, with even a little bit of power in their hands, so I'm going to do whatever the hell I want too."

She chewed on her sandwich and looked at some children playing at the edge of the park. Then she swallowed and turned to me. "I get it that you're furious and I completely understand you want revenge, but I don't want you to go through with this. Brent Lucan is not just any ordinary man with a nine to five job. He's not just a ruthless billionaire, but the freaking heir to the Dukedom of Leighton. Being involved with such a man is not a joke. You could get seriously hurt. And the jealousy? Oh my God, it's going to be through the roof."

"No one will know about it."

"What?"

"Well, except Judi." I grinned. "I might even send her some photos."

GEORGIA LE CARRE

"You're going to go out with Brent Lucan and you think no one is going to know?"

"Okay," I conceded reluctantly, with a sigh. "You're right. He's the next Lord of Leighton. His dating life will make the news, and I'll forever be in the spotlight while I'm with him."

"When are you going to tell your Mom?"

"I don't know, but not yet. Maybe next week."

"So you're going to lie to her until then?"

"I guess so. Telling her at this stage feels like I'm jumping the gun. What if it all falls apart in the next few hours? I'm supposed to meet him tonight, so I'll be telling her I'm spending the night at your place, so if she calls you …"

"Right."

"Sorry to drag you into my shit."

She shrugged. "It's okay. Just don't want you to get hurt," she muttered.

"I do have to keep our agreement."

"Do you?" she asked softly.

I stared into my best friend's worried eyes and told the truth, "I want to."

FREYA

Despite the cold, I was excited as I sighted the magnificent cobalt blue and silver vessel, waiting gracefully by the dock. "Wow, that's a ship!" I gasped.

"It's not. I hear it can only accommodate sixteen people," Michael said, pulling the car door open for me, leading the way towards the waiting yacht.

We took our shoes off and boarded the vessel. We were met with attendants who after taking my parka, offered a selection of little delicacies adorned with caviar, strawberries, nectarine, basil and tomato. They looked delicious, but after stuffing the two in quick succession into my mouth, I forewent the glass of champagne offered, and asked for water.

My eyes caught the piano by the corner, the exquisitely patterned carpet and of course, the glass staircase that I guessed led up to the deck. "When will Brent be here?" I asked Michael.

"He has some business to finish off at the office, but he

should be on the way in no time. Please call for the staff if you need anything more." He showed me to the room we would be staying in and soon took his leave.

The staff announced that food was available if I should need it, but I was too exhausted from the stress of the day to ignore the luxuriously silky bed calling to me. I laid across it and shut my eyes for a quick nap, and only came awake when I heard someone walking around in the room.

At first, I was disorientated and alarmed, because I didn't immediately remember where I was, but then I sat up and saw Brent with ear pods on speaking in extremely low tones.

I wondered once again if the path I had decided on would be one that I would eventually regret. It still wasn't too late to turn back. Then as he pulled the dress shirt off his back, the ridges of toned muscle which seemed as if they had been sculpted into his flawless olive skin flexed—all thoughts of escaping disappeared from my head.

I clenched my thighs at the sensual ache that was beginning to throb between my legs.

He turned around to catch me watching him.

The anticipation of being with him again, was almost excruciating. Lifting myself off the bed, I heard him say, "I'll call you back in a couple of days."

"You were tired," he commented as he pulled the devices out of his ear setting them on the lounge table. His watch followed.

"I was," I responded. "Brent, I'm searching for an internship, and I ... uh ... I also have an examination this week so I might not be able to see you often. After tonight, I need to study for it."

He took his seat on the bed to untie the laces on his shoes.

My heart pattered treacherously away in my chest. How could sexual attraction, I wondered, be this profound? I tried to appear calm but every moment now seemed to me to be a charged, breathless countdown to having his hands on me.

"Where are you looking to do your internship?" he asked.

"Merrill Lynch."

"Well, if things don't go according to plan, you have a position at my company's accounting department. I'm sure you'll be able to pick up quite a few valuable insights into your field."

I was quite certain this was a terrible idea, but I didn't tell him that. "Did you get my mother's boutique back from Judi?"

"Yes, your mother can trade as normal tomorrow. Her rent is paid for the next quarter too."

"Thank you so much. I really appreciate the help."

"I'm sorry Judi involved your mother. It was not fair to drag her into it."

"Yeah, but life's unfair," I said, my voice unconsciously bitter.

"But it's still good."

"Sometimes ..."

"Come," he called.

I knee-walked on the bed towards him, feeling suddenly nervous. "You bought this yacht two years ago, didn't you?" I babbled.

Not till I was a few inches from him did he respond. He reached behind me to gently grab the tie that held up my ponytail and in one gentle pull, he had my hair cascading down my shoulders. "I did," he responded as his heavily lidded eyes roved all over my face. "How did you know?"

"I read about it a while back. Very little is known of it especially the interior. You requested the use of—"

He slipped his tongue into my mouth and I had never received a clearer order to stop talking nonsense. I melted into Brent's arms as they slid around my waist and completely forgot there was anything I ever wanted to say. It felt as though my brain had shut down.

I put my hands around his neck and met the caress of his tongue with mine. When he pulled away for a brief second, I leaned forward blindly, eagerly again. At his soft chuckle, I opened my eyes and realized, as I stared into his glorious eyes that I had *so* missed him. I hadn't even realized just how much until now.

"Show me your body, Freya. I've missed seeing it."

Immediately, I stood in front of him and started to work my way down the buttons of my shirt. I pulled my material apart, and my breasts clothed in a seductive black bra were exposed. He immediately leaned forwards, cupping the mounds through the material and sucking on the creamy flesh.

His touch set my blood on fire and a purr slipped out of me

as my head fell back. His fingers unbuttoned and unzipped my jeans. I felt the material slide down my legs. My panties followed. He reached behind me and my bra snapped open. Then he pulled back and looked at me, his eyes half-closed and full of lust.

My nipples hardened and I grew self-conscious so I grabbed the band of his trousers, unbuttoned his pants, and slipped my hand into his briefs. He was already rock hard. I grazed my nails through the light dusting of hair on his groin before curving my hand around his smooth solid length. It filled my hand with the evidence of his desire for me. My confidence soared. Perhaps it was because we were both now in agreement of what our relationship would be to each other, so there was no need to hold back or pretend.

I dropped to my knees and began to unzip the fly of his trousers. Holding onto the edge of his trousers and briefs, I pulled the soft woolen material down his thighs and lifting his feet, jerked them off.

Then I lifted my gaze back to his erect cock, I couldn't look away from it. It was like a work of art. So straight and strong. I wrapped my hand around the thick shaft, snaked with pulsating veins. A quick glance upwards told me he was waiting to experience what I could do to him.

I took the mushroom head into my mouth.

I sucked gently on the beautiful, pink crown and heard his breath quicken. His eyes were now shut, his head thrown slightly backwards with his hands half clenched into fists.

I continued on.

Hollowing my mouth, I pulled in as much of him as I could

take until his cock hit the back of my throat. Upon retreat, I gently scraped by teeth down his silky-smooth flesh. His groan floated above me. I felt his hands slip into my hair. I grabbed his shaft by the root and fisted him as my mouth sucked on him with a forceful rhythm.

I felt him grow thicker and longer in my hands, the thrusts of his hips growing stronger with each passing moment.

"*Fuck*," he cursed.

I tilted my head to lick, kiss, and nibble along his length. I recalled a tip Ella told Maddie and I decided to try it. I sucked hard on his balls, and then pulled ever so gently. His grip tightened in my hair, and the burst of pre-cum spilled into my mouth so the tip was gold. I had done something right.

It thrilled me and urged me on, his dirty curses above my head turning me on so much I could feel my sex start to throb. I loved that I could bring him this much pleasure as he had done to me countless times and at the sight of strained veins along his temple, I grabbed hold of his thighs and encouraged his rapid thrusts into my mouth. With my tongue and lips, I worshipped and savored his cock, my head bobbing to the sensual rhythm of his hips as he fucked my mouth. My head was now held in place by his hands as he chased his climax.

When he exploded into my mouth, I was taken aback with the force of his spurt, the release so thick and strong it filled my mouth and flowed down my throat.

"Don't swallow," he growled. "Open your mouth and show me."

I opened my mouth and showed how he had filled it. His hand replaced mine as he finished himself off, releasing more sprays of his orgasm unto my face and hair. He was barely conscious of what he was doing, his entire frame bent with his toes clenched at the sweet agony of his release.

His breathing was hard and how I loved what I could do to him. He looked so beautiful to me in that moment as I licked my lips clean, relishing the taste of him. He rubbed his seed into my skin. I knew what he was doing. He was marking me as his. His scent made me heady and I wasn't ready to move away just yet. He was still magnificently hard so I reached forward and licked him clean, hot wet kisses lapping every bit of him up, till he was glistening with wetness from my mouth.

His eyes opened then, sparkling and full of wonder as he pulled me to my feet and dropped me into his lap. "Fuck, I'm sorry," he said. "I got so carried away."

"I love it that you got so carried away. You're always so controlled."

"What are you talking about? I'm never controlled around you. I'm like a keg of dynamite. One little spark from you and I'm off."

"No way. You're always telling me you need me just for sex."

"Can you blame a man for saying that to you?"

I grinned. "Did I do good today?"

"You were awesome, but the magic was not in your technique," he said.

I stopped to pull up his head so I could meet his gaze. "What do you mean?"

"I fucking exploded in your mouth," he said. "Doesn't that hold all the answers?"

"No, it doesn't. I'm dense. Explain it to me."

He nibbled on the tip of my nose. "You drive me fucking crazy, Freya," he murmured. "I don't know what it is about you, or why. Your technique wasn't new, but I've never come that hard in anyone's mouth."

"Do you masturbate thinking of me?" I asked.

"Yeah, do you?"

"Yes," I admitted.

He pushed my legs apart and looked down at my wet sex. "Do it now."

I began to circle my clit. Then I gave him what he wanted. He wanted to see me fucking myself. I plunged my fingers into myself. With a groan, he pushed my fingers away. His mouth landed on my pussy and my back arched off the bed.

"Fuck," I breathed, as my knees knocked together, trapping him between my legs. His warm wet tongue dug into my cunt.

I almost pulled off his hair as he threw my legs over his shoulders so my ass was lifted clean off the bed to give him as much access as he needed. Soon, his fingers were thrusting in and out of me with his mouth licking and sucking on the engrossed bud of my sex.

I writhed on the bed as though possessed as my controllable

cries of pleasure were torn from my lips as he devoured me relentlessly.

"Brent," I gasped as my climax started.

"I never knew you had such a dirty mouth," he said to me, as he gently licked my pussy.

"I never knew I had such a dirty mouth," I whispered, drained of energy. Until I met him, I would never have thought I would say, 'fuck my pussy, Brent' or any of the other equally filthy things I cried out in the throes of my climax.

I felt his rock-hard dick slide into me. At first, he was careful at how tight I was, but as soon as my body adjusted to having his massive girth inside it, he held onto my waist and rammed all the way into me.

As he buried his face in my breasts, suckling and fondling the heavy mounds, my hips bucked with delicious pleasure as I savored his complete possession of my body.

My mind was long gone. All I could do was feel, my fingers clenching the sheet underneath me, my bones moving like rubber as I met every thrust of his, and his cock slamming deeper and deeper into me.

He fucked me so viciously, that at a point I believed my spine would be permanently set in the arched position that my frame had twisted in. My back was no longer touching the bed and his strength and virility was more than I could bear.

"Just like that ... Just like that," he muttered, as I pushed my hips towards his thrusts.

"*Oh, God.*"

All I could hear was his voice … from a distance as he completely overwhelmed me with burning red lust.

"Open your eyes," I heard him rasp out but it was damn near impossible.

"Open them," he growled.

My eyelids opened to gaze into his golden eyes.

The bed rocked with the force of his thrusts, and the wet sound of our flesh slapping echoed around the cabin. As he chased his climax his thrusts grew harder and faster, and I thought I wouldn't be able to contain them.

We heard and felt nothing else beyond the intensity of our desire and when I came, all I could register were my hands above my head, and my fingers linked almost painfully in his. Something was exploding in me that I could not contain. He cursed and sunk his teeth into my shoulders to muffle his cry. I held onto his head desperately feeling as though I would shatter if I didn't.

I heard him roar out my name as I writhed and screamed, my own orgasm quaking my body to it's very core.

He forced his tongue into my mouth. I sucked it and wrapped my legs around his hips, refusing to let go and that was how we both came back to earth.

It was a slow descent, but the lingering effects powerful enough to render us both speechless and motionless for a long time. When he began to move to separate from me, I let him go, gasping, as his slick wet cock slid heavily out of me. I turned to my side to hide whatever the emotion that would betray the depth of my feelings.

Brent wouldn't allow it. He came right up to me and pulled me into his body. Tucked into him, I was sure that no other place on earth would fit me more perfectly. The steady rise and fall of his chest and his warmth completely encapsulating me ... lulled me to sleep.

Just before I slipped into unconsciousness however, I was sure I heard him say, "You're mine now, Freya Anderson."

FREYA

The next morning, I awoke to an empty bed. After untangling myself from the stained sheets - yeah, we got up to more sex during the night - I got to my feet and groggily looked around for my clothes. They had been taken away and in their place, a warm robe had been draped across the lounge sofa.

I quickly put it on and went in search of Brent.

As I walked, I looked through the windows to see that we were now far off shore as there were no more buildings in sight, but the vast ocean. This wasn't good, as I needed to return to my still very messy life and even more frantic mother who probably expected me to come home soon as it was Saturday. I had no classes. I hurried and that was how I tripped over the doors ledge and fell forward.

My knees connected with the hardwood floors, and I groaned in pain.

"What the fuck? Freya?"

I lifted my head to see that I had made a grand entrance into the main cabin where Brent had been having a breakfast meeting with Michael by his side and two other men in suits. I immediately jumped to my feet and spun around to properly tie the silky robe that I now noted clung to every curve of my body.

Worse, I was completely naked underneath. I wanted to bury myself at the thought that I had just given his associates an early morning show. I was so embarrassed. I felt like the empty-headed bimbo he'd brought along for light entertainment. "Excuse me," I said and turned around to leave, but Brent's familiar grip caught my arm. I still wouldn't open my eyes to look at him, so he turned me to face him.

"We're alone," he said, "open your eyes."

I popped one open to see if he was lying to me, and it was clear the men had left. Immediately, I pounded my hands on his chest in frustration. I thought it was just us and the crew. "Why the hell are you having a meeting so early in the morning?" I cried. "And how the hell did they get here?"

"Speedboat," he answered, amused.

Well, I was not amused. I felt humiliated and more than ever, I felt as if I did not deserve to belong in his world. I was from a family of a ruined reputation and that was okay with me, it was my cross to bear and I had carried it this far just fine. Being with him however filled me with the fear that I would begin to be judged as unworthy all over again.

I hated it.

Twisting my hands from his grip, I tucked my hair behind

my ears. "We need to head back to shore. I have to see my mother and I have a test to prepare for in two days."

"We're heading for Scotland," he said. "The isle of Harris. I have a castle there."

My head shot up in shock.

He was not joking. "We sailed away during the night."

"Why would you—" I began but took a deep breath and decided to let it go. "Can we return?" I asked. "You can't just whisk me away like this, I have a life too."

"No problem. We'll just turn and be back in a few hours," he responded as the amusement left his face and he became distant again, just like when we had first met.

I didn't want that. My hand reached out to touch him, but I couldn't make it go all the way. It fell to my side and he walked away from the room and me.

All I could do was watch him leave.

His departure completely soured my mood, as I didn't know when I would see him again. I was so tempted to go in search of him to cancel our return to land, but I had already laid my bed. I came out to the dining area hoping I would see him. Instead, I was told to take my seat as a platter of fruits, yoghurt, scones, croissants, eggs, sausages, bacon and toast were laid out on a buffet.

"Please help yourself to anything you want, Miss Anderson," a male attendant said.

I chose just a scone. I didn't have any appetite for much else.

Then I went back to bed. Hours passed. I felt sad that Brent was a free agent and able to go anywhere and do anything he wanted and I on the other hand had responsibilities for my mom and my classes and couldn't just disappear on a whim.

I was lamenting over my dead phone battery when Brent came into the room and announced our arrival back at the Thames. He had changed from the breezy white linen shirt he had had on before to a black turtle neck jumper and thick massive jet black Parka. "Time to go," he said.

I almost didn't hear him. All I could do was stare dumbstruck once more, at just how handsome he was. I didn't look like that when I wore my Parka.

"Freya," he called.

I jumped up from the bed, already dressed. He turned to leave and shortly, we were riding at the back of his town car.

I remembered then that there were quite the number of things I wanted to speak to him about. I snuck a glance to see that he had his glasses on and was going through a small folder of documents. I wanted to speak, but I felt so nervous. I couldn't understand myself. I had spent the night in his arms ... With him, I had been more intimate than I'd ever imagined possible, why then, did I always manage to alienate him when we were out of bed? If only I had not fallen, become embarrassed and lashed out at him. It wasn't his fault that I was so clumsy.

Eventually I got my mouth to work. "Brent."

He turned to me.

My breath caught at how handsome he was with the low winter sunlight slanting in through the window and turning his eyes into molten gold. "My mother's store ... do you know if everything went okay today?"

"It was reopened this morning, and it was as if yesterday never happened."

"Thank you again," I said, turning my face away.

I told him to drop me a short distance away from my home. Soon the car came to a stop and for a second, I wondered if I should try to repair the tense silence between us before I left the car. But I didn't know how to properly say goodbye to him and I would probably make a mess of trying to apologize, so I just thanked him for a nice time and grabbed the door handle.

He caught my hand just before I could pull it and kissed me with breathless abandon. My eyes fluttered closed, my heart raced, and my lower belly came awake with pure unbridled desire.

He broke it off before I could lose myself in his taste. "I'll see you later," he said.

The question escaped my lips before I could stop it, "When?"

"Come to me tonight."

"I have to study for a test tonight, but message me?"

He nodded and I threw my arms around his neck for one last lingering kiss. Just before I broke away, I planted soft kisses along his jaw and buried my nose in his neck for one last shameless whiff of his scent before I exited the vehicle.

I returned to an empty home and was incredibly relieved. After I charged my phone, though I was blasted with the seemingly unending alerts of calls and text messages. I called Maddie first to calm my nerves down.

She greeted me with a scream. "Where the fuck where you? How could you be out of reach? You idiot. Your mother's been calling me and I've had to tell her all kinds of lies."

"I'm sorry," I apologized, "my phone died."

"God, you're so damn annoying. Your mom was going crazy when she couldn't reach you."

"I told her that I would be staying at your pla—"

"Well, she wanted to fucking talk to you. What excuse do you think I could give as to why you couldn't come to the phone even after she told me to wake you up that it was important?"

"What excuse did you give?"

"I told her you were sick, and then she wanted to come over."

I gasped. "So what happened?"

"I had to ruin my reputation and confessed that I lied. That you were actually on a date. That you have a boyfriend."

"What?"

"What else could I do? She waited to speak to you when you returned, but then she didn't call again, so I'm suspecting she's sharpening her knives. Freaking call her." She hung up the phone on me.

I was left staring at it. I jumped when it began to ring again, and was surprised to see it was Maddie again. "Yeah?"

"What happened last night? I mean are you okay?"

"I am," I began. "We sailed towards Scotland. I'll explain later."

"Fine. I'm still too angry to listen to you now, but call me when I'm back from work."

"Alright, I'm sorry," I said.

She grunted before hanging up.

FREYA

A few hours later, I arrived at my mother's boutique to see her attending to an elderly woman in a gorgeous white suit and three pearl beads around her neck. She had the most gorgeous head of curly white hair that I had ever seen and for a moment, my gaze was fully on her before it fluttered over to my mother.

I met her completely furious pair of blue eyes on me and instantly looked away. After briefly chatting with Martin, I passed the time browsing through the racks of clothes and pretty soon, I heard the click of her heels as she headed over to me.

"You're no longer under my control anymore, are you? You're completely on your own now, right?"

"Mom," I began and felt her glare begin to dig a grave underneath me.

"How dare you be out of touch for so long?"

"I'm sorry, my battery—"

"I have to know where you are at all times," she cried.

I could see that my absence and the loss of contact with me had visibly shaken her, more than I would have expected, and I understood why. After my father's death, we had stuck closely together and she had remained especially paranoid that she was going to lose me too for the longest time. Her old fears were beginning to return. Especially, at all the unexplainable events that had been happening in our lives recently.

"I'm sorry," I said again.

I could see that she was near tears and just as I reached out to her, she brushed me off, and disappeared into her office.

I turned to meet Martin's concerned look. My heart felt heavy with remorse.

"It's okay. She'll be fine," Martin assured me

I settled on the love seat in the rear of the boutique and brought out my books to study for the internship test I would be having the following day.

After a while, she came out. "What are you still doing here?"

I jumped up from the chair. "I'm studying. And waiting for you."

"Oh, what are you studying for?"

"Internship test tomorrow."

She frowned. "Haven't you already secured one?"

My brain raced to recollect what lies I had invented about the situation. I was so bad at this. "Uh, ever since the funds got delayed, I've lost faith in them so I'm trying to find a new one."

"Who helped with the boutique then?"

"Oh that. I got some short-term funding from the professor. He spoke directly with the landlord. That's all sorted now," I said quickly.

She nodded then looked at me and expressed her grave source of concern. "What boy were you with yesterday?"

"He's from my ... umm ... class," I said. "But he's not my boyfriend, or anything. We just stayed late at his place to study together. "

"If you were at his place then why didn't you charge your phone there?"

"I'm sorry. I was careless, I won't do it again."

With a sigh, she looked down at the catalogue she was holding and I knew then that I had been forgiven. "I'll be staying late again at his place ... to study."

"Why can't you study at home?" she asked with a childlike trust in me.

I promised myself that this would be the last time I lied to her. I was going to tell her about Brent. I had to. I didn't want her to find out from someone else. "I'll fall asleep. This is an important test."

"Fine," she agreed. "Keep your phone on though."

"Yes ma'am," I responded and went forward to give her a hug.

"Freya?"

"Yeah?"

"Thank you so much for what you have done. I don't know what I would have done if your professor friend had not stepped in and helped."

I smiled at her. "That's all over now. Don't worry about it anymore."

I took myself off to a Starbucks and spread out my books to study. A few hours of studying and I was filled with restlessness. Perhaps I was just bored, but as the moments passed I found myself staring at my phone and checking for messages. I knew that we were not in the kind of relationship that warranted constant communication, but it would have been nice for him to send a short message to tell me that I was on his mind. He never stopped being in mine. At about five o'clock, I was just returning from a refill when I saw my phone beeping with a new message.

With my heart in my throat, I placed the glass down and grabbed my phone. It was Maddie.

When will you be home?

Disappointed, I answered her and pushing the phone away, returned to work. Five minutes later, my cellphone beeped again. Thinking it will be Maddie again, I glanced at it uninterestedly ... and time stopped.

It was Brent.

Where are you?

I wanted to ignore it, just for a little bit, so I didn't look so eager, but it was impossible. Within minutes, I had the phone in my hands and was drafting a reply.

At Starbucks at South Kensington. Studying for my test tomorrow.

His text came again. *How long will you be there?*

My fingers flew over the keyboard. *Very late. I'll take a cab home.*

I don't know what I expected but whatever it was, it wasn't his reply. *I'll join you.*

FREYA

I had to rub my eyes to be sure I had read the message clearly. Two more hours passed and there was still no sign of him. I rested my head down on the table to cool my brain and when my eyes fluttered open a few minutes later, Brent Lucan was standing over me, a cup of coffee in his hand. I hadn't even seen him come in.

"Hey." His voice was breathy, almost soundless but I heard it all the way deep in my heart.

He was wearing a baseball cap on his head and the same dark attire he had had on that morning. He looked nothing like the powerful magnate the world was accustomed to, but every girl's impossibly handsome crush from secondary school. That unattainable dream was right now beside me and staring into my eyes.

"What are you h-?" I tried to ask but my brain was fried. I turned away and tried to get my breathing under control.

"You're exhausted," he said. "Shouldn't you head home to rest?"

"No," I disagreed. "I have a bit more to go through."

"Okay," he said, and turning towards the computer he had opened in front of him, left me to my work. I couldn't understand how he expected me to concentrate with him sitting so close beside me that I could feel his warmth. If I were honest, I didn't want him anywhere else either, so I placed my headphones in my ears, turned the volume up, and tried my best to ignore him. A little while later, I felt him pull a bud from my ear and place it in his to hear what I was listening to.

He looked at me, his brow cocked in surprise. "Chinese instrumental?"

"It calms me," I replied.

"You started listening to it because of Maddie? She's Chinese, isn't she?"

"Not at all, she doesn't like instrumentals. Her mother used to play it a lot in the house though when we were in secondary school, so that's how I—" Something suddenly struck me. "How do you know about Maddie?"

He returned his gaze to the dark page of codes he was writing on his own screen. "You don't expect me not to know as much as possible about you before proposing a relationship with you do you?"

The pen fell from my hand.

He smiled as he caught it just before it rolled off the desk. "Close your mouth, Freya."

As I watched him, I knew what I wanted to ask but I didn't know how to put it in words. My brain wouldn't work so instead, I looked away and thanked him for saving my pen. Of course, he would know everything about me ... I remembered his brother's words. *He's not an ordinary person. He's calculated, precise ,and never careless. Every move he makes means something and is properly thought out.*

It made me wonder then what he was doing here. What sitting beside me right now in this cafe meant. Did he want to get closer to me, or was he trying to get me to perceive him in a certain light? My guesses didn't make sense and they were draining the energy I had reserved for studying. I turned to him. "Why are you here?"

"I'm working," he answered. When he realized I was still watching him he turned towards me too.

"I know, but you never do things without a reason. You could be working on your own but you're here where it can't be as comfortable as your study. I'm just curious why."

His smile spread into a full grin then as he leaned back into the chair. "What makes you think I never do things without a reason? I'm a human being."

"Well, you're the only one who thinks that," I muttered and returned my gaze to the book open before me.

"What do you mean?" he asked.

I shut the book and turned to him. "You're calculating, aren't you? You plan every single move you make."

He blinked.

"Right?" I prompted.

"Okay," he responded.

I got the impression he was just humoring me. "Forget about it," I said and returned to my book.

"Yes, I am quite structured," he explained gently, "and me being here right now, is quite impulsive for me I have to admit, but I wanted to be near you." He leaned in, his nose to my neck. "To wallow in the scent of your skin."

I felt my bones begin to melt. It was as though his words had conjured up a bubble around the both of us that kept the rest of the world around us outside and silent. It was as though we were the only two that existed in the world right now.

My head slanted to catch his lips, the slight taste of him shooting red molten desire straight to my core.

I pulled away, worried that he would be too uncomfortable with such displays of affection in a public place, but as I licked the taste of him on my lips, his hand went around my neck and pulled me forward. He slipped his tongue into my mouth and I saw stars.

Few seconds later, and I couldn't even sit still any longer My knuckles were white from gripping his sweater. He broke the kiss then and my forehead collapsed onto his chest. I was out of breath and my heart was beating like a drum. "How far away is your car?" I asked.

"If I take you out of here, I cannot guarantee that you will return."

"I don't care."

"If you fail the test, will you come work for me?"

I immediately straightened and leaned away without meeting his eyes. His slight chuckle was pure music to my ears.

FREYA

The following day, I stepped out of the test halls in the Merrill Lynch headquarters in Oxford, quite surprised at how well the test had gone for me. Pulling my phone out of my backpack, I switched it on, my teeth nibbling on my nail as I held my breath for Brent's good luck message.

There was none. Of course. He wanted me to fail so I would go work in his company. I called Maddie.

"Hey," she answered.

"I'm done," I said, "where are you?"

"I'm at home."

"Why are you whispering?" I asked.

"Ella's here," she responded. "And she's completely ballistic. She's been crying for an hour."

"What happened?" I asked.

"David cheated on her," she replied.

I sucked in my breath. "I'll be there as soon as I can," I said and was immediately on my way.

When I arrived, Maddie immediately warned me to keep my voice down. "She just fell asleep in my room."

We crept into the kitchen for a cup of tea, and Maddie filled me in on what had happened. There was an alert from my phone and though I was dying to look at it, I forced myself not to look.

"Are you expecting someone?" she asked.

"No!"

Her eyes narrowed at me and then glanced down at my phone. "Is it your test? Will the results be out today?"

"No, that will be next week."

"That's Brent, isn't it?"

"Could be," I said as nonchalantly as I could and glanced at it. My heart jumped to see that he had indeed sent me a message.

How did it go?

It amazed me how I couldn't stop my smile at the inconsequential message. A few seconds later, I pushed the phone aside and glanced up to find Maddie's face filled with irritation.

"Did you spend the night with him yesterday, again?" she asked.

"Of course not, I had to study. But he did stay with me at the cafe until late. He left just before midnight for an early meeting today."

"I don't like this," she said. "And I don't like him." She paused. "Are you at least protecting yourself properly?"

"Of course I am," I responded. "I'm on birth control. I started it right after my period and I made sure we used a condom for a week after."

"And are you taking it? Religiously?"

"I'm not a child, Maddie," I responded.

"I hope so, or you'll be pushing one in a pram." She looked at her watch. "Anyway, I got to go now. I promised someone at work I would go around. You can wait here for Ella to wake up and take over in listening to her rants when she wakes up."

A new message arrived as Maddie flounced out, and my heart began to race in anticipation.

What do you want to eat tonight?

I responded immediately.

Chinese. You want me to come over?

His reply was back in seconds.

Of course. I only let you go last night because of your test, which I should have told you, you wouldn't need to take.

At the bold statement, my eyebrows furrowed into a frown.

What do you mean?

His reply was cryptic.

I'll tell you when you get here. See you at eight. Shall I send a car?

FREYA

Ella woke up suddenly and I spent an hour consoling her. The poor thing was really devastated by the betrayal, but the beauty of being Ella is bounce. After a while, she talked herself out of her pain. Then she hugged me and told me she would be fine, actually, she would be better off without that shitbag.

I took a taxi to Brent. He surprised me by answering the door himself. I was used to being welcomed by his assistant, Michael, so I was a bit taken aback, but my brows shot up when I noticed the black and white striped apron hanging from his neck.

"Come in," he said with a smile.

I shut the door and followed him over to the kitchen.

There were groceries on the counter and Brent was toiling away washing vegetables under a running water faucet.

"Um," I began, not quite sure how to ask, "What's going on?"

"You said you wanted Chinese food. I'm making it for you."

I covered my mouth with my hand to hide my amusement.

Leaning against the counter looking delicious as fuck in his olive-green jumper, he raised an eyebrow at me. "Is that mockery?"

"No," I denied immediately.

"You don't believe I can do it. I'll show you."

I watched as he brought the washed vegetables over to the massive island and produced a chopping board from underneath. I was surprised he even knew where anything was. Pulling a knife from its holder, he placed the carrot on the board and butchered the poor vegetable in half. I couldn't hold back my laughter anymore, and he seemed to grow even more offended.

"Calm down," I said and placed my hand on him flirtatiously to stop him from using the knife anymore.

He glanced down at the hand and his eyes darkened. "If you don't let go right now, your ass will be the menu for tonight."

My hand instantly left his as my face flushed red, but the image of my ass on his beautiful face while his tongue devoured me immediately became all that I was hungry for.

The knife clattered onto the counter and I took a step backwards. Just like that, the air had changed between us from playful and casual to charged with sexual tension.

"I'm really hungry," I muttered, my eyes fixed on his.

"So am I," he said, "but no longer for sweet and sour chicken."

"Sweet and sour chicken sounds amazing."

"I'll buy it for you, then," he said, as my back collided with the counter.

"I want to see you cook," I said breathlessly.

"I'll make you an omelet tomorrow morning."

My lips puckered into a pout and he was on me before I could blink. The strength left my knees, but as though he now expected the crippling effect that he had on me, his hands gripped my body and held me in place.

His tongue tangled with mine, sucking, stroking and teasing, coaxing the ache that had been constantly simmering through my veins even at the mere thought of him all day, into raging fire. I couldn't get enough of him as I lifted my leg so I could grind my tormented sex against his hard bulge. Red, hot lust raged in the pit of my stomach.

"Brent," I whispered, as his warm wet tongue slid over the delicate skin at the base of my neck.

He finished the tease with a lingering kiss. "You're not wearing a bra," he murmured, as he fondled my swollen breasts, drawing my nipples into his mouth, and sucking hard through the light fabric of my t-shirt.

I cupped his head with one hand and then roughly slipped the other into the front of his slacks. My hand closed around his cock. A breathy grunt of approval immediately escaped from his lips. Encouraged by his response, I fisted him and began to stroke him within his slacks. His forehead fell against my chest. I needed him in my mouth right then but the moment I grabbed his fly to unzip, I was pulled away from the counter. My ass was pressed against him. His hands came around and the button of my jeans unfastened.

My entire body quaked in anticipation of his touch. I ground my ass against his crotch until his hand roughly slid into the panties, and grabbed my soaked sex, hard. My mouth opened at the brute pleasure.

"Have I told you," he muttered close to my ear. "That I've never been this desperate for anyone in my life?"

His words made me smile, but I couldn't concentrate as my toes began to curl at what he was doing to my sex. As he traced kisses down my neck, he stroked my throbbing clit in hard circular motions that made my hips dance and twist in delicious agony.

In one swift movement, I jerked my panties from my hips. When they were midway across my thighs, he rewarded my efforts by slipping two of his fingers inside me.

"I want your cock!" I rasped, "I can't wait."

"You have to," he responded lazily.

I felt my head go fuzzy. Burying his head in my neck, he thrust his fingers in and out of me. I used the opportunity to slip his cock out of his pants and slip it in between my ass cheeks. I rocked my hips to the rhythm of his thrusts, as breathing became more and more difficult with each passing moment.

He was so in tune with my body that he was able to sense when I was about to come, or perhaps my mindless thrashing against him was a clear enough indication. He suddenly withdrew his fingers but before I could cry out in protest, I was lifted up and deposited on top of the counter. The cord of the toaster behind me was torn out of the socket and the machine crashed to its demise and so did the jars of ceramic canisters beside me.

At the ear-splitting crash, my mouth hung open and he quickly covered it with his, effectively deleting every thought from my brain as his fingers continued to plunge in and out of me. I was nearly there, my walls pulsating around his fingers, gripping and releasing the thick fingers uncontrollably.

He jerked my thighs apart and swiped his tongue, hard and hot down my sex. I was so wet the juices of my arousal were already trickling down my thighs.

"Fuck me, Brent," I screamed in frustration.

With a hard grip on my thighs, he pulled me to the edge of the counter, and without any warning, obliged my request. He shoved his cock into me.

My moan was throat deep and endless as my hands struck the counter in torment. *"Oh God,"* I screamed, as his thick cock stretched me. Barely coherent, I grabbed his hair as my legs encircled his waist to drive him deeper into me.

He began to pound into me. My hands slid down to cup his wonderfully firm ass. It was flexing and straining as he chased his orgasm. As his thrusts grew harsher, deeper and more frantic, my sex spasmed around his erection.

"Fuck, *Freya!*" he roared into my ear.

Something about the rawness of his tone sent me over the edge. I exploded and it triggered his climax, sending bursts of hot semen shooting into me. His groan was guttural as he emptied himself into me, the sound echoing in the massive kitchen.

I wrapped my hands around his neck as our bodies quaked from the force of our shared explosion.

"You're going to make me lose my mind!" he muttered. "You're going to fucking make me lose my mind." He continued to move, milking every last ounce of pleasure out of both of us as his arms tightened almost painfully around my waist. As though he never wanted to let go.

He pulled me off the counter with him still lodged inside me and my legs in place around his hips.

"Brent, I can't feel my legs," I confessed.

"Don't worry. You feel stronger because I'll feed you after we're done," he said.

"We won't be done today," I responded, surprising myself at my greed for this man. "I want you to fuck me on every surface in this house."

He kissed me with his approval. "That's the plan, but we'll go in rounds otherwise we might both be rushed to ER." He placed me against a door.

I buckled in cradling his head to my neck, as he began to slam into me all over again. The loud smacking sounds filled the room. It was the perfect melody to our union.

FREYA

Two hours later, Brent was lying across the bed next to me, his hand under his head to prop him up and the platter of takeout boxes we had delivered were spread between us.

I was in the olive-green sweater he had been wearing earlier, but he had forced me to sit with my legs crossed so he could look at my pussy while he ate. I was sure that I had never felt more excited to be alive.

"What did you mean earlier?" I asked, chopsticks in hand as I nibbled on a piece of fried dumpling. "When you said that I wouldn't need to take the test."

He pulled his gaze from my open pussy and briefly smiled.

I licked my finger. "What did you mean? Are you expecting me to fail or something?"

"Not at all. Merrill Lynch is known for their impossible working hours. With the demands I intend to make on your

271

body, you might end up feeling too exhausted after a while. Then you'll come join my accounting department."

"You don't wish me well, Brent." I pouted.

He grinned in response, slipping his hand around the back of my neck to pull me in for a quick kiss.

I playfully pushed his face away in protest. "There's food in my mouth."

"So?" he asked, and I just watched him.

"Um isn't that … um…Weird?"

He looked away then and my eyes followed my plastic fork as I stabbed a shrimp leg. "Freya, an hour ago I had your pussy in my mouth. And I've eaten parts of you that you probably haven't tasted yourself."

Oh. My. God. I stared at him. "The things you say."

He laughed and grabbed my ankle.

I began to scream, "The food. The food. It's all going to go on the bed! We can't fuck on food!"

"My bed is big enough for us and the food," he said and tugged me hard. The paper plate fell out of my hands making an almighty mess, as I slid along the bed until he had maneuvered my body until my bare pussy was pressed tight against his hardening cock. It was a most pleasant position so I remained and subtly began to rock myself against him to return the torture.

He held me tightly, his face in my neck. "I can't believe you can still be this shy," he teased. "Especially after our shower, when you said—"

"Dhudndieiekmdgffodim," I sputtered off indecipherable syllables. "I don't want to hear it."

"I doubt you even remember," he said in a low sexy rumble.

"Really?" I asked, slightly curious. "Did I curse at you?"

"Worse," he mocked.

"What did I say?"

He just smiled.

My eyes narrowed. "Are you lying?"

"I don't lie."

"So what did I say?"

"I don't want to tell you," he said, and tried to push me off.

I pushed him right back down by pressing my body down on him.

"Now you're just asking for trouble," he warned.

I brushed my hair over one shoulder and glanced back to hold his gaze. His hands began to rub the skin of my thighs and soon they were softly tracing the outline of my waist. All the hairs on my body rose to attention. "Tell me," I coaxed, intensifying the pressure of my grind against the solid length of his cock.

"Stop it," he groaned, his forehead now leaning on my head, but I didn't heed him. I slipped my hands into his briefs and grabbed his cock. At his sharp intake of breath, I pressed on. "Come on, tell me." I moved back in his lap and positioned his now free cock between the folds of my sex. I teased the jutting head, using it to stroke my clit. I was going to chase my release then, there was no going back. Impaling myself onto that massive cock, I pushed against his chest until his back was down on the bed.

"Ah," I groaned, and how tightly my pussy received him. I felt complete, and he felt right at home within me. I began to rock my hips against him. Rapidly and then slowly at just the perfect tempo, to get me off.

He was breathing hard, his chest rising and falling, as my slick cunt rode him. I could have stayed in that state forever, with the sweetest sensations in the world coursing softly through my body. It was beyond description—a state of almost otherworldly bliss that I never wanted to be apart from. I wondered how I would ever be content again without this, without him.

"What did I say?" I still managed to rasp out, wild with excitement. I rose till he was almost out of me and then slammed back down to his thighs. "I think I can fuck you better than you do me."

"You nearly passed out in the kitchen," he reminded me.

"Arggh," I uttered as I slammed myself onto his cock.

He gave me free rein and I rode him hard, taking his entire length all the way till I could almost feel it in my womb, but it wasn't enough. I could see the green veins bulging across his forehead, and his eyes were clenched shut with pleasure. I loved that I could do this to him but I wanted more.

I leaned forward. "Can you take over?"

Brent grabbed my hips and began to control the rhythm of our mating. My sex pulsed and oozed liquid desire around him, my entire body quivered with my approaching release.

"Brent, oh, Brent," I cried, as we both began to tighten with the incoming release.

He exploded before me. "Fuck!" he roared, striking his hand viciously against the headboard.

It triggered my own orgasm. He reached forward to pull me into his arms, holding unto me tightly as I quaked all around him. Tears filled my eyes at the unending euphoria of our orgasm and I hid my face and whimpers in his neck.

Never had I felt so raw, never had I felt so shaken, and definitely never—had I felt so warm and protected. I realized with a sinking heart, that I was falling in love with Brent Lucan.

He held me tightly in his arms, as we both eventually collapsed and went to sleep, but despite my exhaustion slumber eluded me. I was sure he was asleep which is why when I spoke, I didn't expect a response, "You never told me what I said earlier."

But it came, "You said … *fuck* for the first time," he responded.

I turned to gaze at his peacefully resting face. "What? Just that? What's special about that?"

"Nothing, and everything," he replied, pulling me back into his arms. "I just wanted to tease you. I love teasing you."

I settled into his body and felt the delicately winged demons in my stomach start fluttering. I knew then that I was in trouble. Big trouble.

FREYA

As I exited the Merrill Lynch office, it was already half an hour to midnight. Brent was right, Merrill Lynch really did work its interns to the bone. I felt exhausted and cranky, but the moment my phone began to ring, I quickly searched for it in my purse before the call disconnected. Brent was away on a three-day business trip to New York. He wanted me to go with him, but there was no way I could take time off work.

Praying it was him, I looked at the caller ID and sighed when I saw that it wasn't him. It was an unknown number, which I considered ignoring, but as I was about to take it, the caller disconnected it. "Fine," I muttered, but then, as I was about to slip the phone into my pocket, it began to ring again.

It was the same number, so I clicked accept. "Hello?"

A man's authoritative voice came through, "Freya Anderson."

"Yes, this is Freya. Who is this?"

"I'm Henry Leighton, Brent's father."

I instantly froze, unable to think or move.

He went on, "There's a black Mercedes right in front of your office building. Knock on the window so the chauffeur will pull it open for you. He'll drive you to the Lucan estate. I need to speak with you."

I immediately wanted to decline, because it was so cloak and dagger and because I didn't know if Brent would want me to go see his father without him, but he ended the call. I was left staring at the phone in confusion.

Right before me on the sidewalk was indeed the black Mercedes he had mentioned, so I walked forward until I reached it. I considered calling Brent and telling him about this new development, but he was in another time zone, so I quickly sent him a text, and as instructed, I knocked on the window of the car and got in.

About an hour later, I arrived in the Lucan Estate, and was shown into the grandiose study. As I looked around at the marble and luxurious wood finishing of the room, I wondered if the Duke was aware that I had been a guest in his estate several times in the past with my family. It was like going back in time, but the sensation of nostalgia wasn't completely pleasant.

Almost immediately, as though he had been awaiting me, he rolled into the study in a wheelchair. The moment he caught my gaze, he held it and did not look away until he positioned himself opposite me.

A woman dressed in a black uniform, hands politely held together in front of her, came into the room and stood just inside the door.

"Would you fancy a light refreshment, Miss Anderson?" he asked. "I understand that it has been a long day at work for you." In so many ways, he felt similar to Brent, in their confident mannerisms and intimidating presence.

"Just a glass of water, please," I responded quietly, as I tried to calm the pace of my heart down. I wanted to get this meeting over with as soon as I could. "Why did you request to see me?"

He broke my gaze to readjust the blanket on his lap. "I hear you're in a relationship with my son."

I did not know how to respond.

"Am I wrong?" he asked, his piercing eyes focused on me again.

"Brent and I are ... friends. We've been acquainted for quite a while."

"Oh really," he asked. "How?"

I didn't want to mention my family, but then he knew my surname. There was no way that he wasn't aware of perhaps even more than I was about my father, so I took a deep breath and responded in kind, "I used to come to this manor with my mother on invitation to certain soirées. One of those occasions, I became acquainted with him. That's as far as our history goes."

"You stopped him from harming his brother, did you not?" he asked me.

I instantly stilled. He was aware of everything.

"Neither of them know that I am aware of what happened that afternoon. It was only reported to me by the security team as they caught it on the cameras. I got to know who you were from then. I apologize for your father's passing."

That was it then, there was nothing left to hide.

"Thank you," I murmured. Perhaps this visit was to warn me away from his son, just like it seemed the whole world was bent on doing. I just wanted to go home to bed.

"Could I ask you for a favor?" he said to me.

"Sure, Sir, go ahead." I waited with bated breath for what he would say.

"You say that you and my son are *friends*, but I believe that your ties run deeper than that. Has he ever mentioned his family?"

"No, Sir, he has not."

"I thought as much." His smile was bitter. "Well, if there's anything I have learned in all of my years is that the cajoling power of one woman can be worth the force of ten thousand. Could you please try to re-open Brent's heart towards his family?"

About twenty minutes later, I was shown out of the study, and with more information about Brent that I would probably never have been able to extract from him. I kept stopping the Duke to tell him I had absolutely no power to influence Brent towards reconciling with his family, but he refused to believe me. I could not understand if it was just blind determination, or misguided hope.

As I exited the study, a looming sense of calamity hung over me. Perhaps Brent would get wind of this and it would severely affect the relationship we had with each other. I was never more grateful that he was out of town. I was escorted by a butler, but I was engrossed in my thoughts I didn't notice the man awaiting me at the end of the hall until I almost bumped into him.

I lifted my head, startled and found myself staring into Liam Lucan's eyes. Instinctively, I frowned and took a few steps backwards.

"Wow," he observed. "Surely, I can't be that unsavory to you? Has Brent so thoroughly brainwashed you with his lies?"

I had expected him to be at least courteous towards me, but he wanted war. I didn't however want a verbal exchange with him, so I stepped to the side to walk away, but once again, he blocked my path.

"I'm not done speaking to you," he said.

"Get out of my way, Liam," I spat, and tried to move away again, but he shoved my shoulder to keep me in place and I staggered backwards. My eyes immediately darted over to the aged butler waiting by the corner who stared at the both of us in shock. When he caught my gaze however, he simply lowered his head meekly to the ground. His hands were held in front of him in the same pose as the woman who served me my glass of water.

I'd had enough. "If you touch me one more time, Liam, I will make sure you regret it."

His laughter roared into the hallway. "How? If I may ask. Are you going to report me to Brent? You think because you've become his whore that you can now have anything you want?"

The insult shot pain straight into my body, but nothing could compare to his following statement.

"I cannot believe that after my warnings, you still ran into his arms. The arms of the very man that killed your own father. And you still have the audacity to carry yourself all high and lofty. You're a whore ... Nothing but a cheap, rotten excuse for a daughter and—"

"Master Leighton," the butler suddenly called, panic in his voice.

I thought he was referring to Liam, but when Liam s face became tight with surprise, I turned around to see what he was staring at.

Brent was walking towards us.

I was shocked out of my mind. He was supposed to be in New York.

"Freya, step away," he commanded.

I quickly did as I was told. It all happened so fast, but in one movement, Liam was retreating and in the next, he had been struck violently to the ground, blood pouring out of his nose.

I was so shaken that I couldn't move.

Liam brought his hand to his nose at the pain, and cried out in fury.

Brent had no mercy. He dove at him again and dragged him up to his feet. Blood was running down Liam's throat into his collar. His voice was low and thick with rage but I still managed to hear what he said, "I warned you to stay away from her."

"I'm in my own fucking house!" Despite the blood, Liam laughed cruelly, his hand over his nose. "You have become completely possessed by this whore, haven't you? Well, that's no surprise. My mother did the same to your father. A mind-blowing fuck is beyond reason, isn't it?"

I could see Brent's hand fisting by his side once again to throw him another punch, so I hurried over to stop him, but I was too late.

Liam tried to defend himself, his arms flailing out wildly, but he was once again struck and sent crashing to the ground.

"Stop, please stop!" the elderly butler cried from the distance in a creaky voice.

I'd never seen Brent so furious before and for a moment, I felt as though he would fling me away to get to Liam, so I held onto his hand and pulled as hard as I could so he would turn his attention to me. "Brent," I called, my eyes filled with tears, I understood now where their enmity originated from. "Please stop. I'm begging you."

"Why did you agree to come here?" he spat furiously. With a look that was so dark and cold that it froze me over, he turned and began to walk away.

Liam yelled after him, battered and beaten, but still so bitterly amused, "What are you so afraid of?" he bellowed. "That she'll be poisoned to death just like your mother was?"

I stilled, and so did Brent, and when he turned around to gaze at Liam, I had never been so terrified.

"You'll be in the hospital before the end of the week," Brent said to him. "Let me know how being poisoned to death feels like."

FREYA

"What's wrong?" Maddie asked as she took her seat beside me in the mall.

I turned to her. "Why do you think there's something wrong?"

Her response was to look away and scroll through her phone.

I looked towards the ice cream cart where Ella was buying ice cream for all three of us.

"Why didn't you order rum and raisin?" she eventually asked. "It's your favorite."

I blinked at the question. "I don't understand. Why does that matter?"

"You always pick that flavor. Today, you just told Ella to get you anything."

"Well ... that's because I wasn't even thinking of ice cream."

"Then what were you thinking of?" Her tone was surprisingly sharp.

"Why do you sound as though I did something to offend you?"

"Are you pregnant?" she blurted out.

I almost choked. "What the hell? Why would you even think that?"

She regarded me and eventually accepted that I wasn't putting on an act to cover it up. "Fine," she conceded.

"Where did that come from?"

"You haven't noticed how exhausted you are these days? And how you're constantly eating something? You always look as though your mind is a billion miles away. And now you won't order ice cream with alcohol in it even though it is your favorite and you always have it."

"And so your conclusion is that I'm pregnant?"

"Well, what else could it be?"

"I'm not pregnant, okay?" I growled at her, turning my face away.

"Okay then," she said. "When the ice cream comes, you'll take a bite out of my rum and raisin to prove it."

"Whatever."

She put her headphones on to her ears.

I had a problem, but it wasn't that I was pregnant.

I turned to her. "I haven't spoken to Brent in three days."

"And?" she asked. "Is that a big deal?"

I couldn't take it. We used to be so close and now she was always angry with me. I felt as if I wanted to cry.

She turned to me. "Did you two fight?"

"His father summoned me to their manor three days ago," I said.

Her mouth fell open. "The Duke himself?"

"Yeah."

"I smell drama," she said, and retrieved a bag of skittles from her purse. She tore it open and began to munch on it. "What happened? Did he warn you off his son, or something?"

I sighed at her and focused my gaze on nothing as I thought back to that night.

"Come on you have to talk. You can't start and then stop. Is that how you and Brent got into a fight? What happened?"

"He was furious that I had accepted the call and gone over to the manor, so when I tried to stop him from hitting his brother, he flung my hand away and stalked off. Since then, I haven't heard from him."

"I don't follow," she said.

I wanted so badly to share what his father had told me about the enmity between them but I hesitated since it was intimate details about Brent's family matters. I focused on what was really bothering me. "He was meant to be in New York for three days, but I suddenly saw him in the house."

"Where does the hitting his brother, and you getting involved come in?"

"His brother provoked him," I said vaguely, "but the reason I'm angry is because he lied to me that he was still in New York and since then, he hasn't called to explain or apologize. He even flung me away when I tried to bring him to his senses, and then drove off from the manor without me. The butler had to call a taxi to take me home."

"Wow!"

"Since we've been together, there's not a single day has ever gone by without us speaking ... until now.

"Hmm ... you've also be spending almost every night in his home?"

"I will not respond or go to him, unless he explains or apologizes."

"Good," she said hardily. "You still have your backbone. I thought love had melted it all away."

I scowled at her just as Ella returned with three ice cream cones.

We took them from her and Maddie instantly pushed hers towards me, her eyebrows raised. "Take a bite," she insisted.

I did as she asked and shook my head at her.

"If you're careless, I won't forgive you," she muttered to me. "I need you to get out of this scot free. It's already gone on for much too long."

"What did I miss?" Ella asked.

FREYA

We arrived back at Maddie's apartment to find ten bouquets of what looked like a hundred white roses in each one outside our door.

Ella squealed with delight, but Maddie scrunched up her face with distaste.

I knew they were for me and my heart had started to beat really fast. I stared at the extravagant act of apology— dumbfounded.

Ella instantly ran up to it. "You are secretly dating someone, Maddie?"

"Those are not for me," Maddie said icily.

Ella turned to me. "Oh my, are these from the Duke then?"

"Maybe?"

"Let's look for the card and take them all in."

"I hate roses," Maddie spat. "I don't want them in my apartment."

GEORGIA LE CARRE

"Oh, Maddie, stop being such a killjoy," Ella sang.

Maddie and Ella went into the apartment.

I quickly searched the bouquet for a note. I found an envelope and as I opened it, I immediately recognized his handwriting.

I'm sorry, Freya. Call me. Please.

I couldn't help the warmth that flooded my chest at the message, and although I was still furious at him, I felt my anger start to dissipate like air out of a balloon. I wasn't ready to call him yet, though.

"Freya," Ella suddenly screamed from the living room, startling me.

I walked in through the door. "Why are you screaming?"

Both Maddie and her were bent over and looking at something on her phone. They turned to me with wide eyes.

"What is it?" I asked.

Ella came forward. "Brent's brother is in the hospital," she said.

I instantly stilled. I was almost too afraid to ask. "W-why?"

"It doesn't say. He was in a restaurant and suddenly collapsed. It's everywhere online."

Ella looked towards Maddie. "They aren't close, are they? Will he be heavily affected by this?"

I rose up to my feet. If only they knew what was in my head. "I have to go," I started to say, but the room started spinning from under me, and before I knew what was happening, I felt myself falling.

When I came to Ella and Maddie were watching over me, their eyes filled with concern.

Stop shaking me, I wanted to say, but I couldn't find my voice.

Maddie eventually brushed Ella's nervous hand away and sat me up.

Looking around, I realized I was on the floor. "I fainted?"

They nodded.

"How long?"

"Almost a minute," Ella cried.

Maddie calmly watched me. "Haven't you eaten today? Why the hell would you faint?"

"Perhaps I stood up too quickly," I said and with their help, I made it to the sofa. When I saw the quiet shock on Maddie's face, I added. "And I haven't eaten much today."

"What about yesterday?" Ella asked.

"I can't remember."

"Let's go to the hospital," Maddie said, and began to pull me up.

"There's no need," I responded. I had to go to Brent. I needed to find my purse, but my vision was still a bit hazy. I saw my purse on the table. "I'm leaving."

"You're fucking not!" Maddie glared at me. "We're going to the hospital."

"I'm fine," I said and started to stand.

"You're going to him, aren't you?"

"She's worried about Liam and what effect it will have on Brent," Ella tried to explain to Maddie.

This wasn't true at all. I wasn't worried, at least not for Liam.

I was terrified for Brent.

FREYA

W hen I arrived at Brent's home, I stood by the cast iron gate and dialed his number.

"I'm here," I said and instantly I was granted access.

He answered the door, dressed in nothing but a pair of dark slacks. They had been hastily thrown on, the button was still undone, revealing the light dusting of hair on his groin.

I couldn't take my eyes off it. How I had missed him. I pulled my gaze up to his, and saw the remorse in his eyes.

"I'm sorry, Freya," he said.

I nodded and walked into the apartment. I stood in the middle of the living room.

"Do you want a drink, or are you hungry?" he asked.

I shook my head. I still didn't know how I was going to ask him about his brother. Perhaps my aloofness and silence would guilt him enough to respond to me the way I wanted but I was aware that I was treading on dangerous ground. Brent Lucan was not a man to be easily toiled with.

"I was on a day trip to Edinburgh," he said. "And I just returned. I was about to take a shower. Will you wait?"

I nodded and listened. He did not close the door and I could hear the sound of the water. I stood there for a few more minutes, then I stripped off my clothes and headed over to his bathroom.

He was in the pose I'd seen him in countless of times. Head bowed, as the scalding hot water pelted down onto his head.

I pulled the door open and he straightened. I didn't look at him.

"It's too hot," he said, and quickly lowered the temperature just as I stepped under the cascade.

I shut my eyes while my head got soaked and water flowed down my body. I tilted my head away from the cascade to lather the shampoo in my hair and he tried to take over, as he had done countless of times before.

"It's fine," I said and brushed his hand away.

I could feel him behind me, naked, vulnerable, and apologetic, but I knew that he would not remain too long in that state. When he lowered to place his chin on my shoulder, his hands sliding around my waist to glue me to him, I allowed him to hold me. After rinsing the suds from my hair, I turned around to face him then, and looked into his eyes.

"I'm sorry," he apologized again. "I was so furious. I felt as if you had betrayed me. You knew how I felt about Liam and yet you wanted to give them your ear, but I shouldn't have left you there. I sent the driver back with the car for you and took a taxi myself, but you had already left."

"Why didn't you call me afterwards?" I asked.

He hid his face in my neck as he spoke softly, "I was still mad. I couldn't believe it when I saw your text coolly telling me you were going over there half-an-hour later. You have no idea how dangerous it was. Liam could have harmed you. What better way to hurt me than to hurt you."

"I didn't call because you were supposed to be in New York." The accusation was clear.

"I wanted to surprise you," he said. "I rounded up all the meetings early so I thought I'd fly in and surprise you, but then I got the text to say you were going to the manor. It was a blow. I couldn't believe it. I became paranoid. I knew they were trying to convince you that I killed your father, but I didn't, Freya. I swear on my life, I didn't. I could never have done that to you."

My heart melted in his embrace. God, I loved this man so much. I turned around and wrapped my hands around his neck and immediately, he picked me up. My legs encircled his waist as he leaned me against the tiles.

My hips already writhing against his hardened cock.

I brushed his hair away from his face, my hand softly caressing the sides. I didn't know how to ask the question that I really wanted to, and I didn't know how to take it if the answer was as I suspected. I chose to hold onto my dream for just a bit longer. I took his lower lip in mine and nibbled softly on it.

He didn't rush me and let it go at my pace, but when I slanted my head to slip my tongue into his mouth - the desire that I knew he was restraining with all his might - was unleashed. It had been almost a week since we had last been intimate, and it was a lot to bear given the way we had become so attached to each other.

He kissed me as though I would disappear at any moment, desperately, breathlessly, intensely. The whole time stroking and sucking on my tongue and lips with such fervor that I could barely keep up.

"I fucking missed you, baby," he said, as he lowered his head to cover my breasts with his mouth.

I whimpered against him, unable to maintain any element of control I had possessed before making my way here. "I missed you too," I whispered.

He chuckled. "Me or him?"

"Him," I replied.

"Ouch," he feigned hurt.

I half scowled at him.

He pulled slightly away and slipped his cock into me.

I realized all over again that I was addicted to him. The gratification of that first plunge was borderline crazy-good. It felt like all the parts of me had received a bolt of energy and had come alive once again. My eyes rolled into the back of my head.

Brent groaned like a beast and he did not need to say a word, I knew. I understood. We were overtaken by the ferocity of our lust for each other. He began to move inside of me. His thrusts were deliberate and purposefully rhythmic, as though he had all the time in the world to savor our union. As if he was content with the gentle waves of ecstasy that rocked through both of our bodies as my sex grappled with his cock and milked it ferociously.

He scraped his teeth along my neck and it made me shudder, but soon I lost the will to take things slow. My hand slid over to his hard buttocks to force his hips to meet the hastening thrusts of mine. "Fuck me!" I shuddered, my nails digging into his ass to contain the bursts of pleasure that were shooting through every vein in my body.

I thrashed against the tiled wall, with Brent growing harder and thicker as he pounded into me with a ferocious urgency. I tried my best to keep my back arched from the wall. My buttocks were turning sore by their constant contact with the tile.

His explosion triggered mine, and I screamed out at the blast that violently shook both of our bodies. His growl was animalistic as he jerked and fought to find his breath against me. He faltered then, his knees giving out and almost sending us both crashing to the floor but luckily, he caught the rod and held us up with his strength.

I couldn't register anything else afterwards, until I felt myself being deposited on the bed along with him. My legs remained around his waist, refusing to part as he settled us, and brushed my hair away from my face.

"Let's go again," I cried, and his smile brought tears to my eyes, I didn't want to let him go. I couldn't let him go.

"I'm not going to fuck you to death. You look tired," he said.

"Yes, I am exhausted today," I confessed.

295

It had become so easy to think that this man I was so intimate with was just an ordinary man. But now more than ever it worried me that perhaps I had been in a bubble for too long. I wondered if he could sense the dread that was brewing inside me. That underneath all the mindless pleasure—I was terrified. In the throes of passion, it had been easy for the world to fade away, but now I did feel frightened.

He pulled me tightly into his arms to fall asleep.

My greatest fear was that I would lose faith in him. If he admitted to me that he had indeed driven his brother to the brink of death like he had sworn a few days earlier, it would be the end of us.

I was now aware of what had created that mind of revenge within him, but the brutality of the act in itself against one's kin - no matter how severe the circumstances - I didn't think I could excuse it.

FREYA

The next morning Brent beat me to the punch.

I was complaining to him about the crippling work-load at the office when he suddenly said, "Are you going to tell me what my father said to you?"

"He thought I had some influence over you and he wanted me to use whatever power I had with you to get you to forgive your brother." I felt the change in him as the words came out of my mouth. Even though I was still physically with him, I could feel his gradual withdrawal, and it stung. "I told him that it was not true," I added.

He didn't say a word in denial or agreement. Instead, he asked, "Is that all he said?"

"No," I responded. "He told me about your mother, that he loved her, but then through poor judgment he got into an affair with her best friend, Liam's mother."

"Poor judgment?" He scoffed bitterly.

I could feel the bile in his tone and I didn't know how to respond, so I just went on, "The affair went on for years until Liam was about fifteen, and then he got tired of being *hidden* away. He threatened your dad that he would take their existence to the press if he didn't give them a home too, so he eventually let them move into the manor. He said that the relationship between the two of you was terrible especially as his mother used to be so close to your mom. She had always wondered why she had lost touch with her closest friend only to see her years later as her husband's mistress. She didn't take it well and neither did you. He said you were furious at him for hurting her. She got sick and he couldn't figure out why, but then you started spouting that Liam and his mother were poisoning her."

"And what did he say about that?"

"He said it was hard to believe."

"Was that all?" he asked coldly.

"Yes," I responded.

He got up from the bed and started pacing the floor.

"He said there was no evidence. It was just a child's fury and pain and that you've nursed that misgui—" I stopped and rephrased. "You've nursed that thought all these years. That it has only turned you revengeful and bitter and ruined your life. He said you ran away to Tibet, and refused any wealth from him. You were determined to make it on your own. And the first time in a decade you visited on his birthday, it was only to threaten Liam."

He walked up to me and looked down at me, and I didn't like

the dark look I saw in his eyes. All I could do was apologize, as I sensed that he especially hated that his father had revealed all these family secrets to me. "I'm sorry, I shouldn't have gone there. I had no right to interfere in something that is so painful for you."

"Yes, you shouldn't have gone. You are supposed to be on my side. If I can't trust you to believe me …" He turned to leave.

I had never felt so inconsequential as I did now. "Brent," I cried out. "I need to ask you something."

He had been just about to head into the bathroom so he stopped to listen, but didn't turn back to look at me.

"Did you …" I began. "I saw the news before I came, about Liam. He collapsed in a restaurant."

He turned slowly and stared at me.

I looked back at him hoping he would tell me he had absolutely nothing to do with Liam's collapse, but his gaze remained set in stone.

"Did you have something to do with it?"

"There you go again. That is none of your business, Freya," he grated coldly. "This is between my family and me, and I don't want you to be involved."

Suddenly, I felt nauseous, so nauseous I had to jump out of the bed and sprint for the bathroom. He stood at the door as I emptied my stomach into the toilet bowl. I felt dejected and on the brink of tears.

"Are you alright?" he asked quietly.

I refused to meet his eyes. "It's none of your business," I replied, and rising to my feet, I exited the bathroom, grabbed my clothes, and was out of the house in no time.

He tried to stop me, but I screamed at him to fuck off.

FREYA

On the train home, I began to shudder.

All I could hear was the whizz of the train as it sped past the stations and the cranking of the mechanism underneath. Every time the hydraulics hissed to pull the door open, I gazed at the influx and exit of people without seeing anything. A crippling suspicion had taken a hold of me from the moment I had left Brent's home.

But it couldn't be possible.

Maddie had brought it up the previous day. At that time, I thought she was being silly. Pulling up my phone again I searched different sites for the early symptoms of pregnancy and was hit with all my current symptoms. My breasts were swollen and tender and I was beginning to spot. All of these however had been the usual symptoms before my periods for as long as I could remember. What was new however, was the constant exhaustion, the fainting spell the previous night, and vomiting.

It was easier to believe that it was triggered more by Brent's aloofness than what these damn sites were pointing me to. The train stopped once more and a new influx of commuters boarded. The breeze brought to me a strong whiff of garlic, and I instantly doubled.

My hand flew to cover my mouth as I retched. The person beside me instantly leaning away. I jumped to my feet just before the doors closed and sprinted from the train. I panicked as I realized I wasn't going to make it to the bathroom. As I spun around in despair, tears stinging my eyes, I caught sight of a trash can by the corner and made it just in time to spew my guts into it. By the time I was done tears were running down my face.

"Are you alright, love?" a kindly woman asked.

"Yes, yes, thank you," I said and moved on quickly.

I found the toilet and after washing my mouth, I exited Hyde park station. I walked along the park, seeing nothing until I got to High Street Kensington. I walked into a pharmacy and bought a pregnancy kit.

Then I boarded the next bus, found a seat at the back, and shut my eyes as I rode home. My mother was at work, just as I had expected so I went immediately to bed, and slept until the evening.

When I awoke that night, I retrieved the plastic bag and headed into the bathroom. My stomach and nerves were in knots that felt as though they could never be untied. I gazed at my phone on the floor before me, feeling more alone than I had ever felt before. The only person I could call would be Maddie. She would scold me, for sure, but she would be my rock.

To my surprise, I heard my mom arrive with the sound of her throwing her keys on the coffee table and her footsteps heading over to the kitchen.

Immediately, I jumped to my feet, grabbed the plastic bag containing the test and buried it deep in my wardrobe. I went out to join her and tried my best to completely put it all out of my mind.

From the time I began my period at thirteen, it had never been regular. The nausea and fainting were just a by-product of bad eating and the complication that was Brent Lucan. Nothing more.

I wasn't pregnant.

Of course I wasn't. I took the morning after pill after that one time we did it without a condom and after that, I went on the pill. So ... of course, I wasn't.

FREYA

Later, I went back to my bathroom and took the test. I
didn't know what to do. I found myself walking down
the road to the bus stop. I sat down, took out the test, and
stared at the blue line.

I was carrying Brent's baby.

The bus that I usually took to the office came and went. I
looked at the people sitting inside it. They seemed peaceful. I
put the stick back into my purse and started to walk blindly.

What was I going to do?

Obviously, I would keep it. Whether Brent wanted it or not, I
was keeping it. I was so deep in my own world I jumped
when my phone rang. The noise jarred me to my very soul
and I quickly fished it out and clicked accept to stop the
sound. "Hello."

"I see you got bad news," Judi Mirren said, and I was so startled I nearly dropped my phone. For a second, I was totally
confused. How could she know? Then I looked around me.

"Or is it good news?" she asked.

"What the hell? Do you have someone spying on me?" I demanded.

"Of course," she confirmed sweetly.

I was so furious I couldn't speak.

"I can see you're still in shock," she said. "So, I'll just say what's needed. Get rid of the child. Brent will have absolutely nothing to do with it and neither will your mother, I imagine. It's going to be an impossible pill to swallow when she finds out that her daughter has been fucking the man who killed her husband and ruined her family, wouldn't it?"

My teeth were clenched and my hands were trembling with fury. I didn't have to hear this. I was about to end the call when her next words stopped me cold.

"You poor thing. It must be awful to be stuck in such situation," she crowed. "By the way, you do know he fucked me, don't you?"

"What?" the word was torn out of me.

"I told you Brent Lucan wasn't an ordinary man. He wanted you and you rejected him. What did you think would happen? Did you expect that he would give up on something he wanted? You're a child if you think that. His ability to read through people is uncanny. Do you really think I closed your mother's boutique on my own? These were his words concerning you, 'Family is worth more to her than anything else. Close down her mother's store, and she'll come running to me.'"

I retched, feeling all over again as though this time I might actually spew my insides to death.

She went on, "You heard the news about his brother Liam, didn't you? It's no coincidence, and I'm sure you are aware of that. Erase him out of your life and move on."

"And you?" I asked. "Are you so threatened by me that you have to monitor me so closely?"

"I'm not threatened," she retorted. "I'm impatient. I want my lover and business partner back. The only way to hold onto such a man is to allow him to go after whatever cheap trinkets claim his fancy. Quickly wrap up this joke of an affair you have with him and send him back to me."

Then the phone went dead on me.

FREYA

I kept my little secret to myself all day.

Now it was late evening and I was in front of the stove, two sausages sizzling in olive oil, and two slices of bread toasting nearby. It had been incredibly hard and discouraging to work up an appetite for anything, as the faintest of smells triggered the most infuriating bouts of nausea.

The excuse I had given my mother as to why I was suddenly home was that I was suffering from exhaustion and I needed a rest because I had a big presentation coming up at work.

She had accepted the excuse without qualms.

She was the last person who could know about my condition. At the same time, I realized she was the one that it would be most difficult to hide it from. The toast dinged its completion so I headed over to retrieve the browned slices. Just then however, the doorbell rang. Eyeing my sausage and judging it a few minutes away from done, I hurried from the kitchen to the door. I pulled it open ...

Brent Lucan was standing before me.

I reacted without thinking.

I slammed the door so forcefully shut that when he shot out his hand to block it, he winced with pain. It only took a moment for him to recover before he applied his strength behind it and with one shove I was displaced. He stepped into the apartment, his annoyed gaze on me as I retreated. "What was that?"

I quickly tied the thick robe across my body to hide the worn flannel shorts and white t-shirt I had on underneath. He was dressed in a superb dark suit and cashmere coat. "What are you doing here? You can't be here."

With a silence that made it hard for me to breathe, he regarded me, his gaze hooded and distant. "Why did you not answer my calls? Are you okay?"

"I'm fine," I said quickly. "Please leave. You really can't be here. My mother will return at any time."

My urgency however didn't seem to hasten him. He slipped his hand into his pocket and stared into my eyes.

I glared back in response, refusing to be intimidated, but it was near impossible not to.

"Something's burning," he said.

I jumped. In an instant, I was scurrying back to the kitchen to lift my pan off the stove. My sausages now burnt black and doused in smoke. I dropped it into the sink, and covered my mouth to keep from inhaling the smoke but it was close to impossible. I don't know why, maybe because my hormones were all over the place, but seeing the burnt sausages made me want to burst into tears.

Tears stung my eyes. "Can you please leave?" I choked out.

"You can't keep doing this," he said gently. "You can't keep running away every time we have even the slightest argument."

I wiped my face and straightened my back, my gaze on the sink full of dishes and my burnt breakfast. "I didn't run away," I replied. "I had to leave."

"And when are you coming back?"

I didn't respond.

"I hate walking on eggshells around people," he said. "When I'm with you, I don't want to be careful. I don't want to be mindful of every little thing that I do for the fear that it would offend you. So tell me, what triggered this bout of anger this time around?"

I spun back around to face him. "Nothing," I responded. "I just wanted to leave ... and I don't want to come back."

The frown on his face was so deeply etched into his forehead, he almost transformed into a different person right in front of me. "What does that mean?"

"I don't want to do this anymore," I said, my gaze somewhere just above his shoulder.

The way he smiled, his gaze dropping to the ground as though I were kidding myself made me very afraid.

I held my breath, waiting ... for what he would say.

Finally, he spoke, "Okay." Then he turned around to leave.

I was taken aback.

As he disappeared from sight and headed towards the doorway, I stared in shock.

It was over? Just like that? New tears filled my eyes and rolled down my cheeks once again and I couldn't even be bothered to stop them. I wanted to go after him, to stop him. We couldn't be over ... I didn't know how to get over him, or if it was even possible. I looked down at my still incredibly flat stomach and wondered why I was so scared to ask ... that we be more than we were now.

Judi's words came clearly to mind and I was reminded once more of why.

Brent was lethal and ruthless. To the world, to himself, to those he loved and to those he hated. He lived by his own rules, with little regard to anyone or anything else and nothing could break that. It was hopeless.

Suddenly, there was the sound of footsteps marching towards me, and I looked up surprised, wondering who had barged into the apartment.

Brent appeared, the counter separating us.

"Brent?" I whispered

He stared at my soaked face and walked up to me. "Why are you crying, Freya?"

I cleared my throat to find my voice. "Hormones," I said to him. "Don't mind me. Why did you come back? Please leave."

"Freya," he called out my name.

I took a deep breath as I knew I couldn't take his presence anymore because I was a breath away from pleading with him to create a space for me in his heart, but at the same time, given the history with him and my father, I didn't know if that was even a feasible or a righteous request.

I turned back to him and for a moment, my vision blurred. I staggered backwards, gripping the edge of the counter behind me to stable myself. "For Pete's sake, Brent, just *fucking* leave."

"Freya, what do you want? Is that what you really want?"

I lifted my gaze to his at the question, but he knew just as well as I did that my mouth wouldn't move. I could never ask him the things I wanted to. Did you ask Judi to take over my mother's boutique? Did you sleep with her? Do you know I'm pregnant?

"Are you doing this just to see how much you can torment me? How far you can go and I will still come back begging for more?" he asked, his voice low, but it was clear he was doing his utmost to control his temper.

I blinked, my gaze expressionless.

"Is it about the money? Do you want more?"

I felt as though someone struck me in the head with a hammer, my eyes widening in such shock that he could still say this to me after all this time. I did not know what I grabbed and it was only after I had flung it towards him that I saw that it was the ceramic vase of wooden spoons.

Brent dodged the incoming attack and we both watched as it crashed into the wall at the opposite end of the room and shattered into pieces.

"You bastard!" I cursed. "Yeah, it's the money. I want more. I want everything you have. Give me that and I'll come back to you!" I was panting so hard with fury that I could barely speak. When he just continued to glare at me, I lost it and screamed at the top of my lungs. "Get out of my fucking home!"

Brent Lucan took one last look at me, and stormed out of my sight, slamming the door behind him.

I sunk to the floor, more dejected than I had ever felt before in my life. I fell asleep right there, and when my mom returned home that was the state she found me in. Ceramic shattered on the floor, spoons everywhere, a kitchen in complete disarray and her daughter semi coherent.

I vaguely remembered pushing her gently away as she tried to help me to bed, and then I fell asleep. I awakened later, overwhelmed with grief. I covered my mouth with my hand as I fought not to choke from the rawness of the wounds inside me.

My heart felt worse than it had when I had lost my father. As though yet another vital part of it had gone missing, and in its place was just nothing, and it would forever remain that way. I kept my voice as low as I could when I called Maddie. "Maddie," I choked.

She was asleep and it took a little while for her to perceive my state. "Freya," she called, her tone alarmed.

"He left," was all I could say. "He left."

"I'll be there in half-an-hour," she said to me, and ended the call.

Half-an-hour later she barged into my toilet and found me just sitting on the floor too shattered even to cry. There were tears in her eyes, but her lips tightened in fury, as she took me to bed. I managed to find sleep in her arms.

FREYA

Ella, Maddie and I were rounding up at Nandos when my mother's call came. It was authoritative and curt, and it alarmed me.

"What's wrong?" Maddie asked.

"It was Mom," I responded. "She said to come home right now, then she hung up on me."

Maddie's eyes narrowed.

"You guys stay and finish up. I'll go and see what's wrong."

"No, I'll take you back. I'm done anyway," Ella said.

They dropped me off home and drove off reluctantly.

When I got into the living room, I saw my mother seated on the sofa, staring into thin air. The moment she sensed my arrival, she got up and I saw that her eyes were reddened from crying.

"What's wrong, Mom?" I called as I hurried to her.

When I reached her, she struck out her hand and slapped me across the face.

I staggered a few steps backwards with the force of it. With my hand to my face, I stared at her in shock. She had never, ever hit me in my life. "Mom," I breathed.

"Are you pregnant with Brent Lucan's child?"

I collapsed onto the sofa then as she came to stand before me.

"Tell me it's not true," she said. "Tell me it's not true that you sold your virginity ... in an auction!" she screamed.

I felt my heart break.

"You stood on a stage, naked, for men to ... to ..." she couldn't go on. She got on her knees and placed her hands on my knees. "Brent Lucan bought you," she said. "You slept with him and that's how you got the money. That's how you got tangled up with him. I told you to stay away from him ... I told you what he did to your father. It's okay if it happened once ... I am a useless parent, I couldn't provide for us so you did what you thought was right for us. But you went back to him? How could you do this?" she wailed. "Freya!"

"Who told you this?" I asked, finally lifting my head to stare into her haunted eyes.

"What does it matter?" she said. "Just tell me it's not true."

I knew without being told it was Judi Mirren. I rose to my feet and stepped away from her. "It is true," I responded." All of it, and I'm sorry."

I started to walk away then but she threw a cushion at me.

"How dare you walk away? Are you saying that right now you're—you-you-are really pregnant?"

I stopped in my tracks. "I am."

"And when were you going to tell me, or were you never going to tell me about it?"

Silence.

Her eyes widened. "You're not thinking of keeping it?"

I did not answer.

"Let's go! Right now," she said.

I turned to her. "Go where?"

"To a clinic. We need to make an appointment to get rid of it. I'd rather you killed me than have a child by the man who killed your father."

"Why do you keep saying that?" I cried. "You told me yourself, that you weren't sure."

"I don't care what the details are. All I know is he was involved, and he gave your father nightmares."

"Why would Dad have had nightmares, if he were completely innocent?"

She was stunned by my words. "What are you trying to say?"

"All the fingers point to him. Why have we then always seen him as the sole victim? Maybe he was wrong ... maybe—"

"Shut up!" She screamed. "Shut your mouth. And so what if he was wrong? And so what if he is guilty? You are his daughter. He deserves your loyalty. Our loyalty. Brent

Lucan drove him to his death. I will never be in any way associated with him, and neither will you. We're going to get rid of that child as soon as possible. The boutique has started to do well now, so we will work out a payment scheme to pay him back every dime he gave you. Then we're going to move past this. He will never be associated with us."

"I know that," I exploded. "I don't want him to be either."

"Then why do you still want to have his child? Are you in love with him? Are you hoping that you two will be together?"

I hung my head.

"That will never happen," she scoffed in mockery. "He won't even want to have anything to do with it. You were probably just a conquest to him ... a sick game he couldn't resist playing—and it makes me want to kill him." Her head fell as she held her hand to her chest. "I am so sorry ... I'm just so angry. So hurt for you."

I knew exactly the kind of pain that had gripped her. It was deep ... emanating straight from a place in the heart that felt as though it could never be reached to be soothed. Just like a knife you wanted to pull out, but knew if you did, the wound would make you bleed to death.

In that moment, I knew what my next step would be. "Mom, Brent is not going to be in my life, but I'm keeping my child ..."

She rose up and the look she gave me was terrifying. It felt as though I was looking at a stranger. "Do you know what a child is going to do to you? Especially at your age? There are no options here. You're getting rid of it. Nothing of his will ever remain in our lives."

"I'm financially secure now, Mom. I'm sorry, but I'm keeping my baby." I turned around to leave.

Her voice softened into a tone that I couldn't ignore. "Freya," she called. "I can't stand by and watch you become tangled up with that man in any way. He is ruthless. And even if you decide to keep the child, in the future, when he finds out about it, he might end up taking it from you and leaving you with absolutely nothing but fury and regret. Wash your hands of him and move on with your life. I beg of you."

My head felt like it might split into two as I continued on my way to my room.

"Freya," she called after me. "Freya!"

I slammed the door shut and locked it behind me.

FREYA

I was awoken by Maddie's text later that evening.

Are you in love with him?

I gazed at the message. As I was contemplating even responding to it, another one came in.

Your mom called me.

She says your door is locked.

You might not want to talk right now but call me soon. Please.

My debating came to an end then. I picked up the phone and called my best friend.

Her voice was careful and soft as she picked it up. "Your mom is livid. I've never ever seen her like that before."

"Me neither," I responded. "Did she tell you everything?"

"She did. I won't berate you yet for keeping it from me, but you can be sure that is coming."

Somehow, I smiled. "Yeah?"

"Yeah ... I imagine you're already so upset right now."

I breathed deeply.

"Why are you hesitating?" she asked.

A long time passed before I could respond, "I want the baby, Maddie."

"Why?"

"Because it's mine," I sobbed.

"Do you want me to come over?"

"No," I said quickly. "The phone is better."

"Do you want to be with him?"

"I do, but I don't know if I'm allowed to want to be with him. Apparently, he scares everyone around me."

"Does *he* want to be with you?" she asked.

A little laugh bubbled out of me. "The way I behaved when he came around, probably not."

"You need to speak with him, Freya," she said.

"And say what? 'Hey, I think I'm in love with you but I'm scared that you're a psychopath?'"

"That sounds fine to me," she responded. "He'll probably say, 'I am a psychopath and I'm incapable of loving anyone'. Doesn't that solve everything? You'll stop doubting yourself, and you'll be able to move on. Problem solved."

When I didn't respond, she went on, "Are you scared of being rejected?"

"I don't expect anything from him."

"I know you don't, but you have to hope. And the baby ... that gives you a greater chance."

I hated everything she was saying, but I couldn't deny the truth in her words.

"Speak to him, Freya, so that you can move on. You mentioned that he scares you ... why?"

"Well, you all keep warning me away from him, for one."

"Forget about us," she said. "Why does he scare you?"

I pondered on the question for so long, and she waited patiently until I responded.

"He feels like a timer in my hand," I explained. "Everyone says that it's a bomb, but all I see is my new favorite toy. I don't ever want to let it go but at the same time I keep wondering, when is it going to explode in my face? What scares me is that if I had to choose, if I forgot everyone else and chose, I would choose to be hurt rather than let it go."

"Okay, big question for you. Everyone is saying he is a psychopath, but has he ever hurt you?"

"No. In all his actions, he has always been caring and protective."

"You have your answer then," she said. "Don't listen to us. Go ahead and try. Don't hold back and especially, don't make assumptions. You're young and this is your first relationship so of course, you're gonna act a bit childish, but you'll get there. Go see him and get the facts out of him and then you'll know exactly how to proceed."

FREYA

Two days later, Liam Lucan died of liver failure.

I did not even get the news until that evening after it had thoroughly circulated the office and news outlets that his half-brother, Brent, had chosen instead to attend a conference in France than the funeral. That evening, feeling a bit sick, I sat at my desk as the sun went down.

It's only polite to express your condolences, I tried to convince myself, but I knew that it was perhaps the last thing that he wanted. Still it was a good chance, and I chose to take it.

He picked up on the third ring. "Hello."

I was so surprised to hear his voice that for the first few seconds, I completely forgot what I wanted to say.

"Hello," he called again.

"It's Freya," I said.

"I know," he responded, and it made it easier for me to breathe.

"I uh, I wanted to apologize ... I mean I'm very sorry for your loss."

"I didn't lose anything," he said.

My mood instantly darkened as the reality of his words dawned on me. "Your brother just died," I reminded him.

"Freya I'm very busy right now. Do you need something?"

"Yes!" I replied. "We need to talk."

"Alright."

"When can we meet?"

"I'll be out of the office in an hour."

His office would have been the best meeting place, but I was skeptical about being in his territory. "Do you want to meet in a cafe? It might be a bit risky for you especially—"

"It's fine. Send me an address."

"Alright," I replied, and he ended the call.

When I arrived, he was already waiting with a cup of coffee. Only when I took my seat did I realize that he was speaking to someone on the phone via the ear-pod in his ears. His eyes followed me as I took my jacket off and sat down, and he only ended the call just as I gave my order of a latte to the waiter. My nerves were fraught as I briefly busied myself with checking my phone for alerts, and by the time I looked up, his hardened gaze told me that it was time to speak.

"I won't take much of your time," I began. "Judi called me, and told me that you told her to take over my mother's boutique."

He watched me, and didn't say a word.

"Is that true?" I urged.

"It is," he answered.

I gasped with shock. I really thought she'd lied.

He took a sip of his coffee, lightly brushed away the stray strands of hair that had fallen unto his face, and returned his gaze to me. He looked at me without any element of remorse.

I sat back, amazed, a thousand words that I wanted to say to him passing through my mind but I didn't even know where to begin. "Brent, do you truly not see anything wrong with that or do you just not care?"

"It was wrong," he admitted.

At this admittance, I almost pressed my hand to my chest in relief. He wasn't completely insane.

"But it was the only way I knew to get you."

"Brent, you cannot possibly think that it is okay to toy with people like that."

"What do you want from me, Freya? I've had a long day. Do you want me to apologize?"

"I don't need your apology," I replied. "You can keep it. I do however want to know exactly how much you paid for my mother's arrears. I'd like to return it back to you."

This was not how I had planned the conversation to go, but I watched in horror as it all twisted away from me.

"You're pregnant, aren't you?" he stated.

I froze.

"Were you planning to ever tell me about it?"

"How did you know?" I declared.

His smile was bitter. "Judi told me because she had the impression I would hate the idea so much I'd make you get rid of it."

I bit my lip. "And that's what you want?"

"No, I want you yo have the child."

My heart stuttered to a stop. "What?"

"I'll support you," he said. "I'll be there every step of the way. I'll ensure you'll have all that you'll need so that the child does not hinder you in anyway. You're still incredibly young."

My head swirled around with confusion. "Brent, what would have happened if I didn't call you here today? You're not just finding out now, are you? If you chose to remain silent then why are you speaking about it now?"

"Freya," he said. "I don't know what you want. I've asked you before, but you chose to push me away instead. You've constantly chosen to push me away. Am I that unsavory to you?"

I was struck at his words. Tears filled my eyes and I didn't bother to hide them. "Can you blame me? Look at the things that you do!"

"Like what?" he asked.

"You got Judi Mirren to take over my mother's boutique."

"I wanted you."

"Is what you want all that matters? How can I be with someone who is so …" I searched for the words. "Unfeeling? You almost shut down my mother's business."

He didn't blink so I decided then that as long as he was listening I was going to say all I wanted to. "Did you sleep with Judi Mirren after we got together?"

He frowned. "I told you. Judi and I haven't been lovers for years, but after what has happened with you, I've completely cut my ties with her. We're nothing to each other now."

I felt relief flood through me. "Brent, you scare me."

"Freya, I know who I am, and I will not apologize for it. Yes, I took control of your mother's assets because I wanted you, but if I didn't sense any interest from you whatsoever I wouldn't have. Your reasons for holding back were based on your groundless and misinformed perceptions of me. I was fucking crazy about you, and hearsay was not going to stop me. And yes, I had quite a lot to do with the destruction of your father's company. He stole a product from a kid and then got rid of him. That kid's name is Bernardo Barros. He had only an elder sister whom he was fully dependent on. They lost their parents two years earlier. He had to drop out from university while his sister had to constantly hold down two jobs. In order to change their lives, he developed the VR program which is like nothing that exists in the world and your father wanted to steal it from him. I was a competitor at first. I was in contact with him too and suddenly, I couldn't reach him anymore. He disappeared and after I found out what your father had done, I directed my attacks on his company. Yes, I wanted to destroy him, just as he had so mercilessly done to someone else. I'm only sorry that he took his life, and it in turn affected you and your mother so terribly."

I didn't know how to respond. I felt like I was being hit with too much information so instead, I recorded it all and gave up on trying to process it in the moment. "What about Liam?" I asked. "He died today... and you told him that he would. Does that mean ... you had a hand in it?"

Something shifted in his gaze as he watched me. "Liam poisoned my mother, Freya," he said. "Slowly and ruthlessly. He blamed her for my father's maltreatment of his mom, and deemed himself fully entitled to everything that came with being the Duke of Leighton's heir. And so he got rid of her, without thought, and would have done the same to me if I had been gullible enough. So tell me," he said and leaned in, his fingers linked together as he rested his elbows on the table. "If I did in fact have a hand in his death, what would be your verdict of my actions in this case?"

"You might not have been able to forgive him, but ... this was too far."

"According to whose standards? Yours? I watched my mother die. She was perfectly healthy before they came along, and then she began to develop sudden lesions on her skin. She was constantly in pain, constantly vomiting, and for the weeks leading up to her death, she became bedridden and died a slow and painful death. We couldn't find any proof, until one day one of the housekeepers disappeared and she left me a note explaining all that Liam had instructed her to do over the course of a year. I watched him closely thereafter and that was how he was found out. My mercy to Liam was that I left his mother out of it."

"Well, he's gone now," I said. "Does that console you?"

"It does. My only lament is that he *is* gone. He can no longer feel any pain."

I didn't have a word to say, so I just watched him, my heart bleeding for the boy that he was. The image of him the day he had almost killed Liam in their home came to mind and more than before I could understand the pain, I had seen in his hollow eyes, and the fury in his trembling hands. Right now, he was a grown man, fully confident but bearing wounds that only a few knew about and even fewer could understand. My heart hurt with the need to soothe it all away, but I knew that it could never happen. The wounds ran too deep, and had so molded him into whom he had become.

With a crumbling heart, I lowered my head and spoke with my heart, "What I want, Brent, is you." The moment the words fell from my lips, I dropped my head at the complete vulnerability. "These words are not enough," my voice broke. "I want you, your wounds, your arrogance, your passion, everything that you are. Is that an impossible request?"

"No. It isn't."

I raised my head and stared at him, my heart beating so fast I could hear it in my temples.

"Freya, I want to try for us and our baby." His voice sounded strangled and torn out of him. "I just can't let you go." He raised his head.

My heart almost stopped at the sight of his reddened eyes.

"Deep down I always wanted you. I always remember the fire in your eyes all those years ago. I tried to pretend to myself, but it was always there. No woman was right because she was not you. I want to give you everything, Freya. All of my heart. I want to be everything that you'll ever need, but I'm not confident enough. My father loved my mother, Freya, but in the end, he completely destroyed her. I never want to do that to you."

His eyes were swimming with tears, but he refused to blink. He just stared at me right in the eye as he had always done. My chest filled with pain for him. He seemed so strong and aloof on the outside, but he had deep feeling.

Tears rolled down his cheeks. "I just can't let you go, Freya. Life would be torture without you, so I'm going to do everything in my power to be a better man than my father was. But I don't completely trust myself … I might hurt you. And the thought scares the shit out of me."

I reached up and wiped the tears from his cheeks. Not even in my wildest dreams did I think a time would come when he would cry for me.

"Will you teach me? Please teach me how to be who you need me to be, Freya. Otherwise, I don't have a chance."

Slanting my head, I kissed him, softly, breathlessly, wholly.

His eyes remained shut as he savored my taste.

I watched him, my heart melting within my chest. I broke the sweet kiss. "You're going to screw up," I said. "A lot, but I'm going to be there no matter what. We're going to make this work."

His eyes fluttered open, and I saw the fear in them. "I know. Promise me that you won't ever give up on me?" He raised his hand to my cheek.

I held onto his hand as it cradled my face, and reveled in his warmth. "I won't," I responded.

"I love you, Freya Anderson."

"And I love you, Brent Lucan."

"Will you marry me, Freya?" he asked.

My eyes widened. "What?"

"That's the only way that I can be assured that you'll be in this with me, until the end."

"My mom will kill me," was all I could say.

"I'll spend the rest of my life trying to win her over."

I kissed him long and deep and when we finally broke apart, I whispered the words that would forever bind me to this man whom so thoroughly owned my heart, "Yes. I'll marry you."

"We have a baby on the way and a lot of work to do before that," he said to me. "I want to know everything about you. I want to know what pisses you off, what makes you happy, what makes you excited … I want to know everything."

"Well, that's easy," I replied, my lips twitching with amusement. "You."

His brows furrowed in confusion, but when my jest finally clicked, he stood up, lifted me away from the ground and buried his face in my neck to hide his smile.

EVELYN ANDERSON

ONE MONTH LATER

"Would you like another glass of champagne, Mrs. Anderson?"

I opened one eye and smiled. "I don't mind if I do."

"Just relax and I'll get someone to bring it to the waiting area for you." The quiet sound of her soft-soled shoes faded away.

I closed my eyes and sighed with contentment. It'd been so long since I was treated like a queen. It felt good. Really good. For a while there, I thought I would never have this luxury in my life again, but as my mother would sing to me, Che sera sera. What ever will be will be. Without any warning, my daughter was marrying a billionaire duke and suddenly, she was insisting that I go for 24 carat gold and caviar facials.

Irina, the beautician came back. "Okay, it's time to remove your masque now."

"Is it? This bed is so comfortable I was about to fall asleep."

She laughed easily and as she worked, she chatted about her

noisy neighbor who played the drums till late at night, depriving her of her sleep.

Her movements were precise and efficient and soon she was done. "Finished," she declared in her lovely accent. "Have a look." She pressed a button and the bed I was lying on became a chair again.

I leaned forward and peered at the large mirror on the wall opposite. The treatment cost the earth itself, but it really did make one's skin glow.

"Doesn't your skin look amazing?" she gushed.

"Yes, it does," I agreed.

"I always say there is nothing like the pulse heartbeat machine to boost collagen production and take years off a woman's skin."

I wasn't going to argue with her about that. I got out of the chair as another member of the staff appeared, carrying a tray with my glass of champagne on it. "This way, please, Mrs. Anderson."

I was lead to their waiting room. It was beautifully and extravagantly done up in cream and gold. There was a vase on the low coffee table that hadn't been there before. It was beautiful and I immediately made note to find something similar for my boutique. I lowered myself down on one of the cream couches and leaned back.

The woman left the flute of champagne on the low table. "Would you like to book your next appointment now?"

I smiled. "Why not?"

She came back with a diary. We settled on a date that was convenient to me and Irina.

When she left, I took a sip of the cold liquid. Delicious bubbles broke on my tongue. Ah, this is the life.

As I placed the glass back on the table, another client of the salon came into the room. I recognized her instantly.

Diana Merrick, wife of Robert Merrick who was an 'old friend' of my husband. She took a double take when she saw me, then she quickly recovered, and gave me a brilliant smile.

Of course, I smiled back, but my smile did not reach my heart. When I was down and out, she had snubbed me. Actually, turned her back on me while I was halfway through a sentence. It was not even like I asked her for a loan or help She just didn't want to know me because I had fallen from grace.

"Hello, Evelyn," she greeted brightly.

"Hello, Diana." My voice was equally false.

"It's nice to see you here ... again."

"Yes, there was a time, only very recently, when I couldn't afford to come here." I pretended to laugh. "Actually, I still can't. Thank God for my daughter. She insists on paying for me to come here once a month."

Diana Merrick shifted uncomfortably on her sofa. "Ah yes, Freya. She's getting married soon, isn't she?"

"Yes, that's right. They are going to have a spring wedding."

She cleared her throat. "Is it going to be a big wedding?"

"Well, my daughter wanted it to be a small wedding, just the family, you know how she is, but Brent wouldn't hear of it. He said he wanted the whole world to know who he was marrying, so my poor daughter has had to settle for an absolutely massive society wedding. Can you believe it?"

Diana swallowed audibly. "Oh! A society wedding. How nice!"

"Don't tell my daughter that. She hates the idea. Thank heavens for Brent."

"Robert's always had a soft spot for Brent Lucan. Says he has a good head on his shoulders. We should all have dinner one day. Maybe the three of you can come over to my place."

I smiled. Yeah, I bet you want to have Brent come over so your slimy husband can pitch him all night long. "Yes, Brent is rather wonderful."

"I suppose you must be proud of your daughter. He's a fine catch."

"To be honest, I wasn't keen at all when my daughter told me he'd asked her to marry him, but I'm starting to see how blessed I've been to have him come into my life. I mean, what's not to like? He loves my daughter to bits and he can't do enough for me." I gave another false laugh. "He moved me out of my tiny apartment into an absolutely massive house in Mayfair. Then he goes and buys both Freya's best friend's houses in Knightsbridge there, so they could be close to Freya too. I know he has a reputation as a stone-cold businessman, but really he so sweet when you get to know him. I'm sure he's going to be a wonderful father too."

"Yes, I heard you moved," she said lamely.

I could see how jealous she was.

"Er ... have the invitations for the wedding been sent out yet?"

This was my moment, my little revenge. I looked her in the eye. "Yes, I believe so."

She tried not to show her disappointment. "Oh. That's good."

I opened my purse, pulled out my cellphone, called my driver, and told him to bring the car around. Then I stood. "Well, I should be going. Have a nice day, Diana."

I sailed past reception out into the bright sunshine.

My driver was already waiting outside. He jumped out of the car and opened the back door for me. I slid in like a Queen, and he closed the door for me with a soft click. My Bentley pulled away. As I settled into the plush leather, I smiled. The expression on Diana Merrick's face when I told her the invitations had gone out and she hadn't got one.

Ha, ha!

Life was good when your daughter was marrying a billionaire Duke.

Life was very good.

BRENT

THREE MONTHS LATER

The Cathedral was so full of flowers their delicate perfume filled the air. The pews were packed with hats, dresses, and suits of the who's who of high society. Sunlight slanted in through the stained-glass windows and gave the lofty space an otherworldly air, as if magic was going to happen.

I shot my cuffs nervously.

From the corner of my eye, I could see my father. His face was expressionless. At first, I did not want to invite him, but Freya said the only words that could have changed my mind.

"I don't think we have the right to deprive our child of his grandfather."

I turned around now and looked directly at him. Our eyes met and he nodded at me. He looked sad and old. His mistake was willful blindness. Like the woman who refused to see her husband's infidelity even though she was staring at his credit card statement and seeing hotel bills from her own city. It was hard, but I was slowly learning to forgive him. I was learning to see him not as the selfish man who thought he could have his cake and eat it too, but as an old man who deeply regretted his mistakes and his arrogance. I nodded back at him. He was sorry and who was I to judge when I had made so many mistakes myself? Let me not be him in my old age.

My eyes moved towards the front row.

Evelyn was wearing a cream suit and sitting with her head held high. She looked happy. I had worked hard to make her happy. Yes, it's true, I destroyed her husband, but she didn't know what I knew about him. If she knew the truth about him, she would hate him. I would never tell her what I knew. Why ruin the illusion? Why fill her with regret and confusion? Regret was an awful thing.

Martin, her PA was sitting next to Evelyn. I liked him and had a lot of time for him. He was loyal, and that was a rare thing in this world.

The music changed. It was nearly time.

I pulled my eyes towards the entrance of the church. My hands clenched helplessly. I still couldn't quite believe I had caught something as fine and wonderful as Freya Anderson in my torn and rotting net. It was like a dream.

When I looked back on my life before she came into it— I realized it was as if I hadn't been truly alive. Powered by hate and consumed by thoughts of revenge, all I did was work. Day and night. I built an empire with my hate. You'd think that was a good thing. It wasn't. In some backward societies, they tie fireworks to the tail of donkeys. Then they light them and the donkeys run to get away from the fireworks.

That was me. A donkey with his tail on fire running faster than anyone else thought possible.

Until Freya.

She put out the fireworks.

Sometimes, I remembered that night of the auction and felt furious with myself. I wished I had called her into my office and fucking just given her the money. Instead, I watched the poor innocent lamb take her clothes off on a stage. I allowed her to sell herself as if she was a piece of meat. I allowed those men to look at her while her legs were wide open.

Once I apologized to her, but she refused to accept my apology. That's the thing about Freya, she's a warrior. She told me she wouldn't change a single thing of our past. She said we had to go through that humiliating, horrible time to find the real people we were. That before a piece of metal can become a sword it must go through a baptism of fire. That was our baptism. We walked through fire to reach each other.

A murmur rippled through the congregation.

I knew I wasn't supposed to turn around and look at her. I was supposed to wait until she got closer, but I'd always done things my own way. I turned around and watched her arrive at the entrance.

A sigh went through my body when I saw her. All my nervousness fled.

She was shining like an angel. God, everyone should be so lucky to see her gracing this aisle. She was so fucking beautiful.

Through her veil, our eyes met.

The music stopped, the whispers of the crowd faded away, and time stood still.

I felt a sensation of déjà vu.

I'd done this before.

With this woman.

In another life, another timeline, another dimension we've already stood this same way and looked longingly at each other. We are old lovers. That was why we could never get enough of each other. Why our lust burned like a lamp with endless fuel. We would go on forever. Even after we left these bodies. Our love was beyond time and space. Our love would never die.

She smiled at me and I felt my eyes burn with tears of joy and pride. I had been blessed with more riches than any human had a right to, but my life was empty until she came. She was mine. Only mine. Now and forever.

Then she began to walk down the aisle. This moment would be forever burned into my brain. Her hair was done up in glowing little curls that bounced with every step she took. When she got to the altar, her uncle lifted her veil.

Yeah, this was *my* bride. It was about fucking time I put my ring on her finger and gave her my name. And later tonight … I had a surprise for her.

I was taking her to the Blue Butterfly. She was about to taste extreme pleasure.

EPILOGUE

FREYA LUCAN

I came awake so early it was still dark outside. I turned my head and looked at Brent. He was fast asleep, his breathing even and calm. He must be exhausted after last night. Maddie wouldn't believe it if I told her, but we spent hours and hours not fucking, but making love. Don't get me wrong, I love fucking Brent, but last night Brent took me to the Blue Butterfly.

And the Blue Butterfly was not about fucking.

It was about a whole other thing. Something that neither Maddie or Ella had ever experienced and I could hardly wait for them to get hitched to someone special so I could send them off to the Blue Butterfly to experience extreme pleasure. Every time I went there, I was shocked all over again at what an intricate machine the human body was and how many hidden secrets it held. We know so little about what goes on in our bodies. I admit, the first trip I took there, I was skeptical. Being naturally suspicious of anything I didn't understand, I thought it was bullshit.

Then an old woman with a prune face told me to touch my thumb, index and middle finger together. "Now hold your hands with your palms face down on your thighs and breathe."

I did as she told me to.

"Remember how you feel," she said. Then she had me do the exact same thing, but with my palms facing up.

"Breathe again."

It was a shock to close my eyes and realize that just by turning my palms upwards it affected my body access oxygen in a subtly different way. I knew then, I had lived in my body for twenty-one years but I hardly knew it.

Then she smeared my whole body with a thick, heavily perfumed oil and proceeded to use a razor blade to remove the layer of oil. Her skill was such that I felt the blade like a feather on my skin, sweeping, sweeping and whispering lightly. Her hands moved so quickly and she seemed to pay so little attention to what she was doing I was certain she was going to rip my skin to shreds, but I came away with not even one cut.

The oil had a strange musky smell. Brent had already warned me that it was an aphrodisiac, but I did not expect it to so completely take over my senses. Once Maddie, Ella and me ingested magic mushrooms in a club and suddenly we were no longer in a seedy club with dirty floors. We were in a world of intense colors. The aphrodisiac was the same. It changed everything. Brent and I went for it for hours and hours and every second was intensely beautiful.

In the pale light of the morning, I reached out and touched

Brent's face. All my life I had dreamed of a man like him, a perfect Prince, a hero. God, I loved him so much.

He opened his eyes. "Hey Beautiful," he mumbled sleepily.

"Hey Handsome," I whispered back.

"I dreamed about you."

I smiled. "Oh, yeah. What was I doing?"

His eyes were half-closed. "We were having sex."

I laughed. "You lack imagination, Lord Lucan. We have sex all the time. Why do you have to dream about it?"

He stroked my hair back from my face. "We dream about the things that we cannot get out of our minds. You live inside my head, Freya. Every day, I fall deeper and deeper in love with you. I can't imagine my life without you."

"Oh, Brent. You cannot know how grateful I am that Ella told me about your club, and I went there to sell myself to some fat billionaire."

He grinned. "Are you calling me fat, Lady Lucan?"

"You know very well, you're not fat. As a matter of fact, it's me who is getting fat."

He frowned. "You're not fat. You know how I feel about it. I would prefer if you put on more weight. I liked you best when you were pregnant with Lance. I loved the way your belly was so full and round with our child, and how heavy and swollen your breasts were. I used to spend hours sucking them."

I looked into his eyes. "Well, in that case, you're going to like my body very soon."

He jerked into a sitting position, his face incredulous. "What?"

I laughed. "Yeah."

"Yeah, what?"

"Yeah, I'm pregnant."

"What? How long have you known?"

"I knew last night."

He grabbed me and held me close to him. "Freya. I swear, there is no man that could possibly be happier than me. I love you so much."

"I love you too, Brent. So much."

"I think we should christen this piece of good news, don't you?"

"I think so too," I agreed. "And I think you better hurry before Stanley wakes up."

"Right," he said, and got very busy between my legs.

The End

Find out more about the Blue Butterfly Club here:
Dirty Aristocrat

COMING SOON...SAVING DELLA-RAY

CHAPTER 1

Della-Ray

"What?" I croaked.

The cashier pulled my MasterCard out of her card reader, and stopped chewing gum long enough to say, "I said, your card has been declined."

I felt my face burn with embarrassment. I wanted to run out of there and never go back, but this was now my local. Tightening my hold on my niece's warm sweaty hand, I swallowed the shame crawling up my throat and said, "It can't be. I just got paid. Can you please try it again?'

Her bored eyes were a dull amber as she held my card out to me. "There are lots of people waiting behind you, ma'am. I know a declined card when I see one."

I forced a smile. "Please. Sometimes it doesn't go through on the first time, but if you try it again it does. I work in bar and it happens to my customers occasionally."

She looked at me blankly.

I let go of Jess and leaned towards the cashier. "Just one more time, please. I'm pretty sure it will go through."

"Go on. Give her card another try. We haven't got all day," the woman behind me said.

I turned to meet the queue of eyes watching me with various expression, impatience, annoyance, curiosity, and outright pity. "Sorry about this," I said with an awkward smile to no one in particular.

With a long-suffering sigh, the cashier slid my card back in. As I tapped in my pin number I could feel the sweat begin to gather under my arms. Silently, I prayed the card would go through. Otherwise Jess would be eating peanut butter sandwiches for dinner tonight.

The cashier turned the face of her machine in my direction. "Declined," she said loudly, as if she was pleased to have proved me wrong. "Martin!" She bellowed. "Can you come here for non-payment re-shelving."

"Coming," a male voice answered from somewhere at the back of the store, but I didn't bother to wait. I picked up my card from the cold steel counter, straightened my back and gave Jess the sweetest smile I could muster. "Let's go, Sweetie."

Gage

I looked at the blonde child's head bobbling innocently. Then I looked again at the girl. Her face was flushed with embarrassment, but that smile she turned to give her the child. There was something majestic and noble in it. I saw that selfless smile once when I pulled a woman out of a burning car. "My baby. Is my baby safe?" she asked. When I said yes, she smiled like that just before she breathed her last. I stared at the girl in fascination. She was too thin and her clothes were clean, but well worn.

Let it go. Let it go.

She was not my problem. Her check would clear in a couple of days and she would come back for the groceries. Not the end of the world. Definitely I shouldn't get involved. No way. Not with a girl like that. One look at her and I knew she would be a big complication. I didn't need even small complications.

"What about the groceries, Della?" the little girl asked.

I saw her take the child's hand with infinite tenderness and something happened inside me. I felt a tug in my chest. Like the first time I looked into the big, bottomless eyes of a child whose father I had just killed. He didn't cry. He didn't scream. Just stared at me as I walked away. Something inside me broke. I was never the same again.

I didn't consciously plan it, but suddenly I had pushed my way to the front of the narrow aisle. She looked up at me, frowned and pulled the little girl to her.

I put my carton of milk on the counter and dropped some twentys next to it. "Add this to her bill."

The cashier's eyes widened. "You want to pay her bill."

I didn't answer her. I didn't even wait for my change. I needed air, even if it was suffocating hot noon air. I grabbed up my carton of milk and walked away without looking at the girl. I couldn't look at her. I couldn't get involved. There

347

should be no blowback from this. It could mean the difference between life or death for her and me.

Della-Ray

I watched his damp cascade of dark blonde hair, the black T-shirt that showed his strong back; the tightly muscled and inked arms, and the stone washed blue jeans that hugged his lean hips as he strode out of the store.

"Ma'am, take your groceries, please," the cashier prompted.

I was bright red as I turned around. "I...I..."

"He paid for it all so can you just take it and leave? There are a lot of people waiting."

"Just fucking take it," someone spat from the queue.

I snatched the $62.30 worth of groceries and hurried out of the store. Jess pulled on my hand and I looked down at her. She was smiling happily.

"There he is," she sang.

I followed her pointing finger to see the biggest monster of a bike I'd ever seen, packed on the curb. It was jet black with polished metal that was blinding in the sun and blood red rear lights. My eyes were riveted to the man who sat on it, as he tipped his head and downed the 500ml carton of fresh milk he'd just bought. I felt my brain turn to mush.

"Big bike. Can I go on it?" Jess squealed excitedly.

The man pulled back his head, and with the back of his tattooed hand he wiped the milk off the light dusting of dark blond stubble across his face.

His gaze met mine. There was no friendliness, no smile. In fact, it was a do not approach look.

It had an opposite effect. I was immediately jolted into motion. "Wait here," I said to Jess, and marched across the sidewalk into the parking lot. I stopped a safe distance away from him.

"Excuse me, but..." I nudged my head towards the full plastic bag in my hand. "I can't accept this. I have to pay you back for it."

His gaze darkened with displeasure.

"I...I mean, I truly appreciate it. Thank you so much for helping us, but..." I glanced down at the bag once more, then at my niece. She was watching the man with open unbridled interest. When I lifted my head again I saw that he was watching Jess too. I stiffened defensively, out of habit as I usually did, ready to tear his head off if he made any snide comments whatsoever about my angel.

"I have to pay you back," I said more loudly.

Completely, ignoring me, he bent his leg, fired up the beast of a bike, and revved it. Thunderous noise filled the hot air.

Seeing that he had no intention of responding to me I went closer. I was determined to pay him back. Only when I was this close did I noticed the ocean blue of his eyes, the slight scar that was hidden in the light stubble along his left jaw and the wild, untamed beauty of the man. He was so, so, so beautiful.

"My pay check was supposed to have cleared yesterday. Something probably went wrong, but the moment I'm able to resolve it I'll immediately transfer your money. Can I please have your bank account details?"

For a moment, he regarded me with disinterest, then, the rude brute started to reverse back. Before I could stop myself, my hand shot out.

He broke his gaze from mine and let it slide to the pitiful hold I had on his thick, tattooed forearms. I snatched my hand away as if burnt. I hadn't even realized I had done that. "I'm sorry-"

He gave me a 'I-thought-so-look', and continued his prep to leave.

"Look, I'll leave the groceries here if you don't allow me to pay you back," I said to him.

"Do what you want with them. They're yours." His voice was deep, gravely with something dark and dangerous running underneath.

"Don't you see, I cannot accept them," I replied. I was getting frustrated. "Especially since you have refused to give me a way to pay you back?

"I don't want money, sweetheart...but if you really insist on paying me back, you could let me fuck you," he drawled, his eyes so blue and piercing it as if he was trying to look into my soul.

The bag fell from my hand. He held my gaze as I stared, wide eyed at him. I felt my lips began to tremble, and I saw his gorgeous eyes drop to my mouth. Some strange expression flashed in them. I should have said something rude. Something cutting, something to put him in his place. The arrogant bastard that thought I would have sex with him for

$62.30 worth of groceries, but I couldn't. For the first time in my life, I wanted to…I wanted to fuck a total stranger.

Without a word, I turned around and headed back to my niece.

As I reached her I saw the empty carton of milk fly in an arc and land inside a rubbish bin by the side of the road. Then I heard his beast of an engine roar harder and zoom away into the distance. I couldn't help turning around to glance back to the spot he had occupied. The bag was on the ground. Together with my niece, we retrieved the cherry tomatoes that had rolled out of the pack. Jess spotted one that had rolled underneath a vehicle and she immediately got down in the dirt and belly-crawled under the car after it. I should have told her off, but my heart was pumping in my chest and I could still feel my palm tingling where it had touched his warm skin.

"Got it," she shouted happily, and jumped to her feet.

"Good girl," I said automatically, and stroked her sweet moon face.

He had ridden off into the sunset, but I had every intention of finding him and paying him back. This was a small town and there was no way a man like that wouldn't be known by everybody.

Preorder Saving Della-Ray
Here
My Book

351

ABOUT THE AUTHOR

Thank you so much for reading my book. Might you be
thinking of leaving a review? :-)
Please do it here:

Highest Bidder

Please click on this link to receive news of my latest releases
and great giveaways.
http://bit.ly/10e9WdE

and remember
I **LOVE** hearing from readers so by all means come and say
hello here:

Made in the USA
Monee, IL
28 March 2021

63893706R00215